a story of music

A Story of Music

HARRIOT BUXTON BARBOUR
WARREN S. FREEMAN

Illustrated by GEORGE McVICKER

REVISED EDITION

Summy-Birchard Company
Evanston, Illinois

Library of Congress Catalog Card Number: 58-10464
Revised Edition Copyright © 1958, by
SUMMY-BIRCHARD COMPANY

Copyright, 1937, 1950, by C. C. Birchard and Company
International Copyright Secured
Printed in the United States of America
Standard Book Number 87487-033-X

CONTENTS

FOREWORD

SINCE the first edition of A STORY OF MUSIC was published in 1937, the world, and the world of music, have seen many changes. In this Second Revised Edition we have tried to reflect some of those changes. All the record listings are new, and CHAPTER XVIII, "Music in the Twentieth Century," has been enlarged. We hope that these revisions will help you to make better use of this book.

A STORY OF MUSIC tells how music grew with mankind. It tells of music from the time of the earliest men, whose music had to be useful—a rhythm to drive away evil spirits, or a trumpet call to battle—through the days when music was the plaything of princes, to the present, when music can be everyone's pleasure. The story of musical form is told in the lives of its greatest masters, from Palestrina, who made music of many voices into an art fit for angels, to composers of the present who sometimes borrow ancient tribal rhythms to express the complexities and tensions of our times.

By careful choice of anecdote and historical background, these lives are used as a means of picturing the social customs which often have changed the form of music. You will see how Handel, broken in heart and purse by the fickle nobility for whom opera was only amusement, took oratorio from the dim quiet of little chapels and made it a great art for the people. You will meet Haydn, liveried servant to Prince Esterhazy, turning out compositions on command, and perfecting sonata form out of his genius and his great need for an artistic way of making a few musical ideas appear many times in different dress.

After you have seen how the great German masters built music into forms as beautiful and lasting as the stone castles and churches of their country, you will find what gifts other lands have brought to music. You will hear musicians telling of the witchery of Spain or the tragedy of Poland in the stately or stirring rhythms of their folk dances. You will learn how the French made pictures with their music, blending tones as artists blend colors. And finally you will see how musicians everywhere are trying to express in music the new speed and stress of the machine age, and how our country is on its way to developing a type of music as truly its own as the opera of Italy and the waltzes of Vienna.

Thus, we have tried to show music in its relationship to history, geography, and social progress. It is a story that advances from the time of intricately lovely music in the palaces and simple song in the cottages—from a time when great music could be heard only in great cities—to the present, when, thanks to the invention of phonograph, radio and television, all music can be for all people everywhere.

We have made a book which may be used either as a textbook or library reference on music appreciation. We hope that we have made a book to be read with interest and pleasure apart from teacher or course of study.

HARRIOT BUXTON BARBOUR
WARREN S. FREEMAN

Boston, Massachusetts
May, 1958

a story of music

CHAPTER I

MUSIC BEGINS

THE first people who ever lived upon this earth had music. They heard rhythm in the steady beat of the waves upon the shore, and melody in the songs of the birds. Soon they began to make music for themselves. But the men of these savage tribes were busy people. Every minute had to be spent in a struggle for life—building shelters for their families, hunting for food, and fighting wild animals or the men of enemy tribes. Their music, like everything else in their lives, had to be useful.

HOW EARLY MUSIC WAS USED

When they beat upon their drums of hollowed logs or wooden frames covered with skin, it was not just for the fun of hearing the sound. It was because the different rhythms of the drum beats would stir the hearts of the people. The slow, somber throbbing would make them mourn the death of a chieftain; a brave, brisk rhythm would urge the warriors on to battle; faster, wilder beats set them whirling and leaping in a dance of victory. When they made flutes of reeds, it was not for sweet music, but for the calls of a shepherd to his flocks or the signals of a leader to his men in time of danger.

They did not have singers to give concerts for people to hear and applaud. Their only songs were the soft lullabies of a mother trying to soothe her baby to sleep, or the chant of an

1

old man, reciting the deeds of heroes of long ago. There were
no books or writings to record history in those far-off days.
There were only two ways in which they could keep great happenings from being forgotten. One was to draw pictures on
the walls of some cave. The other was to sing the story around
the fireside to the children for generation after generation.

THE FIVE TONE SCALE

The music of all the people of ancient times was monoto-
nous; only a few notes used over and over again. Even the
Chinese, who from the earliest times made beautiful poems
and paintings and cities with strong walls and bright porcelain
towers, used only five notes in their music—our *do, re, mi, sol,
la.* This same five-toned scale is found in many very old folk
songs of other lands.

EGYPTIAN AND HEBREW MUSIC

When the early peoples became safe enough and rich
enough to build palaces for their kings and temples for their
gods, music played a greater part in their lives. In the hidden
chambers of the great Egyptian pyramids, men of today have
found beautiful flutes and harps, and wall paintings showing

how the Egyptians worshipped their gods and mourned their dead with music. Perhaps the Hebrews learned their music in the land of Egypt where they were held captive before Moses led them safely through the Red Sea waters. Many of their musical instruments, like the psalter, were like those pictured in the Egyptian pyramids.

We read in the Bible, especially in the psalms or hymns of King David, who was a famous singer and harpist, how the Hebrews used music in the worship of God. "Praise the Lord with harp; sing unto Him with the psaltery and on instruments of ten strings; sing unto him a new song." The beauty of old Hebrew chants can still be heard in the synagogues.

GREEK MUSIC

Of all ancient peoples, the Greeks had the greatest love of music, and have given the most to our music of today. They had many pretty legends to tell how music began. One told how their mischievous god Pan was the first to make music by blowing through a reed. One day he was chasing a maiden named Syrinx, but before he could catch her, she was changed to a reed through which the wind blew sweetly. Pan pulled up the reed and broke it into pieces of different lengths, which he bound together to make a musical instrument, called syrinx, after the maiden. This was supposed to be the first of all wind instruments. From that little syrinx, blown by every shepherd boy, grew the mighty organ with its great pipes through which air is forced from bellows, pumped first by hand, and now by electric motor.

The Greeks also had a stringed instrument called the monochord, which taught later people a great deal about music. You can make a monochord by driving a nail at each end of a thin board or shallow wooden box and stringing a wire, gut string, or even elastic, tightly between these two nails. When you make the string vibrate by plucking it with your finger, you produce a musical tone. Now hold the string down to the board at just half its length. When you pluck one of the halves, you will get a tone an octave higher than that made by the whole string. If you press your finger at different places along the string, the different lengths, when plucked, will give different tones. You will see that the shorter the string is, the higher the tone it gives when it vibrates.

The reason is that the tone is made by vibrations in the air, and the faster the vibrations are, the higher is the pitch of the tone. A short string vibrates faster than a long one, and so makes a higher tone. If two strings are of the same length, but one is thicker or looser than the other, the thick, loose one will vibrate more slowly and give a lower tone.

HOW OUR STRINGED INSTRUMENTS ARE LIKE THE MONOCHORD

All the stringed instruments follow this rule. In those like the violin and 'cello, where all the strings are of the same length, some strings are thicker than others, or more tightly strung to give them different pitches. The player makes still other tones by shortening the strings with his fingers, as in the monochord. In instruments like the harp or the piano where there are strings for each note, the shortest string is for the highest note, and the strings become steadily longer and thicker as they reach the bass.

In wind instruments, the tone is made by a column of air vibrating in a tube. In the syrinx or in the organ, where there are many tubes, the smallest give the highest tones. In those like the trumpet or flute, where there is only one tube, there are keys by which the player can shorten the column of air in the tube.

Apollo was the Greek god of music, and every year there was a great music festival in his honor. In the beautiful white-columned temples, priests would sing or chant hymns in his praise. Crowds of happy people would travel the road past silvery-green olive orchards or dark groves of cypress to the celebration in the great stadium.

MUSIC IN THE GREEK DRAMA

There were poets who strummed on lute and lyre as they sang of the adventures of heroes and gods. There were contests of flute players. There was also drama, with the characters in smiling or frowning masks to show whether they were comic or tragic, and the heroes striding about in clogs with thick wooden soles to make them seem taller and grander than common men. All through these plays, a chorus would sing or chant something to suit the happenings of the play. Sometimes this chorus was divided into two parts, and one would sing and be answered by the other. This use of music with drama was the forerunner of our grand opera.

THE GREEK MODES

The songs or chants of the chorus were in the different modes or scales which the Greeks used to express every feeling. They invented a system of four notes called a tetrachord. By putting two tetrachords together they made scales which they called modes because each one was supposed to express a different mood, such as the Doric for courage and the Mixolydian for fear and surprise. Some seem very strange to us now. But the Lydian mode, expressing peaceful pleasure, had half tones between the third and fourth notes of its tetrachords, and so was exactly like our major scale today.

EARLY CHRISTIAN MUSIC

These Greek chants in the temple and the drama were the most important of all the very old music because they have given the most to later music. When St. Paul set out to carry the news of Jesus Christ around the world, he founded his earliest churches among Greek peoples. It was only natural that they should combine their old temple chants with the Hebrew hymns taught them by Paul in their new worship. At times, ancient church choirs were divided, and the parts sang in response to each other as in the Greek chorus. Later in Rome, the Christians used much the same chanting, for the Romans had learned all they knew of music from the Greeks whom they had conquered and used as slaves to tutor their children.

When Christianity first reached Rome, the little groups of Christians had to meet secretly by night in the underground passages called catacombs, where the Romans buried their dead. Here they chanted their hymns very softly, so that the pagan Romans would not hear them and drag them out to be crucified or thrown to the hungry lions in the arena. As time went on, more and more brave men and women joined the new church.

A noble Roman lady who was a fine musician gave up her life for the new faith. She is known as St. Cecilia and became the patron saint of music and musicians. Many artists have pictured her playing the organ, harp, or viol. At last, even Emperor Constantine became a Christian. After that, the new religion was free to spread all over Europe.

Now chants were sung full-throated by robed monks and nuns in their cloisters, and by choirs of boys in the beautiful stone churches and cathedrals. At first, each church had its own chants, sung in its own way, by singers good and bad, who could put in any notes they pleased. The result was probably quite confusing, and not beautiful. At length, Pope Sylvanus decreed that singing in church was to be done only by trained choirs, and the result of this decree was the establishment of music schools in all the churches. After a while, St. Ambrose formed rules for the making and singing of chants, so that they would be alike everywhere, and later Pope Gregory changed and improved the chants. Gregorian chants were formed upon modes, not exactly like Greek modes, but like scales played only on the white keys of a piano.

HOW THE SCALE BEGAN

Up to this time, there had been no written music. The chants were taught by ear to one choir after another for generation after generation. There were not even names for the tones of the scale. The choir boys used to sing a little Latin prayer to St. John, that he might keep them from having sore throats and hoarseness. The first syllable of the first line was *ut*; the first syllable of the second line was *re* and began a tone higher; the third, a tone higher still, was *mi*, and so on up the scale. Eventually, one of the choirmasters began to use these Latin syllables to represent the tones to which they were sung. Since then, the syllables from the little prayer have been used for the tones of the scale, except that almost everywhere *ut* has been changed to *do* (probably from Dominus, the Latin word for Lord) because it is easier to sing.

At last, they began to use little lines above the words, to help the memory of the singer. A horizontal line showed that the voice was to stay on the same tone. One that sloped up showed that it was to rise, and one that sloped down showed that

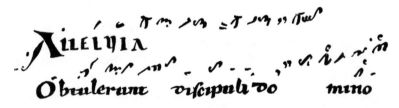

it was to fall. But these lines did not tell on what tone to begin, or how far up or down to go. Then someone had the idea of drawing a red line above the words to stand for *F*, and later a green line for *C*, so as to give a rough idea of pitch. Afterwards, two more lines were added, and a variety of signs, called neumes, were used for notes at different times and different places. Neumes look very strange to us now, especially those called the "fly-track" and "horseshoe and nail," which quite lived up to their names. Little by little, easier and clearer ways of writing music were discovered until at last they used the one we have today.

CHOIR SCHOOLS

So the churches of the Middle Ages gave us our way of writing music, the names for the tones of our scales, our first music schools, and the beautiful Gregorian chants which are part of the service of Catholic churches today. We shall see that many of the greatest musicians, such as Palestrina, Haydn and Schubert, received their first training in church choir schools. There are still famous choir schools in some of the churches.

MUSIC OUTSIDE THE CHURCH

But there was also song in the world outside the great gray churches. Knights rode forth in shining armor to win back the Holy Land from the heathen Moors, and they had their songs of brave deeds far away, and golden-haired ladies left waiting in old stone castles. The people working in the fields to raise food for the monks, knights, and ladies, and carrying the stones to build churches and castles, also had their songs of love and joy and sorrow. They especially liked to sing as they danced on holidays. The musicians of the knights and people were called minstrels in England, trouba-dours and jongleurs in France, and minnesinger and meister-singer in Germany.

THE MINSTRELS

The troubadours and minnesinger were of knightly rank and composed their own songs of love and courage. But often they could not play an instrument, and would hire minstrels or jongleurs to accompany them on the lute or harp. If one of these noble musicians did not have a good voice, he would get a minstrel to sing for him. Or if he wished his songs to become known, he would send out several wandering musicians to sing them.

There were also hundreds of minstrels and jongleurs who were not employed by any knightly musician. They wandered from city to city, to all the court celebrations where rich men and nobles might pay generously for jollity and song. They were also to be found at all the great fairs, going through their tricks to please the crowd, along with the camels, monkeys, dancing bears, and other trained animals. They were not musicians only. An old manuscript tells us they were supposed to "invent clever and amusing games to please people, throw and catch little apples on the points of knives, imitate the song of birds with their voices, pretend to attack a castle, jump through four hoops, play the cymbals, guitar, and bagpipes, and compose a lively jig."

These minstrels carried the songs of the people, also news, gossip, and lovers' messages, from one place to another. Although they were dearly loved by the common people, they were like tramps, without honor and without homes. The law gave them no rights at all. Even if they were wounded by a sword, they were not allowed to strike back at their attacker, but only at his shadow.

THE MASTERSINGERS

But at last they grew so in number that in the tenth century, guilds or unions of musicians were formed, like the guilds of tradesmen. In Germany, the members of the musicians' guild were called *meistersinger* (mys-ter-zing-er) or mastersingers. There were rules of their craft to be learned, and examinations and contests of skill. We shall see later

how the great German composer, Richard Wagner, used the
contests of the mastersingers in his opera, "Die Meistersinger
von Nürnburg" or "The Mastersingers of Nuremburg" and
the songs of the knightly minnesinger in "Tannhaüser."
(Tahn-hoi-zer)

THE MIRACLE PLAYS

The early minstrels and jongleurs also gave plays on religious
subjects in the church-yards on Holy Days. Those represent-
ing Bible stories were called mystery plays and those founded
on the lives of the saints were known as miracle plays. In
some of them, there was more entertainment than religion.
The devil was represented as a comic character with horns,
a tail, and a bright red beard, and the people would drive him
around with sticks. However, these plays had musical inter-
ludes, sometimes songs by a chorus, and so made the con-
necting link between the old Greek drama and grand opera.

FOLK SONGS

The songs of the knights, troubadours, and common people
are called folk songs. Except for a few songs of the trouba-
dours, no one knows exactly who first composed and sang
them. We only know from what country they came. Folk
songs often have strong rhythm because many times they
were used for dancing. They were generally in major and
minor keys, like our music today, instead of the old church
modes. Their melodies are usually simple, and easy to sing.

BINARY FORM

In church music, the melody flowed on and on, always
changing with the words. The folk singers would make up
a lovely bit of tune that they would like so well that they
would sing it again. Then they would use a second musical
theme and would repeat that, too. This use of two musical

sentences repeated is called binary or two-part form. Most of our popular songs are in this form, that is, they have a verse and chorus.

TERNARY FORM

Many times, the singers of folk songs liked their first theme so well that they would come back to it after the second, making what is called ternary or three-part form. Thus, if we call the first musical theme A and the second B, in a song in binary form these themes would be arranged in the order —A-A-B-B, and in ternary form A-A-B-A. Form is to music what rhyme is to poetry. Later we shall see how the simple binary and ternary form of the folk songs grew into the greater forms of the suite, rondo, sonata, and symphony.

THE FIRST PART MUSIC

Music now had rhythm, melody, and form. But it was a long time before it occurred to anyone to sound two or more different tones at the same time to make *harmony*. Then a monk named Hucbald divided his choir in two parts and had one sing the melody four or five tones lower than the other. This kind of music was called *organum*. Although it would sound very queer to us today, it is important because all our harmony grew from it.

COUNTERPOINT

Next, instead of having the two parts of the choir sing the same melody several tones apart, a composer would invent a different part called the *descant*. This was sung either above or below the *cantus firmus*, as the original melody was called. Often the descant was a sort of aimless wandering among sounds, like the sound of shepherd pipes; but little by little the kind of musical writing called *counterpoint* was developed. The name means "note against note." In counterpoint, one melody is accompanied or harmonized by another melody, somewhat as if one singer hummed the Dvořák "Humoresque" while the other sang "Swanee River." In another kind of counterpoint called *canon*, a tune was made to accompany itself, in the manner of a round like "Three Blind Mice."

These are only simple illustrations of a very complicated art. There was a school of musicians in the Netherlands who developed counterpoint to a very high degree. They would harmonize a tune with itself turned backwards, and that was called crab canon. Or they would write music with as many as forty melodies going on at the same time. Probably because most of the music of that time was for the voice, the different parts or melodies in counterpoint were called voices. Hence, all that sort of music was called *polyphonic* from Greek words meaning many-voiced.

The Netherlanders were so interested in weaving and interweaving their tunes, turning them backwards or upside down, that their music is more like a difficult cross-word puzzle or a problem of mathematics than anything people love to hear. Later writers like Palestrina and Bach learned to use the discoveries of the Netherland school and make a simpler polyphonic music woven of lovely melodies.

RHYTHM

Music is still made up of rhythm, tempo, melody, form, harmony, such as is found in the very earliest music. Rhythm is a grouping of heavy and light beats. For example, a waltz rhythm has one marked beat followed by two lighter ones. In a march, every other beat is heavy, to mark when the marcher is to put his left foot forward. The tempo or time of a composition means the rate of speed at which the music travels. It is *rhythm* which makes the difference between a march and a waltz, but *tempo* which makes the difference between a military march and a funeral march.

In a piece with a certain rhythm, we find the same number of beats in each measure, but not always the same number of tones. Sometimes one note is held over for two beats, and sometimes two or more short notes come on a single beat. This gives every piece of music a *rhythmic pattern*. We can see what rhythmic pattern means by comparing two pieces. *America* and the *Star-Spangled Banner* are in the same rhythm (three beats to the measure with the first one accented) and about the same tempo. Yet if we tap out every note of each with a pencil, we never should mistake one for the other. Each has its own rhythmic pattern, by which it can be distinguished.

MELODY

Melody is a series of musical tones sounded in succession to express some musical meaning. Melodies are often called musical sentences. It is interesting to see how a composer puts musical tones together to express feeling. A series of short phrases is more exciting and is often used for gay or lively music, while a longer or more flowing phrase is used for music that is gentle or dreamy.

HARMONY

When two or more tones are sounded together to make *harmony*, there are two kinds of harmonic effects. Those that are pleasant and restful to the ear, we call *consonances*. Those that sound unpleasant or exciting are called *dissonances*. Good music is made up of both consonances and dissonances. A music of all consonances would be as dull as a diet of nothing but cake. A music of all dissonances would be very ugly. Much modern music has more dissonance than consonance, and it is sometimes hard for us to get used to listening to it.

Perhaps the reason is that formerly composers received their inspiration from nature, while now they are often inspired by artificial things, including machinery. Where the composer once heard only the ripple of brooks or song of the birds, he now hears the crackle of electric sparks, the grinding of brakes, or the deafening roar of an airplane motor. More probably, the spirit of modern invention, which has led men to conquer even the sky and the waters of the sea, is leading musicians to seek ever new and daring combinations of tone.

The Record Lists

The recordings suggested at the close of each chapter of this book are intended only as a general guide to the instructor or the home listener. An extensive choice is offered on the assumption that if one recording is not available, another might be. Many fine recordings adapted to educational purposes were not in print at the time these lists were compiled (May, 1958). Consequently, though mentioned in the text, they are not included in the lists. They may, however, become available in the future; the teacher who wishes to use them is urged to consult the latest catalogs.

Since the advent of long playing records there has been a tendency not to index the shorter musical compositions under their own titles, especially in the monthly catalogs. When seeking such titles, reference to manufacturers' catalogs or the encyclopedic loose-leaf indexes maintained by some music stores may prove helpful. If these aids are not available, recourse may be had to the classified lists sections of the monthly LP guides. This recommendation applies especially to the musical illustrations for Chapter I. The catalog sections on "Folk Music" and "Collections" are rich sources of materials for educational use.

In learning situations where pupil participation is feasible, such participation sometimes may be more rewarding than passive listening to records. Possible activities might include: the singing and playing on various instruments of correlated folk songs, chants, rhythms, etc., from school song books and other sources; live performances by selected class members of excerpts from the art music suggested for listening purposes; experiments in writing music and scoring it for small combinations of instruments to afford an insight into some of the creative processes involved.

With limited in-school listening time, it is not likely that more than a small percentage of the music suggested in this book can be touched upon in the classroom. The pupil may profitably use the extended lists as a basis for constructive extra-curricular listening, or building his own record library.

RECORD LIST — CHAPTER I

The beginnings of music:
Drum rhythms of Africa, etc.
American Indian songs and dances
Chinese folk songs and dances
Hebrew chants, folk songs and dances
Hymn to Apollo
Gregorian chants
Russian liturgical music (the early chants)
"Sumer is icumen in"
English medieval songs (12th and 13th centuries)
Folk songs, ballets, and madrigals of various countries

Machaut, Guillaume de (c. 1300-1377)
Motets, ballades, virelais and rondeaux

Wagner, Richard (1813-1883)
Die Meistersinger (The Master Singers of Nuremberg) —
Dance of the Apprentices; Procession of the Master Singers;
Walter's Prize Song. (Or use the Prelude to Act One.)

Selections illustrating melodic phrase, rhythm, and rhythm patterns:
All through the Night
America
Auld Lang Syne
Comin' through the Rye
The Harp that Once through Tara's Halls
Londonderry Air
The Star Spangled Banner

Barcarolle, from "The Tales of Hoffmann"— Offenbach
El Capitan — Sousa
Hungarian March (Rakoczy March)— Berlioz
National Emblem — Bagley
On the Beautiful Blue Danube — Strauss

On the Mall — Goldman
Roumanian Folk Dances — Bartok
The Stars and Stripes Forever — Sousa
Waltz from "Swan Lake" — Tschaikowsky
Waltz in A Flat — Brahms
Waltz in C Sharp Minor — Chopin
Washington Post — Sousa

CHAPTER II

PALESTRINA

THE SEARCH FOR NEW WORLDS

CHRISTOPHER COLUMBUS set out to find a new way to the riches of old India and China. Although he failed, he opened a passage to a new world and wealth and adventure greater than the grandest dreams. Soon little brown ships with russet sails were bobbing everywhere over strange seas, sailing around the great globe of the world, discovering new oceans and new routes to old treasure. Stout, bearded men with doublet and sword landed and pushed through wild forests to the gold and silver and jewels of ancient hidden cities.

Yet few people in the old countries knew how the world was widening. There were no newspapers. Printed books were so rare that only rich men and nobles could afford them. Letters were sent by messenger on horseback, and many people lived all their lives without ever receiving one. Perhaps those who lived in seaport cities, where ships came back for new sails and to caulk leaky seams, listened to the tales of the sailors. Or those near the courts of kings would see the adventurers visit the palaces with gifts of gold and bright feathers and dark-skinned captives in chains.

Away from the sea and the court, men worked in their fields all the week and came on Sunday to the churches to rest awhile in the dim, lovely light of the colored windows, to hear the holy words and sweet music, and to bring their hopes and fears and sorrows to God. They did not care whether the earth were round or flat, as long as the good Lord sent the rain to make their crops grow green and the sun to make them grow sweet. For these people, the greatest adventure was a trip to some large city.

PALESTRINA'S TRIP TO ROME

In 1540—about the time that De Soto was braving a barren wilderness from Florida to the muddy Mississippi, seeking for treasure that he never found—an Italian boy left his little town of Palestrina (Pah-les-trée-nah) for a holiday visit to the grand old city of Rome. He said good-bye to his family, to the friendly goat and hens and chickens that ran in and out of the open door. He turned for a farewell look at the white oxen plowing the brown earth of his father's farm and the low stone houses of the village clustered in the shelter of the church.

He came at last to the great city with its ruins of olden days—the broken columns and battered stone gods and ancient walls, like dim gray ghosts. He saw fair ladies and fine gentlemen go proudly in silks and gold and jewels, and he saw the monks and nuns walk quietly and humbly in robes of black and brown and gray. He heard the quick clatter of horses' hoofs as soldiers rode through the hard paved streets, and he heard the beat of the goldsmiths' tiny hammers in the dark little shops where they were making a ring for some lady's little finger or a cross for the altar of some church. He passed by the fountains and statues in the open squares in front of beautiful palaces and churches. As he was passing the church of Santa Maria Maggiore (Sahn-tah Mah-rée-ah Mah-jee-ó-ray), the greatest of all Roman churches dedicated to the mother of Jesus, he began to sing because it was so good to be young and alive in a world full of wonderful things.

Perhaps he sang a lovely bit of old plainsong learned in

the choir of the church at home. Whatever the song was, a
priest heard the beauty of his voice and brought him into
the great church. At once, he gave the boy a place in the
fine choir and called him Palestrina after his native town.
In the choir school, young Palestrina learned to play the organ,
to read music, and to write music. When he was eighteen years
old, he went back to the church in his home town as organist
and choirmaster. There he married and became head of a
family, and there he might have stayed all his life, if the
Bishop of Palestrina had not become Pope. This Pope
Julius knew the genius of the young musician of his town
and took him to Rome as choirmaster at the rich and mag-
nificent church of St. Peter's.

HOW PALESTRINA'S MUSIC WAS PUBLISHED

Soon Palestrina published his first book of masses which
he dedicated to Pope Julius to thank him for his favors.
A mass was the musical setting of the church service, com-
memorating the Last Supper of Jesus with his disciples. In
those days a composer had to pay to have his own work
printed. Then he would dedicate it to some great noble or
churchman. If the patron, or person to whom the work
was dedicated, was pleased, he would send the composer a
gift of money or find him a better position. Pope Julius
appointed Palestrina one of the college of singers of the Sistine
(Sis-teen) Chapel where the services were held in which the
Pope himself took part.

The other singers were very angry because there were
supposed to be only twenty-four members, and these were to
be admitted only with an examination and the approval of
all the other members. Palestrina had to give up his other
work to take the place, and almost as soon as he had done so,
Pope Julius died. The new Pope, Marcellus, was a very good
man and much interested in music. No doubt he would have

helped Palestrina, but he also died after only three weeks in office.

Paul, the next Pope, was very strict and had no love of music. He passed an order that church singers, like priests, should not be married. So Palestrina and two others were dismissed with tiny pensions. The loss of his position was such a cruel blow to Palestrina that it made him quite ill. It left him with no work and scarcely enough money to support his family, and it also ruined his hopes of bringing out more of his music with the help of the Pope or other high church officials. All the time that Pope Paul lived, Palestrina published no music.

Later, he became organist and choirmaster at the church of St. John Lateran, the oldest church in Rome, which was called "Mother of all churches of Rome and the world." However, the old church was now poor and had to take second place to the rich church of St. Peter's. Palestrina was not happy there. He was not given enough money to make music as lovely as he wished for the glory of God. Then he had trouble with those in charge and resigned. After being without work for three long years, he went back as organist and choirmaster to the church of Santa Maria Maggiore where he had first come as a boy. It must have seemed like going home.

PALESTRINA'S WORK FOR THE SISTINE CHAPEL

In the meantime, Pope Paul had died, and the new Pope Pius IV was more fond of music. Palestrina had written a tenderly beautiful setting for part of the Good Friday service, and Pope Pius wanted it to be copied into the great music books of the Sistine Chapel to be used every Good Friday thereafter.

This was the greatest honor that could come to a musician. Usually it was the custom to have a work roughly written

out and rehearsed by the whole Sistine Choir who would decide whether it was worthy of being written into the great books. If the votes were in its favor, the four clerks always employed by the college of singers copied it on huge sheets of parchment in notes large enough to be read by the whole choir at once. These were illuminated in rich colors, and bound into books, many of which are still used today. The great musician Mendelssohn, who lived three hundred years after Palestrina, writes of seeing one of these enormous books carried before the choir as it went in procession in St. Peter's.

This success gave Palestrina new courage. He presented the Sistine Chapel with another mass and more sacred songs, which were also copied into the great books. This music was so lovely that someone said that the different voices rose and fell like angels passing on a ladder between heaven and earth.

In those days, men's grandest plans and the finest work of their hands were all for the glory of God. They built great churches and cathedrals with lacy windows and towers and spires like dreams come true in stone. They adorned all the high places outside, and niches within, with beautifully carved images that would always remind people of angels and saints. The light came in the windows through jewel-colored glass, and the walls were painted with holy pictures lovelier than the world had ever seen.

Music alone lagged behind the other arts. Perhaps the reason was that music is the only art which does not have to imitate nature. In painting and sculpture, the saints could be modelled from good men and the Madonnas drawn after the likeness of fair Italian maidens. In music, men had to make their own rules and discover their material little by little through the ages. We have seen how, in the Dutch schools, they were so interested in rules that they forgot the beauty of music.

ABUSES IN CHURCH MUSIC

Even worse abuses had sprung up in church music. To begin with, the descant, or upper voice, often had four or five notes to one in the lower voice or cantus firmus. The result was a pleasant warbling in which the people could not understand one word of the holy service. What was still worse, the music of many of the masses was founded on folk songs which were more melodious than the church modes. But instead of singing sacred words, the singer of the part with the folk melody would sing the old words of the song. It was as if the tenor of a quartet should sing "Old Black Joe" while all the others were singing "Nearer My God to Thee." This strange custom was followed even in the Sistine Chapel.

THE MARCELLUS MASS

In 1562 a council of churchmen took up the matter of doing away with music composed in counterpoint, or different parts. Many thought it might be well to go back to the old unison plainsong in which, at least, the words would be clear to all, and there would be no excuse for anyone to sing words not suitable to a church service. On April 28, the

Sistine Choir sang masses in private before two cardinals who were to judge whether such music was to be used in the church. Some have said that Palestrina was asked to compose a mass especially for the occasion and that he submitted not one, but three. The one called Marcellus, after the good Pope who had died after only three weeks in office, was selected as a model for all church music, and so saved music for the church.

This story has never been proved true. But it is known that the council to purify music met at this time and three Palestrina masses of about this date have been found in the library of the Sistine Choir. The Marcellus mass was first publicly performed at a great service of thanksgiving in the Sistine Chapel in the presence of the Pope. It was received with great enthusiasm as a masterpiece of church music.

In Palestrina's life, as in the lives of us all, sorrow was mingled with joy and failure with success. Within a short time his wife, son, and two grandchildren died. Although he became once more choirmaster at great St. Peter's, the new Pope Sixtus V was not satisfied with the mass Palestrina composed in his honor and said that Palestrina had forgotten the genius he had shown in the Marcellus. Later he wrote a mass to be performed in his old church of Santa Maria Maggiore for the Feast of the Assumption which celebrates the ascent of the Virgin Mary into heaven. It is so very beautiful that they say it is to music what the Sistine Madonna is to art.

Pope Sixtus was delighted with it and wanted Palestrina to be choirmaster of the Sistine Chapel, but the other singers were jealous, and objected. So in the end, the Pope gave Palestrina the honorary title of Composer to the Papal Chapel, a title which only one other musician ever held after him. Still the other singers were so bitter and envious that when Palestrina presented the Chapel with three new and very lovely masses, they were not used or written into the great books.

Moreover, the patrons to whom Palestrina dedicated his music were far from generous. Seven Popes held office during Palestrina's life in Rome. Although Palestrina dedicated music to all but one of them and also to two dukes, a grand duchess, and a prince, too many of them were like Philip II who sent his thanks and nothing else. In a dedication to Pope Sixtus V, Palestrina mourned that he could afford to publish his work only in a small mean form, and not in a splendid large folio more suitable to music composed for the glory of God. It was very hard for him to see the Spanish musician, Vittoria, able to bring out his work in beautiful illuminated folios under the patronage of the King of Spain.

LAST YEARS

Later he found more generous patrons, and many honors came to him. One of the happiest events of his life must have been when fifteen hundred of his townsmen from Palestrina marched into Rome singing his music, while he directed them at the head of the procession. When he was old, a company of all the best musicians of Northern Italy came to him, greeting him as the father of all musicians and asking if they might dedicate to him a Book of Vesper Hymns. At last, in 1594, he died after a long life of making music for the worship of God. He was buried in St. Peter's and on his tomb were carved the words:—"Princeps Musicae"—"Prince of Music."

RECORD LIST — CHAPTER II

Byrd, William (1543-1623)
        Mass for Four Voices
        Mass for Five Voices
        Motets — various

Corelli, Arcangelo (1653-1713)
    Concerto Grosso, Op. 6, No. 8 ("Christmas Concerto")
    Suite for Strings

Dowland, John (1563-1626)
    Dances for Lute
    First Book of Ayres

Gibbons, Orlando (1583-1625)
    Anthems, Fantasies, Madrigals — various

Josquin des Pres (1445-1521)
    Missa Pange Lingua
    Secular works — various

Lassus, Orlando (1530-1594)
    Masses and Motets — various

Monteverdi, Claudio (1567-1643)
    Lamento d'Arianna (Lament of Arianna)
    Madrigals — various
    Vespro della beata Vergine

Morley, Thomas (1557-1603)
    Elizabethan madrigals — various

Palestrina, Giovanni Pierluigi da (1524-1594)
    Ascendo ad Patrem
    Assumpta est Maria
    Iste confessor
    Magnificat
    Missa brevis
    Missa Papae Marcelli
    Missa sine nomine
    Stabat Mater
    (Other choral works as available)

Victoria, Tomas Luis de (1548-1611)
    Selected works (Vatican Choir)

CHAPTER

BACH

HERE in the new world, people were struggling to make homes for themselves in a wilderness. They had to work from dawn till dusk to raise enough corn to keep from starving and chop enough wood to keep from freezing during the long winter. Then men had to go into the forest to shoot deer and wild fowl for their meat, and they had to defend themselves against savages who lurked behind trees to kill and scalp them, burn their houses, and carry off their wives and children. There was no time for music or painting or any of the arts that make life pleasant.

THE MUSICAL BACHS

Back in Europe, men fought old wars and sang old songs and followed the trades of their fathers in the same old way. In Thuringia (Too-rin-gee-ah), a province of northern Germany, lived a family of musicians named Bach (Bahk). There were Bachs who played the organ in little gray village churches, and Bachs who played the violin in the court orchestras of dukes and princes, and Bachs who were town pipers and made merry music in the streets on festival and fair days. There were so many of them that people called all musicians Bach, thinking that if a man were a musician, he must surely be a Bach also.

Every year the whole family—fathers, sons, and grandsons, uncles, nephews, and cousins—would hold a jolly re-union, usually at Arnstadt. They would begin by singing a *chorale* (ko-ráhl) or hymn and end with what was called a *quodlibet*, in which each one would sing or play whatever came into his head, all at the same time.

THE GREATEST BACH

In 1685 was born the greatest Bach of all. He was Johann (Yó-hahn) Sebastian, third and youngest son of a town musician of Eisenach (I-zen-ahk), a small town in the shadow of the Thuringian forest. As his father and mother were dead when he was only ten years old, he was taken into the home of his older brother who was an organist in a near-by town. There he went to school and learned music from his brother who was a very strict man.

Printed or engraved music then was so rare and expensive that musicians who could not afford to buy it would make themselves copies by hand. Bach's brother had made a manu-script copy of music by all the most famous composers of the time, and this book was very precious to him. Though Sebastian longed to study the music in it, his brother said that he was too young to appreciate it. Whenever the manu-script was not in use, it was kept locked in a bookcase with a wire lattice or grating in front.

Every moonlight night the boy would tip-toe to the book-case. There he would manage to pull the manuscript through the wire grating, taking care not to rustle the pages or make any sound to awaken his brother's family. Then he would set to work to copy it, bending low over the tiny notes in the pale, wavering light of the moon. It took him six months to finish his copy, and the first time he practised it, his brother heard him and took it away from him. Many think that the blindness of Bach's later life was caused by straining his eyes in the moonlight when he was a boy.

FIRST POSITION

By the time Sebastian was fifteen, his brother had so many children of his own that it was hard to find food and clothing for them all. So the lad set out to earn his own living. He and a friend, Georg Erdmann, travelled two hundred miles, mostly on foot, to Lüneberg (Leena-berg) * where they found places as paid singers in the choir of the school of St. Michael. Bach's voice soon changed so that he could no longer sing soprano parts, but he stayed as accompanist at rehearsals and played in the town band that went through the streets at festivals and at New Year's.

Then he became court violinist in the orchestra of the Duke of Saxe-Weimar (Vy-mar). In those days if a nobleman was fond of music, he would keep his own orchestra and chorus at the palace to entertain himself and his guests. From the time of Bach on, for many generations, the dukes at the little court of Weimar were friends to both poets and musicians.

JOURNEYS TO STUDY MUSIC

During this time Bach was studying all the good music he could find, and hearing all the fine musicians in the country. He went to the ducal court at Celles where the band played French music, and he went to the great city of Hamburg to hear the grand opera and the famous organists there. As he seldom had money for fare in the stage coach, he would trudge long miles over dark wooded hills and through sunny meadows and towns. Often he would stand tired and footsore at the side of the road while the coach drove by with its prancing horses and coachman cracking his long whip and the ladies and gentlemen smiling within. Or after he had munched his last crust of rye bread, he would sniff

* In phonetic spelling it is impossible to approximate very closely the sound of the German umlaut.

the fragrance of fat roast duck through the kitchen window of some cozy inn.

Once, coming back from Hamburg, he sat hungrily outside an inn from which floated the mouth-watering smells of a good dinner. Suddenly a window opened, and out fell two herring heads. Herring was at least something to eat, and young Bach scrambled for them. To his surprise, he found inside each head a Danish ducat. This was money enough to buy him a fine dinner and also to pay for his next trip to Hamburg. He never found out the identity of the kind person who had taken pity on him in his hunger.

FIRST CHURCH POSITION

One of his journeys was to Arnstadt, the old meeting-place of his family, to try a new organ. The consistory, or committee of church elders, heard him play and at once gave him the position of organist, making the old organist a sort of assistant to the eighteen-year-old boy.

Soon he was in difficulties. The grand old Danish musician, Buxtehude (Boox-teh-hoo-deh) was organist at Lübeck (Lee-beck), a gray old town on the Baltic Sea, and Bach felt that he must hear him play and learn from him. So he obtained a month's leave of absence from his church and made the two hundred mile journey on foot. Once there, he was so enchanted by Buxtehude's skill and the pleasant evening musicales that he forgot time. Instead of four weeks, he stayed four months.

On his return, he was brought before the consistory and called to account. That was the beginning of trouble. Next came a complaint that "the organist Bach played for too long a time, but being notified of this has gone to the opposite extreme and made it too short." And at last he was rebuked for allowing a strange maiden to come and make music in the church.

The strange maiden was his cousin Maria Barbara Bach. Shortly after, he found a better place as organist in Mühl-hausen (Meehl-hów-zen). His few household goods were moved across the Thuringian plain in a queer old four-wheeled cart drawn by an ox and a pony, and as soon as he was settled, he came back and married Maria Barbara. Organists were not well-paid then. His salary was only about seventy-five dollars a year. However, the young family was in no danger of going cold or hungry because each year he was also given two cords of wood, six bundles of brushwood, twelve bushels of grain and some fish.

CHURCH MUSIC

Even while Bach was in the little towns of Arnstadt and Mühlhausen, he began to compose beautiful music for the worship of God. Since the time of Palestrina, the Protestant church had separated from the older Catholic church. This new church held the belief that music should not be sung by trained choirs alone, but that every man, woman, and child in the congregation should be able to join in the praise of God. For this reason, there was need for music easier to sing.

MARTIN LUTHER AND THE CHORALE

Martin Luther, the founder of the Protestant church, adapted old folk songs to hymn words because they were simple and singable. Thus a song called, "Oh dear Hans, take care of your goose!" became "Oh dear God, this Thy command." Luther was both a poet and musician. When he could not find a folk tune ready made for his chorales (ko-ráhls) or hymns, he would compose one himself on the flute while someone wrote it down for him. The most famous of all chorales, "A Mighty Fortress Is Our God," is Luther's own composition. These chorales were sung in unison with organ accompaniment.

Bach took many of these old chorales and harmonized them in four parts for the choir to sing with the congregation. The beauty of the harmony with the lovely simple melodies makes Bach's chorales take place with the noblest church music of all time. Much of Bach's other church music was founded on the chorale. In those days the organist did not merely play over part of the hymn before the congregation began to sing. He took the melody of the chorale and wove other parts with it to make a lovely tone poem. Bach also enlarged and elaborated the chorale into the cantata which had solo parts and parts for choir and congregation and an accompaniment of string and wood wind instruments.

Beautiful as this music was, there were some in the church who thought that all music was sinful and should be stopped. So Bach was glad to escape the quarrelling and find a place again at Weimar as court musician and organist to the Duke. He kept on making his journeys throughout the country to hear good music or to play a fine organ, and his own fame spread. Once a prince heard him play and was so astonished by his skill that he gave Bach the gold ring from his finger.

BACH AND MARCHAND

At another time, when he was in Dresden to hear the opera, there was visiting in the city a famous French organist and harpsichord player named Marchand. There arose such a heated argument as to which was the better player that their friends arranged a contest between them. A brilliant company of ladies and gentlemen gathered. Bach arrived promptly and so did the judges, but there was no Marchand. They waited and waited. When at last they sent out after him, they found that, afraid of defeat, he had fled from the city by fast coach that morning.

About this time, the Duke's old musical director died. Bach, who had become his assistant or concert master, should have been promoted, but for some unknown reason the Duke gave the position to someone else. So Bach accepted an offer to become musical director to the Prince of Anhalt-Cöthen (Ahn-hahlt-Keh-ten) with whom the Duke was on very bad terms. He was so enraged that he threw Bach into prison to keep him from going to his enemy. There Bach stayed a month. At last, when the Duke found that he could not make Bach change his mind about leaving, he decided that a musician in prison was of no use to him and let him go.

The young Prince of Anhalt-Cöthen was very fond of music. He was a good singer and played the violin, viola, and harpsichord. He and Bach became such close friends that he would not go on any journey without taking Bach with him. As there was no telephone or telegraph then, news travelled very slowly from town to town. After one of Bach's trips with his prince to the warm mineral springs at Carlsbad, he came back to the terrible grief of finding Maria Barbara dead and buried and their children motherless.

SECOND MARRIAGE AND NEW HAPPINESS

After some time he married again. His second wife was Anna Magdalena Wülcken (Vilken), a court soprano. She was only twenty-one years old, but had a lovely voice and was a good musician. It was a very happy marriage. She helped him copy his music and he gave her lessons on the clavichord. There is still in existence a book of tuneful little pieces he made for her and had bound in green leather and gold—"A Little Clavier Book for Anna Magdalena Bach."

Palestrina had believed that the chief purpose of music was to bring God to the hearts of men, but Bach said that the object of music should be the glory of God *and pleasant recreation*. It was while he was at Weimar and Cöthen that he composed the music that has given pleasure to musicians for hundreds of years. There he wrote the six famous concertos dedicated to the Margrave of Brandenburg. A concerto (kon-chért-o) was a composition for different combinations of instruments to play together, or *in concert*. It usually began with a lively section, had a slower middle part, and ended in fast tempo again. The three sections were not separated into *movements* as in a symphony, but were played all in one piece.

THE SUITE

Another form of composition which Bach enjoyed was the *suite* (sweet). The suite, which was begun and developed by the French, was a set of pieces in different dance rhythms. For the sake of variety, a slow dance like a *sarabande*, which was founded on the procession of Spanish altar boys on Holy Thursday, would be followed by a lively gavotte or dainty minuet, and the *pavanne* which imitated the stately walk of peacocks would come next to a whirling jig. In many of the dances such as the minuet, the themes are in binary (A–B) or ternary (A–B–A) form as in folk tunes. In Bach's suites, some of the dances, such as allemands, were composed according to polyphony. That is, the themes are repeated or interwoven in different voices like the canon or "round." In others like the minuets and gavottes, the melody is in binary or ternary form. Bach's most famous suites are the sets of French and English Suites for clavichord.

IMPROVEMENTS IN PLAYING THE CLAVICHORD

Pianos had not yet come into use, and the clavichord was Bach's favorite instrument. Bach made improvements in its playing and tuning which have affected all keyboard instruments. Before Bach's time, a player held his hand flat and used only his three middle fingers because, with the hand in that position, the thumb and little finger were too short to reach the keyboard. This must have been an awkward way to play, and Bach found that by holding the hand raised, all the fingers could be used. After this, much richer chords and more interesting melodies could be written for keyboard instruments.

Bach had also invented the method of tuning called *equal temperament* by which our pianos are tuned today. What gives a tone its pitch is the number of times per second the tone vibrates. Strictly according to mathematics, E♭ has a greater number of vibrations and so is a bit higher than D♯ which is the leading tone, or *ti*, of the key of E. So a musician could not play pieces in both E and E♭ without retuning his instrument, and a piece could never change key in the middle as many do now. But by making the tones just a shade off pitch, Bach found a way of tuning in which the same tone could be used for A♯ and B♭, G♯ and A♭, etc., as in our pianos today.

THE FUGUE

To illustrate this new method, Bach wrote the set of preludes and fugues, one in each key, called "The Well-Tempered Clavichord." The *fugue* (fyoog) is the highest form of polyphonic, or many-voiced music. The word *fugue* means flight, and the name is a good description. A fugue begins with a main theme, usually short and easy to remember. This theme is repeated in a different voice or voices, and the themes are always moving, chasing each other, being woven and interwoven into a lovely pattern of music. To a trained musician, there is no greater delight than seeing how a composer repeats his theme, inverts it, doubles it, turns and twists it, and weaves it into his piece. There are fugues with the theme running on in two, three, four, five, and even six voices all at the same time. Even if we are not trained musicians, it is sometimes fun to see how many times we can recognize the main theme during the course of a fugue.

ST. THOMAS'S SCHOOL

Perhaps Bach might have stayed all his life in peace and comfort with his prince, but at last the prince married a princess who thought only of parties and balls and gay society. She did not care for music at all, and the prince soon lost interest, too. Besides, Bach was beginning to wonder how he could give his sons a good education, for they were brilliant students. After a great deal of thought, he left the prince to become cantor in St. Thomas's School in the old university city of Leipzig.

It was not easy to give up the honor of being director of music to a prince to become singing master in a school. The work was a hard grind. The cantor was supposed to teach singing and Latin, take the boys to church every Thursday morning at seven, and hold examinations one week every month. The boys of St. Thomas's School had to supply music for the services at the four great churches of the city, for weddings, funerals, and fairs. They also had to take part in processions through the streets on holy days. In addition, the cantor had to compose music for the boys to sing on special occasions. His grandest religious music—the Passion Music, or musical settings of the stories of the Crucifixion according to St. Matthew, St. Mark, and St. John—was composed at Leipzig. He never had the joy of hearing them performed by a chorus of really good singers, but only by the hoarse or piping voices of his St. Thomas boys.

The slow processions through the streets in wind and cold and snow and sleet ruined the boys' voices. One of the former cantors had asked the church council to excuse two boys with the best voices from singing in the streets to save their voices for the church. This did not help a great deal. Three times a year, great fairs were held at Leipzig, and merchants came from far and near with fabrics and pottery and jewelry and clocks. Hunters came in from the forests with furs, and peasants brought wood carvings that were wrought by patient fingers in the labor of many months. There were dancing bears in the street, and opera from Italy or France on the stage. The boys with the best voices all left school to sing for pay in the opera, and the poor cantor was left with only the worst singers at a time when he wanted to make the best showing.

On top of all his other troubles, the cantor's pay was very small, although he was supposed to get an allowance of grain and firewood and extra fees for weddings and funerals. Bach once jokingly wrote to his friend Erdmann that when the weather in Leipzig was good, there were fewer funerals and he received less money. It must have been a hard struggle for him to bring up his large family of children, for he had twenty in all—seven born of his marriage with Maria Barbara and thirteen of his second marriage. Even though the oldest of them were out in the world earning their living before the youngest were born, there must always have been many small mouths to be fed and bodies to be clothed.

BACH'S CHILDREN

Yet it was for the sake of his children that he came to Leipzig. Only by living close to a great university could he afford to give his many sons the education he wished for them. There is a pleasant picture of his family life in another letter to Erdmann:— "My eldest son is a student of law; the second is in the highest class (at the university): and my third son is in the second. The children of my second marriage are still young, the age of the eldest boy being only six. But they are all born musicians, and I assure you that I can give a vocal or instrumental concert at any time just with the members of my family. Not only is my wife a good soprano, but my eldest daughter does not do badly."

Though some of Bach's sons studied law, they all in the end turned to music. His greatest pride was the success of his third son, Philip Emanuel, who became director of music to the Emperor, Frederick the Great. Bach was seldom free from trouble with the heads of the school, who did not appreciate his genius. At one time they quarrelled so bitterly that they kept back part of his pay. They even elected another man to be cantor of St. Thomas's when "Sebastian Bach should die." Yet all the musicians who visited Leipzig heard him play and his fame spread throughout the country. Frederick the Great spoke to Philip Emanuel of his wish for a visit from the old musician.

VISIT TO FREDERICK THE GREAT

Now Bach was too ill and weary to enjoy journeying and was in the midst of labor on his "Art of the Fugue." But invitations from a King are like commands. At last, he felt he must go, and set out with his oldest son. Frederick the Great was just sitting down to play a flute concerto with his court orchestra when he heard that Bach had arrived.

"Gentlemen, old Bach is here," he cried and laid aside his flute.

There was no flute concerto that day. He sent for Bach and had the old man brought in just as he was, dusty and rumpled from the journey, without giving him time to change into his neat black court suit. Then the Emperor led him through all the rooms of the palace. The piano was a new invention, and Frederick had seven which he wanted Bach to try. Bach did not like the piano as well as the clavichord and thought it would never be used for any except light and gay music.

At last Bach sat down at the well-loved clavichord and

began to play. First, the King gave Bach a theme and Bach made a fugue from it then and there, while they all exclaimed at his skill. Then Frederick wished to hear a fugue of six voices, and Bach at once composed one while the King cried again and again, "There is no one like Bach!"

BLINDNESS

After Bach had returned home, the King sent him a generous gift of money. If he had received it, there might have been a fine celebration feast of roast goose for the young children still in the home. Certainly Bach would not have had to wear out his tired old eyes etching little lines and notes in copper plates because of lack of money to pay an engraver. But the money was embezzled or stolen on the way and never came. Bach strained his eyes over the engraving of his "Art of the Fugue" until, after an operation, he became quite blind.

He saw the world for the last time in a dazzling flash of light just before he died. During his lifetime, he had been famous more as a player than a composer and some of his best music was never printed. After his death, for a long time his fame and his music were almost forgotten. They say that whenever a boy of St. Thomas's wanted some paper to wrap up a bread and butter sandwich, he would tear a page out of one of Bach's manuscripts. It was not until many years after, when later musicians became interested in his work, that the world realized that one of its great musicians had already lived and died.

RECORD LIST — CHAPTER III

Bach, Johann Sebastian (1685-1750)
    Anna Magdalena Book
    Brandenburg Concertos Nos. 5 and 6
    Cantata No. 4, "Christ lag in Todesbanden" ("Christ lay in bonds of death")

Cantata No. 80, "Ein' feste Burg ist unser Gott" ("A mighty fortress is our God")
Cantata No. 211, "Coffee Cantata"
Concerto in D Minor for Two Violins
Mass in B Minor
Passacaglia and Fugue in C Minor (organ)
Suites for Orchestra Nos. 1, 2, 3, 4
Toccata and Fugue in D Minor (organ)
Two-Part Inventions (harpsichord)
Well-tempered Clavier (harpsichord)—excerpts

Buxtehude, Dietrich (1637-1707)
Choral works—various, including "Missa brevis"
Organ works—various

ANCESTORS OF THE PIANO

A CLAVICHORD

Its strings were struck by a piece of metal.

A HARPSICHORD

Its strings were plucked by a quill or a point of hard leather.

CHAPTER IV

HANDEL

BACH AND HANDEL

In the gray old Saxon town of Halle (Háh-luh), George Frederick Handel was born in 1685. Because he and Bach were both great musicians, were born in the same year in places not more than a day's journeying apart, and were blind in old age, they have often been called the "twins of music." Yet their lives were different, their music was different, and they never met.

Bach labored in a quiet corner of Germany for his beloved music and his many children. Handel never married and lived a life as full of adventure as a story-book—contest, duel, fame and fortunes made, lost, and regained. Bach was the last and greatest of the masters of the old polyphonic or many-voiced music which grew from the music of the great church choirs. Handel was a composer of operas, and all his music was more in the new homophonic style, founded on the solo of the opera.

There were no musicians in Handel's family as there were in Bach's. Handel's father was a barber and surgeon. Those were the days when bleeding was thought to be a cure for all ills, and the operation was always done by barbers. The striped pole was supposed to represent the winding bandages of the surgeon, and is still used as a barber's sign even now when barbers no longer do surgery. Handel's father was quite an important man, because once in a while he was called to the service of the great Duke of Saxe-Weissenfels (Vy-sen-fels) forty miles away. However, like most fathers, he wanted something better for his son and planned to make a lawyer of him.

HANDEL'S CHILDHOOD

As a baby, little George Frederick cared only for toys that would make music—drums, trumpets, or little flutes. At first his father was amused. Then he became alarmed. He thought musicians were poor, half-starving creatures not good for much but playing around the streets on holidays. He would not have a son of his become one of them if he could prevent it.

The musical toys were smashed or thrown away. The boy was not allowed to go into any house where there was a clavichord or any musical instrument. He was even tutored at home so as to keep him away from the grammar schools where music was taught. But the father could not stop the choirs from singing in the church or the pipers from playing in the streets. The story is told that when George Frederick was seven years old, he managed to smuggle a little table clavichord into the attic. When everyone was out of the house or too sound asleep to hear the weak tone of the little instrument, he would steal away to practice in secret.

VISIT TO THE DUKE

A short time later, his father went to pay a visit to the Duke. The boy begged to be taken along. It would be a wonderful trip through the green countryside in a carriage behind prancing horses. Besides, the Duke was a great music lover, and the palace had many fine clavichords in the great drawing rooms. His father sternly refused to let him go. Young Handel did not sit down and cry. He ran after the carriage. He ran and he ran until, when he was about ready to drop, his father noticed him. It was too late to turn back.

The lad received a sound scolding, but he was taken along.

At the palace, he simply could not keep his fingers away from the clavichords. The Duke heard him and was surprised that a child could play so well. He gave the boy a pocket full of money and told old Handel that it would be a sin to keep his son from using such great talent. Let him keep on with Latin and the law, but give him a good teacher of music, too! The advice of a Duke was not to be taken lightly. When they returned home, young Handel became the pupil of Zachau (Zah-kow), the church organist, a good and faithful teacher whom Handel always loved.

FIRST FAME

The teacher was delighted with his new pupil and felt that he could not do enough for him. Handel studied counterpoint and composition, harpsichord, violin, and oboe. At the end of three years, Zachau felt that his young pupil had learned almost all he had to teach. So George Frederick was sent with a friend of his father's on a trip to the great city of Berlin where there was an opera house and many famous musicians. The boy surprised everyone with his skill. All the musicians treated him with the greatest respect except an Italian opera composer named Bononcini (Bon-on-ché-ne). He wrote the hardest composition he possibly could and asked the child to play it at sight. When Handel did so easily, Bonancini was jealous and treated him as a hated rival.

Even the King took an interest in the boy. He wanted to send him to Italy to study and then give him a position at court. Young Handel must have been delighted at the chance, as Italy then was the musical leader of the world. But it would have meant an end to his father's dreams of having a lawyer in the family. Old Handel called his son home in alarm and the lad had to be content with more quiet study under Zachau. The next year, the father died, and George Frederick dutifully carried out his wishes by entering the University of Halle as a law student.

FIRST POSITION AS CHURCH ORGANIST

All this time, Handel had been substituting for the organist at the castle and cathedral. When this organist was discharged for neglect of duty, Handel was offered his place. As he had needed to borrow money from his mother for his expenses, he felt that he should be making a living, and so gave up the law.

For a year, he lived much as Bach did all his days. He played his organ and drilled his choir and orchestra and composed several hundred cantatas, none of which he thought worth saving. Then he felt that he could go no farther in his home town and went to seek his fortune in the great seaport city of Hamburg, where Bach had journeyed to hear the famous organists and the opera.

HANDEL TURNS TO OPERA IN HAMBURG

In Hamburg, Handel became friendly with a dashing young man named Mattheson who played the organ, harpsichord, harp, violin, double-bass, flute and oboe, was a tenor soloist at the opera house and wrote operas himself. Mattheson helped Handel find pupils and a place as second violinist in the opera-house orchestra. He also taught Handel a bit about the new operatic music, while Handel helped him with harmony and counterpoint. The two had a jolly time and shared many adventures.

In those days, when a very famous organist was to retire, there was usually a contest to decide who should be chosen in his place. Once Mattheson and Handel went together by coach as friendly rivals for the position of grand old Buxtehude of Lübeck. When they arrived, they found that one of the rules of the competition was that the winner should marry Buxtehude's daughter. Alas! the lady was not young and she was not fair. Our friends looked and left, and there were two musicians less in the contest.

Whenever Mattheson wrote an opera, he would sing the part of the hero while Handel conducted the orchestra. Then the orchestra leader did not conduct with a baton, but sat at the harpsichord, marking time by striking chords. In his opera "Cleopatra," Mattheson sang the role of Mark Antony. After Antony had died and so was no longer on the stage, Mattheson wanted to keep in the public eye and tried to oust Handel from his place at the harpsichord.

Handel refused to give it up. They quarrelled, and on the way out of the theater, Mattheson boxed Handel's ears. In an instant, both hot-headed youths had drawn swords—which all gentlemen always wore. They began to duel in the market place before an interested crowd. They lunged at each other and at last Mattheson hit. Fortunately, Handel followed the fashion and wore buttons as big as butter-plates upon his gay colored coat. The sword broke on one of these. The shock brought them both to their senses, and they became better friends than ever before.

Handel's own first operas were produced in Hamburg with great success. For three years, he composed and taught and played—and saved his money. He not only managed to pay back what he had borrowed from his mother, but scraped to gether enough to take him on his longed-for trip to Italy.

BEGINNING OF OPERA

All musicians longed to visit Italy and win fame there. Italy has often been called the "cradle of music." Here church music grew to its greatest heights with Palestrina, and here opera was born. In the old city of Florence with its dark towers and stepped streets, bloody wars and great artists, there was a group of noblemen who were interested in the arts of the ancient Greeks. They read about the old Greek drama, with the music of the chorus to help express the feeling of the words. The only music with a play that they knew was the chorus, or musical interlude, which sometimes was used between the different parts of the mystery and miracle plays given near the churches on holy days. These noblemen decided to bring Greek drama to life again. They began to set old Greek stories to music and give them in costume at some gay carnival or the wedding of a fair duchess.

These first operas seemed very queer because the whole story was sung by a chorus, instead of having the part of each character taken by a separate singer. It was hard for anyone then to imagine music different from the polyphonic music of the church choirs. If the god Orpheus was mourning for the loss of his bride snatched away by the king of darkness, his sorrow would be sung by a chorus of twenty.

SOLO, RECITATIVE AND ARIA

At last, someone had the idea of having the part of each character in the story taken by a single singer, and in between the chorus numbers, he or she would sing *solo*, or alone. When the speech of the character was soft and gentle, the words would be half sung, half spoken. This sort of singing, almost like a chant, was, and still is, called *recitative*. Stronger feeling was expressed by a real melody called an *aria* or air.

EARLY USES OF ARIA

After awhile, the aria became used not so much to express feeling as to show off a singer's fine voice. There was the aria in which the singer could, at certain places, put in trills and turns of his own, not written by the composer, who was not considered nearly as important as a singer, anyway. There were arias full of runs and high notes written especially to show all the singer's tricks, and there were arias to imitate birds or hunting calls, with accompaniment by flute or horn. No one singer could have two arias in succession, and the only time there was any chorus or ensemble singing was at the end of each act when it was a rule that all the characters had to be on the stage together. It is no wonder that the stories of the operas never had a chance to be anything but silly and dull. That is why none of the old operas is ever performed today, though many of the finest arias, such as Handel's "Largo," from the opera "Xerxes" (Zerk-sees), are well-loved concert pieces.

FAME OF ITALIAN MUSICIANS

In addition, no matter whether an opera were given in Italy, England, or Germany, the aria was always in Italian while the recitative parts were in the language of the country. The reason was that the most important and highly paid singers were Italian. Native singers simply did not have a chance. A German Emperor even said that he would as soon hear a horse neigh as a German prima donna sing. The great fame of Italian singers has lasted through the years, and in our own country today there are young singers who think they will win greater success if they give themselves Italian names.

Italian teachers were the first to develop ways of training the voice, and these early methods have never been bettered. There are many interesting stories of famous old singing masters and their pupils. The famous singing teacher, Porpora, once had a pupil to whom he gave a sheet of exercises and kept him at them a year. At the end of the year, the pupil asked, "When may I sing?" "Not yet," was the answer, and the poor pupil was made to toil over the same exercise sheet. At the end of the second year came the same question and the same reply. The third year passed, and at last came the despairing question, "Can I ever sing?" and the reply, "You are already the greatest singer in Italy."

HANDEL IN ITALY

This was the Italy, the leader in opera and song, where young Handel went to seek learning and win fame. His operas were produced in the greatest opera houses of the land along with those of Italy's own most famous composer of opera, Alexander Scarlatti (Scar-láht-tee). Everywhere audiences applauded wildly and cried again and again, "Long live the dear Saxon!" A contest was arranged between Handel and Scarlatti's son, Domenico, who was the foremost harpsichordist of his time. It was called a draw at the harpsichord, but Handel was declared winner at the organ. Domenico Scarlatti's music for harpsichord shows how the influence of the opera changed even instrumental music. Instead of being written in counterpoint like most of Bach's music for harpsichord and clavichord, it has one principal part with many runs and trills like an operatic aria. It was Domenico Scarlatti who first introduced cross-hand passages in harpsichord playing, but gave them up later in life when years and good living had made it hard for him to bring his hands across his ample front!

In every city, Handel was given honors by all the music societies, even though he was not old enough to be a regular member. Every visitor to Italy took back home tales of the brilliant young Saxon musician. When at last he left Italy, it was to go to a fine position as director of music to the Elector of Hanover. Hanover was a rich city in the fertile Saxon plain, and its Elector could afford to support at his own expense one of the finest theatres and opera houses in Europe. He paid Handel as his musical director a salary more than twenty times greater than the beggarly bit poor young Bach was receiving as church organist in a country town.

SUCCESS OF FIRST ENGLISH VISIT

Soon Handel was invited to appear in England, and obtained leave of absence to go. England's great composer, Henry Purcell, had been dead for fifteen years, and no one had come to take his place. Italian opera was beginning to be the fashion, and all the lords and ladies were wild to hear the young man who had won such fame in Italy. They thronged to his organ and harpsichord concerts. He was commissioned to write a new opera and composed the music in two weeks, working so fast that the poor poet who was supplying the words could hardly keep up with him. The opera was staged with the greatest luxury. There were even live birds in the garden scenes. A march contained in the opera became the official march of the Life Guards, and the most famous arias were played on every harpsichord in England.

COMPOSER AND PUBLISHER

At that time, a composer had no rights to the publication of his work. Any printer might publish and sell it without paying the composer a penny for the privilege. All the composer could do was to have more copies printed to sell for his own benefit with perhaps new songs or better accompaniments. A printer named Walsh published this opera of Handel's and made fifteen hundred pounds (about $6500). Whereupon Handel said to him, "Next time you can write the opera, and I will publish it."

When at last the time came for Handel to go to his duties with the Elector of Hanover, even Queen Anne herself begged him to come back to England as soon as he could. He spent a quiet year in Hanover, but so many pressing invitations came from London that he asked the Elector for a second leave of absence. It was granted "on condition that he return within a reasonable time."

He stayed the rest of his life.

The pleasant weeks stretched out into months, and the months into years. He knew that nowhere else in the world could he find such honors and such friends. He was commissioned to write celebration music for great state occasions, such as the Queen's birthday. One of his closest friends was the rich and powerful Lord Burlington, who had just built a fine palace in the midst of the green wood and meadow land outside the gray city of London. He liked to have as his guests the poets and wits and writers, and all the most brilliant men of the country, and he asked Handel to live with him.

It was a happy life at Burlington House and Handel was free to do as he pleased with his time. Every morning he had peace and quiet for his work. At noon, he would meet the lord and his guests in the banquet hall for a fine hearty dinner of England's roast beef or mutton or goose with the sauce of much mirth and good cheer. In the afternoon, it was pleasant to walk into London and practice on the excellent organ at St. Paul's Cathedral. In the evening, if there was no opera, he would often present a harpsichord concert at Burlington House, of which one of the lord's poet-guests wrote:

"There Handel strikes the strings; the melting strain Transports the soul and thrills through every vein."

Then, two years after Handel's arrival in England, Queen Anne died, and who should succeed her as King George I but Handel's old master, the Elector of Hanover. Handel remembered the leave of absence long overstayed, and feared the new King's wrath. He kept in hiding at Burlington House, not daring to show his face at court or in the city. At last, a friend thought of a scheme to bring Handel to the King's favor once more.

THE "WATER" MUSIC

The King was planning a water picnic on the river Thames. The royal barge, attended by many other barges, filled with lords and ladies in bright satins and laces under gay awnings, floated slowly on the silver waters between green leafy banks. Suddenly an unknown barge mingled with the others. It was filled with musicians playing the most entrancing music.

The King was charmed and had the music played over three times. He asked the name of the composer, and when he found that it was his old servant, Handel, he commanded Handel to come before him. Then he praised the music and not only forgave Handel, but gave him a pension of $1000 a year.

Handel's "Water Music," as it is called, is often heard in symphony concerts today.

HOMOPHONIC MUSIC

Handel's music sounds much more modern to us than Bach's because it is mostly in the new *homophonic* (one-voiced) style brought in by the opera—that is, single outstanding melody with accompaniment—rather than the older polyphonic style founded on the interwoven voices of the great church choirs. Just as the great test of musicianship in polyphonic music was a fugue, the form of homophonic music which musicians used to show their skill was the *theme with variations*. Bach excited the interest of Frederick the Great by taking a theme and weaving it into a six-voiced fugue. The masters of homophonic music would take a theme or musical sentence, and give it quite simply at first. Then they would show it in all sorts of different forms with various accompaniments, major and minor, slow and fast, merry and sad, and ornamented with all kinds of runs and trills. Some musicians made as many as a hundred variations on one theme—which may have been good sport for the composer but rather dull for the listener after the forty-ninth variation.

THEME WITH VARIATIONS

However, if a theme were given just enough variations to show off its beauty, it could make a very lovely piece of music, and one of the loveliest is that by Handel known as "The Harmonious Blacksmith." The story was that one day as

Handel was taking a walk through an English village, he passed a smithy where the blacksmith was singing lustily in time to the beat of his hammer on the anvil. The simple tune so pleased Handel that he made it the theme for a set of variations. It is a disappointment to learn that there is no truth in the story, and that the name was given to the piece by a music publisher after Handel's death.

However, the melody had a sturdy English folk swing as if Handel might indeed had picked it up on one of his country rambles. He often used bits of songs and street cries that he heard. In writing his many operas, he also often borrowed bits from his own earlier work or even the work of other composers. For this reason, he has sometimes been called the "grand old robber."

But customs were different then. Just as it was considered quite all right for a printer to publish a work without paying a cent to the composer, it was proper enough for a musician to use another's themes as long as he set them to different words or accompaniment and did not simply copy. Wherever Handel borrowed, he also improved. Once, when accused of taking a theme from another musician, he said, "Bah! that pig doesn't know what to do with a good tune."

HANDEL AND OPERA IN LONDON

Most of Handel's life was devoted to the opera. It brought him success, and it also brought him ruin. In Italy, opera was the music of the people. In the opera houses of the Italian cities, the nobles might sit in the gilded boxes, but the poor man might go without bread to scrape together pennies enough to get through the door and stand during a glorious evening of song. He would carry the songs away in his heart and sing them over his work in the streets or the fields. Love and joy and sorrow—every feeling he found expressed in the opera, and opera was truly the folk music of the Italian people.

In England, opera was simply an expensive plaything of wealthy people. They enjoyed making singers and composers contest with each other, as they enjoyed horse races and cock-fights. First, there was a London opera company for which Handel and the old Italian Bononcini, who had treated him so jealously as a boy in Berlin, were engaged as rival conductors. Each conducted his operas on alternate nights to the wild applause of his friends and the hisses of his enemies. At last, the supporters of both arranged a contest in which the two musicians were to write an opera together, Handel doing one act and Bononcini another, while the third act was finished by a different composer. Handel was declared the winner. After awhile the whole company disbanded in bickering and bankruptcy.

THE RIVAL OPERA COMPANIES

Bononcini's followers backed him in an opera company of his own while Handel started an opera company, too. A city which would not give steady support to one opera company could hardly afford two. Both companies were forever failing and beginning anew. After Bononcini had fled from England in disgrace (he had tried to palm off another's composition, word for word, and note for note, as his own), his place was taken by the famous singing master, Porpora.

Handel's companies were always disbanding in failure while he would dash off to Europe to gather more celebrated singers to make a brave new start. It was when he was on two of these hurried trips that Bach tried so hard to meet him. The first time, Bach journeyed to Dresden and arrived just after Handel had gone. The second time, he was too ill to travel and sent his son, Wilhelm Friedmann, to invite Handel to visit him at Leipzig, but Handel could not spare the time. And so the two greatest musicians of their age never met.

TROUBLE WITH SINGERS

Handel had as much trouble with his singers as with his rivals. They all thought that a composer existed only to furnish music to show off their voices. If they did not like his arias, they would simply refuse to sing until he had put in enough trills and high notes to suit them. Most composers meekly let the singers give them orders, but not Handel. When one day at rehearsal a prima donna refused to sing an aria unless he rewrote it, he carried her to a window and held her out, saying, "Madame, you will sing this just as I have written it or I will drop you."

This temperamental lady, Francesca Cuzzoni, and another called Faustina, were Handel's singing stars, and they fought like a couple of cats. Like all opera singers of that day, they were the spoiled darlings of the courtiers, and each prima donna had her followers who thronged the opera hoping to hear their pet out-sing the other. If either thought the other was getting more high notes, woe be unto poor Handel! When they had a duet, he had one repeat the same phrase after the other so that there would be no reason for jealousy. Even so, the two ladies carried their quarrels to the stage one night, pulling hair, boxing ears, and breaking up the performance.

Such a happening, of course, would delight Handel's enemies. They were getting ever more vicious and violent because the rival opera companies were simply used as a way of working off old grudges. If the King and Prince of Wales quarrelled, each would support a different opera company. Opera even got into politics. In one election, the Whigs supported Handel and the Tories the other company.

FAILURE

At last, his enemies began to give balls, dinners, and card parties on the same nights as his operas to keep the nobles from attending. It was well known that Handel loved good living, and a cartoon was published, showing him as a fat hog sitting on a beer barrel and playing an organ hung with sausages, ham and fowl. In short, they did everything they could to ruin him, and they succeeded. He went bankrupt. The husband of one of his singers threatened to have him thrown into debtor's prison. His mind gave way, and his left side and arm became paralyzed so that he could no longer play. He fled to France to the healing baths at Aix-la-Chapelle, a weary, broken old man.

THE STRUGGLE RENEWED

Anyone else might have given up the struggle, but not our grand old fighter. At the end of six weeks, he was already thinking of going back to England to start again. But he had already decided that if he were ever to gain back his fortune, it would not be with opera, but oratorio.

BEGINNING OF ORATORIO

Many years before—in about the time of Palestrina—good St. Philip Neri (Neh-ree) had wanted to make the young people of his church more interested in the stories of the saints and great men of God. So each week he would present some Bible story set to music in the chapel or oratory, as it was called, and thus this form of music became known as oratorio. If the words of the different characters in the story were sung by different singers, as in a play, it was called dramatic oratorio. If the singers just told the story, it was called lyric oratorio.

In the early years of Handel's long life in England, Handel had held the position of chapel-master to the rich Duke of Chandos, "who loved ever to worship God with the best of everything." Every Sunday he would ride to church attended by a hundred Swiss guards. The road would be thronged with the carriages of lords and ladies come in to worship with him in the magnificence of his richly decorated chapel. He had a beautiful organ and a fine orchestra and choir, and it was for him that Handel wrote his first oratorio on the Biblical story "Esther."

NEW SUCCESS WITH ORATORIO

Later he had "Esther" and several newer oratorios performed. They had often drawn immense crowds in spite of attacks by his enemies who claimed that it was sinful to present religious subjects in a theater. Now he felt that he would be more likely to succeed with oratorio than opera for several reasons. First, as there was no action and so no need for costumes and scenery, it was less expensive to produce than opera. Second, as the oratorio was planned in the beginning to let as many as possible share in the worship of God, the music for great massed chorus was more important than that for solo singers. Finally, as there did not have to be any Italian aria, all the words could be in English and understood by all the people.

Little by little, he began to succeed. His friends were warmer and his enemies less spiteful. Perhaps they all admired his courage in starting again in spite of almost overwhelming debt and discouragement. Perhaps, too, as the rival opera company had also failed, he offered the only musical entertainment in London. His concerts—especially those at which he himself would play upon the organ or harpsichord—began to be better attended.

"THE MESSIAH"

Then a good friend, who was a poet, showed Handel some verses which he had selected from the Bible for an oratorio to be called "The Messiah." This was composed of all the noblest verses referring to the coming and life of Christ. Handel composed the music as an act in the worship of God. He worked at a white heat of religious feeling, finishing this great oratorio in just twenty-two days. As he was writing the music for the sad words, "He was despised and rejected of men," a servant found him weeping over his work. And as he reached the grandeur of the "Hallelujah Chorus," he said, "Methinks I did see all heaven before me, and the great God himself."

VISIT TO IRELAND

Handel had been invited to visit Ireland and give concerts in Dublin. He decided to give "The Messiah" its first performance for the benefit of the charities of "that generous and polite nation." The days in Ireland were among the happiest of his life. The whole country was friendly and loved his music. His concerts were crowded, and he made a good sum of money to help pay his London debts. But the crowning triumph was "The Messiah," at which the principal singers as well as Handel were to give their share of the proceeds to charity. So many people attended that special traffic regulations were made for the sedan-chairs in which they were carried to the concert hall. And the ladies were requested to come without the hoops in their skirts so that they would not take up so much room! (The hall was said to hold five hundred ladies with hoops or seven hundred without.)

"THE MESSIAH" IN LONDON

"The Messiah" was as great a success in London. All the nobility was present, even the royalty. During the "Hallelujah Chorus," the King, in his enthusiasm, rose to his feet. When a king stands, everyone else in the room must stand, too. So the whole audience rose, and ever since that time it has been the custom for audiences to stand during the singing of the "Hallelujah Chorus."

No other oratorio has ever been so well loved or so often sung as "The Messiah." It is still the favorite of singing so-

cieties in every town in England and America, especially at
Christmas. Though it was the greatest success of Handel's
life, he looked upon it as a gift to God and turned over to
charity every cent he made from it—even at a time when he
sorely needed money to pay his debts. When a nobleman
complimented him on the "noble entertainment" of "The
Messiah," he answered, "I should be sorry if I have only entertained; I hoped to make men better."

EASIER TIMES

Easier times came with "The Messiah." He no longer de-
pended on the support of the fickle nobility. Instead of selling tickets only in advance by subscription to lords and ladies,
he had them sold at the door to all who would come. The
common people took his music to their hearts. Since then
oratorio has always been one of the favorite musical forms of
the English, and Handel their best loved composer. Those who
listened on the radio to the funeral services of King George V
of England heard him borne to rest to the grandly solemn
strains of the "Dead March" from Handel's oratorio, "Saul."

HANDEL'S GENEROSITY

Now Handel was able not only to pay off his debts, but
also to make a comfortable fortune. The kindest-hearted of
men, he sent generous sums of money both to his own family
and to that of his old music teacher back in Halle and gave
freely to London charities. He also educated a young lad,
Christopher Smith, the son of an old college friend.

BLINDNESS

Like Bach, Handel became blind in his old age. When he
knew that he would never see again, he lost courage for
the first time in his life. But he soon regained his old fighting
spirit and sent for young Christopher Smith who cared for

him as tenderly as a true son. He kept on with his concerts and had Smith conduct and play his organ compositions in his place. Later, he learned to play from memory or make new music at the organ on the spur of the moment—to improvise, as they called it. In his oratorio "Samson" from the story of the Biblical hero who, after his great strength is shorn away with his hair by the treacherous Delilah, is blinded by his enemies, occurs the verse,

> "Total eclipse—no sun, no moon,
> All dark amidst the blaze of noon."

At these words, the sight of the blind old composer waiting to be led to the organ would bring tears to the eyes of the audience.

FAME AFTER DEATH

He died in 1759—eight years after Bach—leaving a goodly sum to relatives, friends, and charities, and his harpsichord and music manuscripts to the devoted Christopher Smith. Smith would not sell them for any amount of money, not even when the King of Prussia offered him a small fortune for them. But toward the end of his life, he gave them to the King of England so that they might be preserved in Buckingham Palace forever. Thus, during the years that Bach's manuscripts lay forgotten in dusty cupboards or were torn up for lunch wrappings, Handel's were guarded like treasures in the palace of a king.

RECORD LIST — CHAPTER IV

Handel, George Frederick (1685-1759)
　　　　Arias — various
　　　　Concerti Grossi, Op. 6 — excerpts
　　　　Harmonious Blacksmith (harpsichord)
　　　　Messiah — excerpts
　　　　Royal Fireworks Music

Semele — excerpts
Sonatas for Flute and Harpsichord — various
Suites for Harpsichord Nos. 2 and 11
Water Music Suite

Scarlatti, Domenico (1685-1757)
Keyboard Sonatas — various
Violin Sonatas — various

CHAPTER V

HAYDN

CHILDHOOD HOME

In 1732 while Bach was drudging away at St. Thomas's School and Handel was in London struggling with his Italian opera singers, another great musician was born. He was Franz Joseph Haydn (Hý-dn), the son of a carriage maker and a cook, in Ruhrau (Róor-ow), a little Austrian market town. Their home was a low thatched-roof cottage, and they were humble people with no money or education. Yet they loved music. The father could play the harp by ear and had a fine tenor voice. Every evening when the day's work was done, he would gather his family around him to sing old folksongs. Little Joseph would saw away with one stick upon another, pretending to play the violin.

One day a distant relative named Frankh, a school teacher and choirmaster in a nearby town, noticed that the little boy kept perfect time. He offered to take the child and teach him music. It was too good a chance to miss, much as his parents must have disliked the idea of sending such a little boy away from home. Six-year old Joseph must have had many miserable hours. Frankh was a harsh man with a vicious temper, and Haydn later said that Frankh gave him more beatings than gingerbread.

But he also said, "I shall be grateful to Frankh as long as I live for keeping me so hard at work."

Frankh was, at least, a conscientious man and kept his

promise to Haydn's parents by spending many hours knocking music into his young pupil. At the end of two years, Joseph was a skillful violinist and harpsichordist and could sing a mass with the choir. Then Reutter (Roy-ter), the choirmaster at great St. Stephen's Cathedral in Vienna, made a tour of the towns round about in search of new voices for the choir. Eight-year old Joseph sang the test piece so well that Reutter cried, "Bravo!" and threw a handful of cherries into the boy's cap.

THE CHOIR SCHOOL

When Reutter returned to Vienna, he took Joseph with him to enter the choir school and sing in the great cathedral with its roof of colored tiles and great columns adorned with many little statues of the saints. The school was much like St. Thomas's in Leipzig. There was so little money for the school that the boys often were cold and hungry. Besides furnishing music for the cathedral, the boys had to sing in street processions to celebrate holy days and royal birthdays.

The boys were supposed to be taught Latin and the regular school subjects, besides singing, violin, and harpsichord. But Reutter was no Bach. Not only was he as hard and cruel as Frankh, but he was also lazy. In later days, Haydn could remember having had only two lessons from Reutter in nine years. All that he learned, he had to pick up by himself. He begged his father for money for books, and although there was hardly money enough for food in the little thatched-roof cottage, his father sent enough for the two books he wanted most.

"By hard work, I managed to get on," he said. "I was industrious when my companions were at play. I used to take my little clavier under my arm and go off to practice undisturbed. Whenever I sang a solo, the baker near St. Stephen's always gave me a cake."

Some have said that Reutter was jealous for fear young Haydn would grow up to be a rival. At any rate, whenever the boy would get a scrap of paper and try to write music, Reutter would jeer and laugh at him. The great Empress, too, took a grudge against the fun-loving lad because of a boyish prank one day when the choir was to sing at the palace. At the first sign of a change in his voice, she declared, "Young Haydn sings like a crow."

His place as soloist was now given to his younger brother Michael who was now also in the choir school. Yet even after his voice broke, he might have found some sort of work as accompanist, as Bach did at Lüneberg, but for a bit of mischief. In these days, if a man did not wear a wig, he wore his hair in a neat little pigtail. One day young Joseph came to rehearsal with a new pair of scissors. The temptation was too great. Snip! went the pigtail of the singer in front of him, and out was thrown young Haydn, after a severe flogging, into the cold wintry streets of Vienna.

HARD TIMES

Seventeen years old, hungry, broken-voiced, without a penny in his pocket or any way of earning one, he wandered along in search of a friendly face. Of course, he would have found a warm welcome at home, but he knew the low cottage was now overcrowded with younger children. Besides, to go back to the country town would mean giving up his hope of writing music. So he trudged on for weary hours until at last he met an acquaintance, a poor tenor singer in the church of St. Michael's. Although this good man earned hardly enough to support his wife and child, he took the young man home to his bare little attic, and there Haydn stayed all through the winter.

He did anything he could to earn a penny. He copied and arranged music for anyone who wished, and played at balls, weddings, baptisms, and even street serenades, often composing the music especially for the occasion. Little by little, the struggling young musician began to be noticed. A kind merchant lent him enough money so that he could afford to move into an attic of his own. Thus, he no longer had to be a burden to his poor friends, and had a place where he could work away from the world, with his battered old clavichord, paper and pen.

In the great houses of Vienna, princes and nobles lived in luxurious apartments on the first floors, merchants and successful poets and singers lived above them, and up under the roof dwelt cooks, footmen, and struggling musicians. Haydn's tiny attic room was dark and cold, and plenty of rain leaked through the roof to drench him in his bed. However, the great court poet Metastasio (Me-tah-stah'-zee-o) lived in comfort on the third floor, and somehow the two met.

HAYDN AND PORPORA

Metastasio found him some rich pupils, and introduced him to the fashionable Italian singing-master, Porpora, the same who had been Handel's rival in London. Porpora made Haydn his accompanist and valet, and took him wherever he went to the estates of noblemen. Besides playing the harpsichord at concerts and lessons, Haydn had to black his master's boots, brush his coat, trim his wig, run his errands, and eat at the servants' table. In return, Porpora paid him six ducats a month and taught him singing, composition, and Italian.

Being with Porpora helped him to become known. He got more music lessons at better prices, and was often engaged to conduct a concert and compose music for some count or baron. At last he became director of music for a Bohemian baron who kept an eighteen-piece orchestra. This nobleman had a rule that none of his musicians should marry. Yet that is just what Haydn proceeded to do.

MARRIAGE

He fell in love with the younger daughter of a wigmaker named Keller, but she was very religious, and became a nun. So the old wigmaker said, "Well, my lad, if you can't have one daughter, why don't you take the other?"

Haydn, with his usual good nature, agreed, and married Anna Maria Keller, who was some years older than he. It was a bad bargain. She was extravagant and a great scold, and thought so little of his music that she used to tear up his manuscripts to use for curl-papers. Fortunately, his marriage did not throw him out of a position, for just then he was offered a much better place as assistant musical director to Prince Anton Esterhazy (Es-ter-haht-zee).

ESTERHAZ

The Esterhazy princes were very rich and powerful. They had control over twenty-one castles, sixty market-towns where peasants and merchants brought their goods to buy and sell, and 414 villages. They loved music and kept an orchestra, chorus, and solo singers. Of course, in those days, a musician was a servant just as much as a valet, cook, or footman. Haydn had to eat at the servants' table and sign a long list of rules, some of which were; to be inoffensive and mannerly in eating, drinking, and conversation; to appear daily, before and after midday, to ask whether His Highness wished to order a performance of the orchestra; and to see to it that he and all members of his orchestra appeared in uniform with white stockings, white linen, and either a tie-wig or powdered hair with pigtail.

Yet he was well paid and well treated, and always had a fine orchestra ready to try out his compositions. After a few years, Prince Anton died. He was succeeded by Prince Nicolas, and Haydn was promoted to the position of director of music. Prince Nicolas Esterhazy was a master after Haydn's own heart, a gay soul, fond of pomp and splendor. He loved to wear a uniform aglitter with diamonds, and he dressed his orchestra in scarlet and gold. He built a new palace with summer-houses and conservatories, and two little theatres, one for operas and plays and the other for shows by marionettes or puppets. The grounds were laid out with flower gardens and deer park, groves, and little caves.

Here he was host to kings and queens and princes and princesses, and the greatest personages in all Europe. It was Haydn's duty to compose and direct music for their entertainment. One of the reasons why Haydn's operas have not lived is that they were mostly written for the tiny theatre at Esterhaz, and sometimes even for the puppet theatre. On the other hand, Haydn did so much for the growth of form in orchestral music that he has been called the Father of Instrumental Music, and this was certainly because he forever had to create fresh musical delights for his fine orchestra to play for Prince Esterhazy's guests.

EMANUEL BACH'S SONATA

He took all the forms of homophonic music then in use, and wove them into something newer and better. We have seen how the set of dances called the *suite* was used for pleasure-music in the days of Sebastian Bach. Bach's most famous son, Philip Emanuel, and other composers of that time developed from the suite a new form called the *sonata* (so-náh-ta). The word came from *sonare* (so-náh-ray), the Latin verb *to sound*, and meant a composition to be sounded by instruments, to distinguish it from the cantata, from the Latin *cantare* (can-táh-ray), to sing, which was a composition to be sung. Emanuel Bach's sonata was a set of short pieces in the same key, a slow one following a lively one for the sake of variety, as in the suite, but they were not all dance forms like the parts of the suite.

RONDO

Another form used for gay and lively music was the *rondo*, which was really like ternary form with an extra theme or two. The first theme A is followed by a second, B, and then A again, as in ternary form. But the piece does not stop there. An entirely new theme is followed by A again so that the whole plan is A–B–A–C–A. One of the jolliest examples of this form is Haydn's "Gypsy Rondo."

SONATA FORM

Haydn's sonatas, which served as models for all later musicians, are in four parts called *movements*. The first, *allegro* or lively movement, is generally in the form developed by Haydn himself, which we call *sonata form*. In *sonata form*, as in ternary form, there are three sections, of course, played without break or pause. The first, called *exposition*, shows the main themes, usually two, the first bold and bright, and the second softer and gentler, rather like a man and a woman. Next, in the *development*, the composer puts his themes through all sorts of clever paces—tosses them from one instrument to another, rushes them along in double quick time, makes one accompaniment for the other—until they seem like circus performers in daring acts and dazzling dress. Last of all, in the recapitulation, they appear to say good-bye as their simple, natural selves once more.

The second, or slow movement of the sonata—an *andante*, *adagio*, or *largo*—is usually either in simple ternary form or else is a *theme with variations*. Next comes the graceful minuet, the only surviving part of the ancient *suite*, and the sonata closes with a gay movement in *rondo* form.

CHAMBER MUSIC AND SYMPHONY

When Prince Esterhazy had only a few guests, he entertained them in one of the drawing-rooms glittering with gold and mirrors, instead of opening his great concert hall. Perhaps Haydn himself would play a new sonata for harpsichord or piano, or with another musician would present a violin sonata. Or perhaps there would be a sonata for three instruments, called a *trio*, or for four—two violins, viola, and cello— called a *string quartet*. Since that time, music written for only a few instruments and more suited for performance in a room than in a large hall has been called *chamber music*. More often, the concert hall was filled to hear a new symphony by the Prince's famous music director and orchestra. *Symphony* is simply the name for a sonata for orchestra.

ABSOLUTE AND PROGRAM MUSIC

Now that Haydn was the sober servant of a prince, all the fun in his nature had to be expressed in his music, and the prince enjoyed a musical joke as well as Haydn did. Music in his time was mostly what we call *absolute music*, which means that it was music for its own sake rather than to illustrate a story or idea like the later *program music*. Yet many of his symphonies and quartets have been given names because of some interesting story connected with them. Such an one is the "Farewell" Symphony.

PRINCE ESTERHAZY AT THE FAREWELL SYMPHONY

THE FAREWELL SYMPHONY

Beautiful as was the palace Esterhaz, the musicians always longed for the prince's return to Vienna where their families lived. Once the prince stayed on and on in the country until it seemed as if the poor musicians would never see their homes again. So Haydn composed a symphony in which the players, one by one, took their candles and tiptoed from the stage until there were only two violinists left in the dim, flickering light. The prince saw the joke, and the musicians had their vacation in Vienna.

For thirty years, Haydn served his prince. The beautiful music he made for his patron's noble guests made him famous all over the world. Kings and emperors presented him with gold medals, rings, and snuff-boxes set with brilliants, and he received invitations to present his music at the richest courts and in the greatest cities. Yet he always kept the simple, sunny nature which made his friends and fellow-musicians all call him "Papa Haydn." And he would not leave his prince, whom he adored, even for a short time.

At last, Prince Nicolas died, leaving a pension to his faithful Haydn. He was succeeded by Prince Anton, who did not care for music and disbanded the orchestra. At the age of fifty-eight, Haydn finally was free to go wherever he wished. Although some of his friends thought him too old to travel so far, he accepted an engagement to appear in London where Handel had had his great success.

THE "SURPRISE" SYMPHONY

In London, his works were received with wild applause, and he himself was entertained and dined by princes and nobles until his health began to suffer from rich food and excitement. He found, too, that the good Londoners' love of hearty dinners did not help their appreciation of music, for they had the sad habit of falling asleep during the slow movement of a symphony. Instead of being angry, Haydn planned a little joke. He wrote the famous "Surprise" symphony in which the slow movement opens very softly. Then, just as the people in the audience were settled for a nice nap, there was a crashing chord to wake them up again.

"That will make the ladies jump!" he said. Yet an English writer thought that the music represented a lovely shepherdess, lulled to sleep by the sound of a distant waterfall, who wakes in alarm at the sound of a gun! So we see that even in absolute music where there is no story, everyone may have the pleasure of making a story of his own to fit the music.

AUSTRIAN NATIONAL SONG

Haydn was deeply impressed with the English national anthem, "God Save the King" (our music for "America"). His own beloved country had no national song. Back in Vienna once more, he wrote the Austrian National Song, "God Love Our Emperor" in which he created one of the most beautiful tunes of any national song. It was sung for the first time on the Emperor's birthday, and he was so delighted that he sent Haydn a gold box with his portrait. Although Haydn wrote other larger and greater works, none gave him so much pleasure as the lovely little melody which became the song of his native land. He played it over every day as long as he lived.

Haydn made a second trip to London. Perhaps now he himself felt that he was getting old for the long journey by stage-coach over rocky roads and the little boat across the stormy English Channel, for he took with him a companion. This was Johann Elssler, son of a copyist of music for Prince Esterhazy, who served Haydn faithfully all his life, copying a good part of his music and caring for him tenderly in his old age. His second London visit was more triumphant than the first. "It is only in England," he wrote, "that one can make so much money in a single evening." He returned to Vienna not only with a comfortable fortune, but with such strange presents as a talking parrot and a dozen pairs of cotton stockings with the themes of his most important compositions woven into them.

HAYDN AND ORATORIO

For the English people, who loved the oratorio more than any form of music, he wrote his two great works, "The Creation" and "The Seasons." In these oratorios, the orchestra for the first time is used not only to accompany the voices, but to paint a picture of nature. These two oratorios became as well-loved as any of Handel's, except possibly "The Messiah," but the labor of composing them used up the last of his strength. With his devoted Elssler, he lived away from the world in his Viennese home, a feeble old man.

The last time he appeared in public was at a performance of the "Creation" arranged in honor of his seventy-sixth birthday. All the great musicians of the land were there. Prince Esterhazy sent his own carriage to bring Haydn to the hall, and as he was carried in an armchair to a seat among the princes and nobles, the whole audience rose. It was cold and drafty in the hall, and the ladies all around wrapped dear Papa Haydn in their dainty shawls and furs. At first, there was silence, but with the grandeur of the passage "And there was light," came a burst of applause.

"Not I, but a Power above created that!" the old man cried.

His friends saw that the excitement seemed to be too much for him and decided to take him home. All crowded around him, for they felt they might never see him again. As he was being carried out, he had his bearers stop a moment and turn him toward the orchestra. Then he raised his hand as if in blessing and a last farewell.

LAST DAYS

It was truly a last farewell. Napoleon's French army was bombarding Vienna, and a cannon-ball fell not far from Haydn's house. The old man soothed the frightened servants who were dressing him, saying, "Don't be afraid, my children. Nothing can hurt you while Haydn is here."

Although he had no fear, he was overcome with sadness at seeing his beloved city attacked and captured by the enemy. For the last time, he was carried to his piano. Gathering his servants around him, he played the Emperor's Hymn over three times with so much feeling that all were moved to tears. Five days later he died.

Record List — Chapter V

Bach, Carl Philipp Emanuel (1714-1788)
    Chromatic Fantasy
    Concerto in D for Orchestra
    Magnificat
    Symphony No. 1 in D
    Symphony No. 3 in C

Bach, Johann Christian (1735-1782)
    Concerto in F for Organ and Strings
    Sinfonia in B Flat
    Sonata in G for Two Pianos

Boccherini, Luigi (1743-1805)
    Cello Concerto in B Flat
    String Quartet in D, Op. 6, No. 1

Haydn, Franz Josef (1732-1809)
    The Creation
    The Seasons

String Quartet in C, Op. 76, No. 3 ("Emperor")
Symphony No. 45 in F Sharp Minor ("Farewell")
Symphony No. 92 in G ("Oxford")
Symphony No. 94 in G ("Surprise")
Symphony No. 104 in D ("London")
Trios for Flute and Strings, Op. 38
Trios for Violin, Cello, and Piano, Nos. 10, 16, 24

CHAPTER VI

MOZART

In 1756, young Haydn was still wandering hungrily through the gay and bustling streets of Vienna, seeking musical odd-jobs to earn his bread. At the same time, in the sleepy old cathedral town of Salzburg about 150 miles away, the Lord Archbishop's assistant musical director, Leopold Mozart, went about his tasks, sure of his daily bread, but probably just as sure that nothing exciting would ever happen to him. Yet that very year, he rejoiced in the birth of a little son to whom he gave the rather terrific name of Johann Chrysostom Sigismund Wolfgang Amadeus Mozart (Mote-zart), and the little baby with the big name was one of the most musical children ever to come into this world.

THE WONDER CHILD

He learned music as easily as other babies learn to talk. He had an older sister named Marianne. When Wolfgang was hardly old enough to walk, he would listen while Father Mozart gave a music lesson to little Marianne. Then he would toddle to the harpsichord and play the lesson over perfectly. By the time he was four years old, not only could he play the harpsichord, but he had begun to compose pretty little minuets, and even a concerto for orchestra.

Without anyone knowing about it, he got a little violin and learned to play it. One day when his father and three of his friends were playing a string quartet in the summer

house in the garden, little Wolfgang surprised them all by
playing the second violin part without a mistake. Then he
played the difficult first violin part as well.

The happy and excited father decided that he could no
longer keep his children hidden in the quiet gardens of Salzburg. Marianne was a very gifted child and little Wolfgang
no less than a wonder, and proud Father Mozart wanted
the whole world to see them. Besides, he felt that if his
little boy became famous while he was young, he might grow
up to find a better place than assistant director of chapel
music to a crusty old Archbishop.

FIRST MUSICAL JOURNEY

First, he took the two children to the musical German city
of Munich, where everyone went wild over them. Then he
thought what a fine thing it would be if they could have a
chance to play before the Emperor and Empress in the great
city of Vienna. So he got leave of absence from the Archbishop, and the little family started down the river Danube
by boat.

They stopped at every town to give concerts in the palaces
of nobles. At a monastery, the boy surprised the good monks
with his skill on the organ, an instrument he had never tried
before. At the custom-house in Vienna, he so charmed the
officials with his little violin that the Mozarts were let through
without delay. People who had heard the concerts they gave
on their way down river were talking everywhere about the
wonder-children. Soon they were invited to play at the homes
of dukes and princes, and at last came the longed-for command
to appear at the Emperor's palace.

The children played before the Emperor and Empress and
all their court. The little boy was put through all sorts of tests.
He played at sight a difficult concerto by the court composer
who turned the pages for him. He improvised beautifully on

one of its themes. He played with one finger and he played with the keyboard covered with a cloth. At last, the Emperor called him a little magician, and the Empress presented each child with a diamond ring, and gave Marianne a white silk dress and Wolfgang a little suit of lilac silk with broad gold borders.

MOZART AND MARIE ANTOINETTE

The Empress was charmed with the little boy because, when he was not at the keyboard, he was such a happy, natural child. He and Marianne were allowed to play with the Princesses Elizabeth and Marie Antoinette (who later became Queen of France and was beheaded during the French Revolution). As they were scampering about the great glittering rooms with vast waxed floors like lakes of ice, Wolfgang slipped and fell flat. When Princess Marie Antoinette kindly helped him to his feet again, he cried, "You are so good and kind. I will marry you when I grow up."

At last, the Mozarts returned to their quiet home at Salzburg with golden ducats, rich presents, and a fame that was spreading all over Europe. Father Mozart now thought the time was ripe to take the children out of the country into the great world, especially to Paris and London. The Archbishop once more gave leave of absence, and the modest chapelmaster and his little family set out on the most amazing tour in musical history.

FURTHER TRAVEL

For three years, they travelled by stage-coach and boat through Germany, France, England and Holland. They stopped and gave concerts wherever a duke or prince was holding court. Noble ladies petted the little boy so much that the father wrote to a friend that he wished they would give the child as many gold pieces as kisses. In Paris, a famous artist painted a picture of the two children and their father, and the

French Empress invited them to be present at a state dinner in the royal banquet hall where the table was set with gold and silver plate and canopied with embroidered silk and cloth of gold. In London, they appeared at the private fête (fate) of an earl where there were fifteen hundred guests and the gardens were lighted by ten thousand lamps. And an English critic wrote, "This child knows by instinct more music than many a chapel-master has learned in a life of study."

The "little man with his wig and little sword" as he was described by someone who saw him, was the rage everywhere. In England, the father was for a time so ill that he could not bear the sound of music, and the boy amused himself by composing symphonies. Later, in Holland when Wolfgang himself became ill, he had a board rigged up across the bed so that he could compose without losing time. Many of his compositions, dedicated to some duchess or queen, were published, and it is hard to believe them the work of a child. When the Mozarts finally returned to Salzburg, it was with enough lace, shawls, silks, gold snuff-boxes, rings, and other gifts to start a store, but very little money. All that they had made in their concerts was used up in travelling expenses.

After a year of quiet study in Salzburg, where one of the boy's teachers was Haydn's brother Michael, they went to Vienna once more. The Archduchess Maria Josepha was to be married to the King of Naples. There were to be all kinds of gay and grand festivities with kings, princes, and nobles from all over the world. Father Mozart hoped that the children would have a chance to play at many concerts.

Suddenly a smallpox epidemic scattered the princes and spoiled all the parties. At that time vaccination had not yet been discovered. All were seized, and many died, including the young bride in the palace. The Mozarts fled from the city, but both children were overtaken by the terrible disease, and for nine days Wolfgang was so ill that he was blind.

When he was well and the epidemic was over, they went back, but all changed. Everywhere there was mourning, and there were no concerts. Then, people were not as excited over the boy of twelve as they had been over the little child. The Emperor suggested that the boy write an opera, as opera was the most popular form of music in Vienna. He was promised a hundred ducats for its production. The other musicians of the city were wild.

"What!" they cried, "shall we see a great master conduct an opera one day, and on the next a twelve-year old child?"

JEALOUSY

It was the first instance of the jealousy that was always to keep Mozart from a position with a sure and comfortable income. There were plots and delays. The opera was never produced, and the Mozarts returned to Salzburg in disappointment for another quiet year of study. Wolfgang was appointed concert-master to the Archbishop's chapel, but without pay.

TOUR TO ITALY

His father soon saw that if the lad stayed in Salzburg long, he would be all too soon forgotten. Another tour was planned, this time to Italy. Italy was musically the most important country in the world. Every city had its own opera house. Italian operas, composers, and singers were in command all over the world, often driving out the work of native musicians. The father thought that if Wolfgang could win fame in Italy, his way in the world would be easy.

So father and son made a tour of the Italian cities. It was a triumph from start to finish. Rich ladies showered him with gifts. He was commissioned to write operas for the great opera house at Milan. In Naples, his playing so astonished the simple folk that they thought there must be magic in his diamond ring, and made him take it off. During Holy Week in Rome, the Mozarts went to the Sistine Chapel to hear a piece of sacred music which had been guarded so jealously by the choir that no copy had ever been allowed. Wolfgang went back to his room and wrote it out from memory.

"KNIGHT OF MUSIC"

The boy was put through all sorts of musical tests, and his father reported that he "did it all as easily as one eats a piece of bread." His greatest feat was to pass in a short half hour a severe examination that many established musicians failed to do at all and so to win his golden spur and the title "Knight of Music."

Not long after his return home, the Empress sent him back to Milan with the commission to write a wedding serenade for the marriage of her son to a princess there. Although it was written in twelve days, in a room with one violinist living above and another below, a singing teacher next door, and an oboist across the street, it was a great success. The Empress in her delight gave him a diamond-studded watch containing her portrait.

THE NEW ARCHBISHOP

Just then the old Archbishop of Salzburg died. The new Archbishop was a mean and cruel man, hated by all who knew him. When he rode through the streets on the way to take office, the townspeople stood in sullen silence. Once a thoughtless boy cheered at the grandeur of the procession and a tradesman soundly boxed his ears, saying, "Boy, you cheer while all the people weep."

For Mozart, the days of travel and triumphs were over, and the struggle for a living had begun. Mozart held the position of concert-master to the Archbishop and wrote much lovely music for the chapel. Yet the Archbishop would pay him only about $5.00 a month so that he still had to depend on his father for support. When Mozart wrote an opera for a carnival at the old German city of Munich, the Archbishop appeared and took all the applause and glory to himself because he had been so kind as to let his servant compose the work.

All requests for more pay were refused. Then the Mozarts asked for a leave of absence so that Wolfgang might look for a place with more pay and better treatment—perhaps such a position as Haydn had with Prince Esterhazy. The Archbishop said he did not wish to have the Mozarts "travelling about begging" while they were in his service and, after a quarrel, discharged both father and son. Wolfgang set out with his mother to seek a place in the world while the father and Marianne stayed behind giving music lessons to help pay for the costs of the journey.

Everywhere young Mozart received many honors and a few orders to compose pieces for special occasions, but no steady position. So he and his mother wandered from city to city. In the German city of Mannheim, he lingered. He had many friends there who ordered compositions and found pupils for him. There was a fine orchestra in which Mozart learned the use of the clarinet, thus getting the idea for his later "Clarinet" Symphony.

FIRST LOVE

Most important of all, there was an opera house where one of the prompters, Weber (Váy-ber), had four fair daughters. Mozart at once fell in love with Aloysia (A-lo-ees-ya), a fifteen year old girl with a beautiful soprano voice. Father Mozart was alarmed for fear his son would marry before he had found a good position. He wrote, urging the young man to try his luck in Paris. Like a dutiful son, Wolfgang said farewell to Aloysia and went on to Paris, disappointment, and sorrow.

The city that had gone wild over the child-wonder had

little interest in the young man. A mighty battle of music was raging between two different kinds of opera, and music lovers had no time or thought for anything else. On one side was the old Italian type of opera, such as Handel had written, which was just a collection of arias loosely strung together on some sort of story. The music of the song, of course, was not to express the feeling of the words, but to show the singer's voice in trills and runs and long-drawn-out high notes. On the other side was Gluck (Glook) with what he called his "classic" opera. Like the very first writers of opera, he believed that music, as in the drama of the ancient Greeks, should be used only to express the feeling of the words. He also believed that the orchestra should be used not only to accompany the singer, but to help paint a musical picture of the setting and the action. He even used all-Greek stories to set to music.

The champions of the two kinds of opera fought their battles with pamphlets and cartoons, and sometimes even duelled with pistol and sword. In the midst of the excitement, young Mozart was neglected. But he listened and learned a great deal so that his later operas combined the best points of both types, and his two masterpieces, "Don Giovanni" (Gee-o-váh-nee) and "The Marriage of Figaro" (Fée-gah-ro) are the earliest operas to be regularly performed today. However, he was no nearer earning a living than before. What is more, his mother died, and he was left alone far from his home.

SORROW, DISAPPOINTMENT AND RETURN

His father saw that there was no use in staying longer or journeying farther. He managed to make his peace with the Archbishop, and get his son the position of court organist. Wolfgang turned sadly homeward. He visited the Webers on the way and found that the fair but fickle Aloysia had changed her mind about him and now received him quite coldly.

QUARREL WITH ARCHBISHOP

It seemed as if the Archbishop had taken the young musician back only to make his life miserable. Mozart wrote a very successful opera which was even praised by the Emperor, but the more famous he became, the worse the Archbishop treated him. He made the now celebrated composer eat with his lowest servants. He made him play without pay at the homes of his friends and refused to let him play in the palaces of nobles where the young musician might have been rewarded richly. At last, after a bitter quarrel, the Archbishop discharged him and had the Chamberlain kick him through the door.

MARRIAGE

Mozart went to seek his fortune in the great city of Vienna. His old friends, the Webers, were there. Aloysia had become the highest paid singer in the Vienna Opera House, but she was now married to an actor named Lange. However, there were still three daughters. Mozart fell in love once more, this time with Aloysia's younger sister, the merry, dark-eyed Constance, who returned his love. Mozart's father objected to his marrying when he had no steady income. Constance's guardian refused to let him see her unless he signed a paper promising to marry her—a paper which Constance promptly tore up saying, "Dear Mozart, I need no written promise, I believe your word." But after many troubles, they were married at last, and a day later a letter came with Father Mozart's blessing.

Like a story-book couple, they were happy with each other through good times and bad. Constance had the knack of telling amusing stories like the princess in "Arabian Nights," and she never lost her gay heart in poverty or ill health. She could manage admirably when there was anything to manage. Too often Mozart would lend or give all that he had to any stranger who seemed in need.

Mozart was one of the first musicians to scratch out a living without having a church or court position—and a poor and uncertain living it was! He gave music lessons whenever he could get a pupil. He held weekly concerts of chamber music in his rooms for which season or subscription tickets were sold. For these concerts, he composed some of the loveliest sonatas and quartets and trios that have ever been written. At other times, he would hire a hall and an orchestra and present his newest symphony to the lords and ladies of Vienna who eagerly subscribed for tickets.

MOZART'S OPERAS

His operas brought him the greatest success. From his stay in Paris, he had learned to combine the best of the Italian and "classic" opera of Gluck. He wrote lovely melodies to show off the voices of the singers and please the ears of the audience. He also made these melodies fit the feeling expressed in the words and even describe the characters of the different people in the story. For example, a love song of the gay, shrewd barber, Figaro, wooing the Countess's maid, Susannah, would be quite different from that of the wicked Don Giovanni who murdered the father of a lady he had deserted and in the end was dragged shrieking into the next world by the old man's statue.

THE OVERTURE

Most important of all were the changes and improvements he made in the overture, or introduction by the orchestra, played before every opera. In Handel's time, the overture was simply some lively music, usually a set of dance pieces, played to keep the audience from getting too restless while waiting for the curtain to rise. Mozart wove his themes of the chief songs and scenes cleverly together—the gay contrasting with the sad—and made almost a little story in music of the whole opera to come. All later composers used Mozart's overtures as models. Not only are his two greatest operas, "Don Giovanni" and "The Marriage of Figaro," performed by all opera companies today, but his overtures are favorite concertpieces of our symphony orchestras.

With all his music lessons and the work of composing and arranging concerts, he was always in a great rush. The day before his opera, "Don Giovanni," was performed, he had not yet written the overture. He worked all night while Constance told him amusing stories and refreshed him with home-made punch. The completed score was hurried to the orchestra with hardly a minute to spare, and they had to play it at sight without rehearsal.

"MARRIAGE OF FIGARO"

Perhaps the greatest success of his life was the first performance of his "Marriage of Figaro." One of the singers wrote, "Never was anything more complete than that triumph. The overflowing audience cried, 'Bravo! Bravo! Maestro!' And Mozart? Never shall I forget his little face lighted up with the glowing rays of genius. It is as impossible to describe as it would be to paint sunbeams." There was so much applause that the Emperor had to forbid encores or the opera would not have come to an end all night.

Still, successful operas could not be written every day, and in between were long, lean weeks. Sometimes friends had to help, or he and Constance would have starved. Once, the landlord came in and found them dancing to keep warm because they had no money to buy firewood. All Mozart's beautiful music never brought him a good court position which would have saved him from worry and kept him from ruining his health from overwork. The reason was the jealousy of the other musicians who were afraid that if they ever gave him a chance, he would get ahead of them all.

MOZART AND SALIERI

His greatest enemy was the director of court music to the Emperor, a handsome Italian named Salieri (Sahl-yáy-ree) who was a learned musician, but not a great composer. He was a great favorite with the Emperor, and used all his influence to keep Mozart down. Even when Mozart was recommended as music teacher to the Princess Elizabeth, Salieri saw to it that the place was given to someone else.

MOZART AND HAYDN

Mozart's only true friend among all the musicians was the greatest of them all, good old Papa Haydn. He was too busy with his own duties at the Esterhazy estate to be of much help. When he was in Vienna, however, he often used to play the violin in the chamber music concerts Mozart held in his rooms. It was at one of these that he said to Mozart's father, "I tell you honestly that I acknowledge your son to be the greatest composer I have ever heard."

Mozart's symphonies were more perfect in form than those Haydn wrote at Esterhaz and far richer in the use of different instruments. Haydn's symphonies were written for an orchestra of mostly strings, such as he had at Esterhaz, while Mozart led the way in the use of woodwinds, especially clarinets. Instead of being jealous, Haydn admired Mozart's work greatly, and his own later London symphonies show how much he learned from the younger musician.

Mozart loved the older man dearly and when Haydn was about to go to London said, "Ah! Papa, you are too old to go out into the world and you know too few languages."

"My language (music) is understood by all the world," Haydn answered.

Still, Mozart said farewell with tears in his eyes, saying that he felt they would never meet again. His fears came true.

Haydn returned safely from London, but he found that his young friend had died.

Mozart, already ill, was working on his last opera, "The Magic Flute," when one day a stranger appeared. He was tall and gaunt and all in gray. He said that he came for a mysterious patron who wanted a requiem mass written as a memorial to his wife. In his illness, poor Mozart felt that the stranger was a messenger of death from another world and the mass was for his own funeral. Later the mystery was made clear. The stranger turned out to be the servant of a rich and rascally count who liked to buy compositions of great composers and pass them off as his own. But Mozart never knew. He died in the midst of writing the mass, and it had to be finished from his notes by one of his pupils.

Salieri remarked, "It is well for the rest of us that he is dead. If he had lived longer, no one would have given us a crust of bread for our compositions."

Constance was too ill to go to the funeral. A violent thunderstorm drove all the mourners back at the cemetery gate. Mozart was placed in a common grave, with some other poor victims of a plague in Vienna, and his burial place has never been found.

Though Mozart was only thirty-six when he died, he had composed some of the loveliest melodies in the world, and was also a master of the difficult old-school counterpoint. His "Magic Flute" overture is one of the jolliest fugues ever written. He accomplished what no other musician has ever been able to do. That is, he left a masterpiece in every branch of music—opera, church music, chamber music and symphony. If he had been given as many years as Papa Haydn, or even Bach or Handel, he might have been the greatest of them all.

RECORD LIST — CHAPTER VI

Gluck, Christoph Willibald (1714-1787)
Ballet Suite (arranged by Mottl)
Orfeo ed Euridice — excerpts

Mozart, Wolfgang Amadeus (1756-1791)
Adagio in C for Glass Harmonica, K. 671A
Concerto No. 10 in E Flat, K. 365, for Two Pianos
and Orchestra
Piano Concerto No. 26 in D, K. 537 ("Coronation")
Violin Concerto No. 5 in A, K. 219 ("Turkish")
Don Giovanni, K. 527 — Overture and excerpts
Magic Flute, K. 620 — excerpts
Marriage of Figaro, K. 492 — excerpts
Mass in C Minor, K. 427 ("The Great")
Piano Sonata No. 11 in A, K. 331
Piano Sonata No. 15 in C, K. 545
Piano Sonata No. 17 in D, K. 576
Serenade, "Eine kleine Nachtmusik," K. 525
Symphony No. 28 in C, K. 200
Symphony No. 38 in D, K. 504 ("Prague")
Symphony No. 40 in G Minor, K. 550
Symphony No. 41 in C, K. 551 ("Jupiter")

CHAPTER VII

BEETHOVEN

It was 1770. In the new world, men were pausing in the struggle with the soil and the forest long enough to grumble about sending money in taxes back across the sea. Still their only music was the droning of hymns in the square wooden meeting-houses, the singing of some ancient English ballad by an old woman at the fireside, or the jolly scraping of a fiddle at a barn dance or husking bee. In the old world, Haydn in scarlet and gold was offering his chamber music and symphonies to Prince Esterhazy's aristocratic guests. The fourteen-year old Mozart was astounding Italy with his skill. And in the pleasant German university city of Bonn on the river Rhine, Ludwig van Beethoven (Lood-vig vahn Báy-tow-ven) was born.

THE BEETHOVEN FAMILY

He was named after his grandfather, who had come from Belgium to be tenor singer in the chapel of the Elector of Bonn, and had risen to be chapelmaster. The father, Johann, was also a singer in the Elector's chapel, and his mother, Maria Magdalena, who had been a cook, was a gentle, quiet woman whom they all dearly loved.

Every year, they celebrated the day of the saint for whom she was named—a custom in some countries instead of celebrating birthdays. Someone who lived in the house where the Beethovens had rooms wrote: "On the eve of the day,

Madame van Beethoven was persuaded to go to bed early. Then music stands were placed in the two sitting-rooms overlooking the street and a canopy decorated with flowers was put up in the room containing Grandfather van Beethoven's portrait. By ten o'clock all was ready. The silence was broken by the tuning of instruments. Madame van Beethoven was awakened, asked to dress, and led to a beautifully draped chair beneath the canopy. An outburst of music roused the neighbors, the most drowsy soon catching the spirit of gaiety. When the music was over, the table was spread, and after food and drink, the merry company fell to dancing (but in stockinged feet so as not to be too noisy) and so the festivities came to an end."

These must have been almost the only happy scenes in poor little Ludwig's wretched childhood. Most of the time his father was too drunk to be kind to his family, or even to care whether they had enough to eat or wear. At first, the good grandfather kept the family from too much suffering, and it probably made him very happy to see that his oldest grandson was musical. But he died when little Ludwig was only four years old. All Europe was still talking about the triumphant tours of the Mozart children. Father Beethoven thought how fine it would be if he could make a wonder-child out of Ludwig, and travel like a prince from city to city, living on his little boy's earnings.

A SAD CHILDHOOD

He dragged the child to the keyboard and kept him there long, hard hours, boxing his ears at every mistake. Often the neighbors would hear the little boy at the harpsichord, sobbing away from weariness and pain. Soon a worthless travelling musician, Pfeiffer (Fy-fer), came to town and was taken into the Beethoven home. He and Father Beethoven would stay out in some tavern drinking until midnight and then come home to pull little Ludwig out of bed and begin a lesson which sometimes lasted until morning.

To make him seem more like a wonder-child, his father lied about his age and, when he was eight years old, brought him out in a concert as a boy of six. But wonder-children are born, not made. For all his trouble, Father Beethoven was never able to make another young Mozart of his son.

BEETHOVEN COMPARED WITH MOZART

To begin with, Mozart was better taught. His practice hours were pleasant, quiet times with a kind father and a beloved sister, while Beethoven's were a torture of hard words and blows. Then, although probably no one has ever written music as truly grand as Beethoven, he never could pour out his musical thoughts as quickly and easily as Mozart. Mozart could write a "Don Giovanni" overture in a single night, while Beethoven, whose mind was slower, but perhaps deeper, once worked ten years on a single symphony. The boy Beethoven won the respect of his home town by his playing, but not excitement enough for a world tour.

A GOOD TEACHER AT LAST

Father Beethoven took the boy from teacher to teacher to learn the different instruments and the art of composition. None of these teachers was at all good until he came into the hands of Neefe (Nee-feh), the court organist and director of the theater at Bonn. He was a good teacher of music, and also a kindly, well-educated young man. This was a bit of good luck for Ludwig. Although there were the finest of schools in Bonn—such as good old Bach would have rejoiced in for his many children—Father Beethoven never thought it worth-while to send Ludwig to school for more than two or three months. Book-learning would not bring in money like music.

For the first time in his life, young Beethoven found lessons pleasant. Herr Neefe was very kind to him and taught him not only music, but some of the many other things in the world. To pay for his lessons, Ludwig would take his teacher's place as organist when Herr Neefe was busy or out of town. When he was fourteen years old, he was made assistant court-organist and cembalist (clavier or piano player) in the theater. How glad the wretched father must have been to see his son's music bringing in some money at last!

VISIT TO MOZART

About this time, he made his first visit to Vienna and played for his great idol, Mozart. Mozart, who thought the lad was only playing a show-piece long practiced for the occasion, praised him politely but coldly. Angry, Beethoven begged the master to give him a theme, and then he improvised variations on it with so much feeling and genius that Mozart stepped to the door of the next room where a party of his friends had gathered.

"Keep an eye on this young man," he cried. "Some day the world will hear of him!"

Perhaps he might have stayed in Vienna and studied with Mozart, but he was called back home by the illness of his beloved mother. Soon she died, and the affairs of the little family went from bad to worse. His father drank up all his salary, and Ludwig's was not enough to support himself and his two younger brothers. Many times they would have suffered want if kind friends had not come to their aid. At last, Ludwig was made guardian of the two younger boys, and half his father's salary was paid to him for their support. Karl was to study music, too, and Johann was apprenticed to the court apothecary.

Ludwig was now playing the viola in the theater orchestra and already publishing some of his compositions. He was also finding many pupils from aristocratic families through his devoted friends, the von Breunings (Broy-nings). The noble Councillor von Breuning had lost his life in a fire many years before while he was trying to rescue someone from a burning palace. He left a widow and four children, the oldest one a year younger than Beethoven. He met them through a university student, Franz Wegeler (Váy-ge-ler).

Frau von Breuning was a charming and sympathetic woman who mothered the sullen, abused boy. When he was discouraged, she cheered him; when he was in one of his wild moods (which she called a "raptus") in which he felt too grand to be understood by anyone on earth, she alone could bring him to his senses. Of the children, the oldest, Stefan, became his closest friend, and he was devoted to the lovely Eleanore. Some say that she was the inspiration for his only opera, "Fidelio," in which the brave and lovely heroine is named Leonora. When he was in one of his black moods, they quarrelled, and she later married Wegeler who became a doctor Yet in time, the trouble was forgotten, and the Wegelers and Stefan von Breuning were his faithful friends to the end of his life.

The von Breunings gave him his first glimpse of a really happy home life. He taught the children music and shared their other studies. He went with them on picnics to the lovely green woods and fields outside the old town, and these jolly excursions were probably the happiest days of his life. Through the von Breunings, also, he met the young nobleman, Count Waldstein (Vahld-shtyne), who gave him a grand piano and many presents of money.

SECOND TRIP TO VIENNA

When, at last, Beethoven saw that he could go no further in his home town and decided to seek his fortune again in Vienna, Count Waldstein gave him letters of introduction to the nobles of that great city. By the time Beethoven reached Vienna the second time, Mozart was dead. But old Papa Haydn, fresh from his first London triumph, was at the height of his fame. In passing through Bonn, Haydn had heard and praised one of Beethoven's cantatas. So to Haydn the young musician first turned for lessons.

BEETHOVEN AND HAYDN

Haydn was long past his first youth and strength, and was working harder than ever before with the composing and conducting of his greatest works. It is no wonder that he did not have much time or energy for correcting lesson sheets. As he only charged the poor young students twenty cents a lesson, he probably felt that he did not have to spend too much time on the exercise papers. But Beethoven was very angry at finding some uncorrected mistakes.

While the old master was away on his second London visit, Beethoven changed to a teacher who was less of a genius, but a strict master of counterpoint. Later he often loudly declared that he had learned nothing at all from Haydn. In time, he must have come to feel that he owed Haydn something for inspiration, if not for corrected exercises, for he dedicated his first piano sonatas to Haydn. And at Haydn's last appearance for the performance of his "Creation," the young master bent and tenderly kissed the feeble old man as he was carried out by his servants.

Never had there been such music as when the princes of Vienna entertained their noble guests in the vast drawing-rooms with gold filigreed and mirrored walls and glittering crystal chandeliers. They had the finest of orchestras and quartets dressed in gorgeous uniforms to play the latest works of the most famous composers. But the favorite entertainment was to match two famous players together in a contest or battle of music. Such contests had been popular ever since the cowardly Marchand had fled from Bach, and Handel had

vied with Domenico Scarlatti. The most brilliant players of
the world came together in the gay concert-halls of Vienna.
Soon the short, stocky youth with the deep-set eyes and unruly
hair (often politely covered by a wig) had met and conquered
all.

The newly invented instrument, the piano, had taken the
place of the harpsichord as the favorite of the drawing-room.
It could be played in a terrific thunder or a gentle murmur,
as the harpsichord and clavichord could not, and so was exactly suited to Beethoven's genius. His was a music not of the
fingers, but of the heart. Other musicians with their flying
fingers could make audiences wonder. Beethoven alone could
make them weep. And when the ladies were delicately drying
their eyes with lacy handkerchiefs so that the tears would not
ruin their powder and patches, Beethoven would break off
with a harsh laugh, saying that what artists wanted was not
tears, but applause.

He became the rage of Vienna. Countesses and princes, and
even the brother of the Emperor, flocked to take lessons of
him. A baron sharpened his quill pens for him, and a princess
went on her knees to beg him to play. One prince kept an
orchestra at Beethoven's disposal to rehearse all his newest
compositions. Another had a string quartet especially for
Beethoven's chamber music. This same prince was a good
pianist and spent hours practising Beethoven's piano sonatas
so that he could play them in public and prove that they were
not, as some critics said, too hard for anybody but Beethoven
to play. He even had the young musician live with him at
his palace and gave his servant orders to answer Beethoven's
bell before his own.

BEETHOVEN'S INDEPENDENCE

Yet Beethoven could not be made into a parlor pet. He
left the prince's palace because he could not stand having to
be at home regularly at half past four to shave and dress for

dinner. He preferred his own lodgings where he could come and go and rise and dress and eat as he pleased. He was very fussy about his rooms and once had a window cut especially to give him more air and a view.

He was forever in trouble with landlords and forever moving about. Whenever he was in the heat of composition, he would

cool his head by pouring basin after basin of water over it until the water soaked through to the rooms below—we can imagine to the delight of landlord and other tenants! Sometimes he moved so often that he did not even bother to have his piano set on legs, but played it sitting on the floor. Because every time he hired new rooms, he had to sign a lease for a certain length of time, he was often paying rent on as many as four apartments at once. Probably this is the reason why, although he made plenty of money, he never had much.

HIS LOVE OF NATURE

In addition, every summer he would take rooms outside of Vienna so as to be near the country he so loved. He enjoyed nothing better than to take a long walk through woods and fields with some good friend, stopping at some country inn to watch the peasants at work or dancing on the green. One day his friend stopped to hear the faint, sweet call of a faraway shepherd's pipe. Beethoven stopped and listened too, then shook his head sadly. For him, all was silence.

HIS GROWING DEAFNESS

When he first knew that he was surely going deaf, he was in despair. Life did not seem worth living. For a musician not to be able to hear the sweet sounds he loves and lives by is the saddest fate of all, worse even than blindness. At first, only a few old friends like Dr. Wegeler and Stefan von Breuning knew of his misfortune. He gave up going to the palaces for the gay concerts he loved so well. He was afraid people would notice his deafness and think that no good work could be written by a musician who could not hear. Then he thought of all the music he wished to write and said, "I will take Fate by the throat."

It was perhaps not so hard for him to write music in his deafness as it might have been for other musicians. To him, music was more than sweet sounds arranged in themes or patterns; it was a language to express his deepest thoughts. He wished to use it only nobly, and did not see how Mozart could write lovely music for the story of a wicked character like Don Giovanni. Beethoven found only one story which he thought worthy of making into an opera—that of a faithful wife, Leonora, who delivers her husband from a prison where he has been unjustly thrown by a tyrant. The story hardly had action enough for a good opera. Though it was made over several times, it never was very successful. But the overtures which Beethoven wrote for the different versions keep all the best music of the opera and are among our best-loved concert pieces today.

THE "CONCERT OVERTURE"

Though Beethoven never wrote another opera, he wrote several of what is known as *concert overtures*. That is, they

were not really *overtures* or *opening selections* to any opera,
but were pieces which expressed in music some story or poem:
such as the "Egmont Overture" inspired by a poem written
about the noble Count Egmont who was beheaded for support-
ing the common people of his country against the tyranny of
Spain.

THE BEETHOVEN SYMPHONIES

Beethoven wrote only nine symphonies. Haydn, as a sort of
symphony factory to Prince Esterhazy, turned out over a
hundred, and Mozart in his short life composed forty-one.
Yet only about a dozen of Haydn's and Mozart's are often
played today, while all of Beethoven's are played over and
over again. Although symphonies were usually *absolute*
music—that is, music for its own sake and not to tell a story
—Beethoven used his symphonies as a means of expressing his
thoughts. His great Third—called the "Eroica" (Er-ó-ec-a),
or "Heroic"—was first dedicated to Napoleon whom Beethoven
worshipped as the deliverer of the common people from the
oppression of kings.

THE "EROICA"

Then Napoleon, drunk with power, made himself Emperor
and tried to conquer the world with his armies which even
bombarded and captured Vienna. While Papa Haydn was
comforting his frightened servants, Beethoven was hiding in a
cellar, his head muffled with pillows, not so much afraid for his
life as the harm the noise of the cannons might do his weakened
hearing. In a great rage, he tore up the first sheet of his
symphony with its dedication to Napoleon, saying, "Bah!
He is no better than other men after all."

THE FIFTH SYMPHONY

His Fifth Symphony has been called the "Fate" Symphony
because it is supposed to represent man's struggle with Fate

and perhaps was inspired by Beethoven's own struggle with his handicap of deafness. The rhythmic pattern of the brief main theme—three short notes followed by a long one—Beethoven called "Fate knocking at the door." Some have thought it was a memory of the drunken knocks of his father trying to get into the house after a night of revelry.

THE FIRST PROGRAM SYMPHONY

His Sixth Symphony, which he called the "Pastoral," expresses his love for the country and is the first *program* symphony. That is, it did not express a feeling to be discovered or imagined by the listener, but something definite that the composer had in mind. To make sure that the listener would understand what he was trying to say, he wrote notes of explanation to be printed in the program. The first movement of this symphony Beethoven called "Joy on arriving in the country." In the second, "By the brook," we even hear the cuckoo call at the close. The third movement—or rather the last three played as one—tells a regular little story. First, the peasants are dancing on the village green. A thunder storm draws near and the merrymaking stops, the dancers fleeing in alarm. The storm comes and passes over, and we hear the shepherd's pipes again and feel the earth rejoicing after the rain.

SCHERZO

In using music as a language to express his thoughts, he sometimes found the old sonata form not rich and free enough. Where the older writers had combined two quite different themes, he often used three or four, but all relating to a single mood or feeling. In place of the usual minuet, he would write a quick third movement called a *scherzo*—or musical joke—not the kind of joke to arouse joyous laughter, but the brave and bitter laughter that hides pain.

BEETHOVEN AND THE ORCHESTRA

The piano was the love of his youth, and on it he could give forth every feeling of his heart. But when he became so deaf that he could no longer hear himself play, he lost interest in it. His piano sonatas have been called the New Testament— as Bach's Preludes and Fugues were the Old Testament—of the piano.

Though no lovelier chamber music than his has ever been written, it was to the full orchestra that he turned for comfort and expression in his great and sad years of silence. Each key had its special meaning for him, just like the Greek modes— D minor for sadness and melancholy; E flat major for light-hearted gaiety, C major for dignity and grandeur, etc. The voice of each instrument in the orchestra, too, had its own message. To him, the trumpet spoke courage and heroism, and he made more use of it than had any other composer.

THE NINTH SYMPHONY

His Ninth Symphony is perhaps the greatest piece of music ever written by man, and expresses Beethoven's idea of life. He used the grandest combinations of instruments, and in the finale even added the effect of the human voice in solo and chorus passages. This great work was performed for the first time at a subscription concert for Beethoven's benefit. Beethoven himself conducted and at the end, there were thunders of applause. Still Beethoven stood facing the or-chestra with his back to the audience until one of the singers turned him around so that he might see the applause he could not hear. When the audience understood, they stopped clap-ping and waved their handkerchiefs wildly.

Beethoven was the first musician to make a good, inde-pendent living. Haydn had been practically a servant; Mozart had nearly starved to death. Although at one time, four noble-men paid Beethoven a yearly sum to keep him in Vienna, after a while one died, and inflation brought on by the war made the money paid by the others worth little or nothing. So Beethoven learned that it was wiser to depend upon himself than others.

His steadiest income came from the publication of his works. The world had changed since the time a composer had his work published at his own expense and dedicated to a nobleman in the hope of a reward. The day had passed when a publisher could make a fortune from a composer's work while the composer did not get a penny, as the English publisher, Walsh, had enriched himself at Handel's expense. Now there were publishers who paid composers well for the right to publish their work, and Beethoven once had as many as seven bidding for a single composition.

BEETHOVEN AND HIS FRIENDS

No musician ever had more success during his lifetime—or less happiness. His friends were good and faithful, but his deafness cut him off from them. Often even his ear-trumpet would fail him, and his only way of keeping in touch with them was by the "conversation book" and pencil he always carried with him. He would see them talking among themselves, imagine they were always talking about him, saying evil things, plotting against him.

One day he would write, "Never appear in my presence again. You are a dirty dog and a faithless fellow." On the next, finding that his suspicions were false and his friend was true, there would be another note, "Dearest friend:—You are an honest man and you were right. I see it now. So come to me this afternoon. Love from your Beethoven." And his friends—fine fellows they were!—always forgave the violent quarrels and stayed with him to the end.

His family life was tragic from first to last. He never married. When he first went to Vienna, he proposed to a singer from his own town, Magdalene Willman, but she refused because he was "too ugly." After that, many times he loved many ladies of noble birth—lovely ladies with lovely names— the Countess Babette, the Countess Julietta, the Countess Josephine, the Countess Therese, and Therese Malfatti, and Amalie Leebald and Bettina Brentano. To them he would pour out his heart in music, and they would take the music, but refuse the heart.

BEETHOVEN AND HIS BROTHERS

As soon as he began to be successful in Vienna, both brothers came from Bonn to sponge on him. They borrowed his money and tried to manage his business affairs, working off on publishers some of his early childish compositions that he did not want published. He set Johann up in the apothecary business. When Johann had prospered enough to buy an estate outside of Vienna, he sent the brother who had given him his start a haughty card engraved, "Johann van Beethoven —Land-owner." Beethoven at once sent back a card with the written words, "Ludwig van Beethoven, Brain-owner."

The other brother took up music not very successfully and died, leaving Beethoven the guardianship of his nine-year old son, Carl. All the love that Beethoven had not been able to give his family or any woman was poured out upon the little boy. One minute he would spoil the child outrageously and the next he was furiously angry at some little fault. Uncle and nephew were always quarrelling and making up. Carl was too young and too senseless to see—as did Beethoven's friends— the deep love that lay under the violent outbursts. And Carl had inherited all the Beethoven weaknesses. He was expelled from school after school. He took to drink and gambling. At last, in serious trouble over gambling debts, he shot himself.

Upon leaving the hospital, he went to the estate of his other uncle, "Johann van Beethoven, Land-owner" to regain his health. Of course, loving and long-suffering Uncle Ludwig had to rush to him and forgive him once more. Beethoven's health was already broken, and this visit probably brought on the end. His sister-in-law put him in an unheated room in the bleak December weather. His brother tried to give him a bill for board. Enraged, Beethoven left in a hurry and rode back to Vienna in an open carriage.

THE END

As he lay dying, it was not the proud princes of Vienna who come to cheer him with gifts of fruit and wine, but the poor pupils and the old friends like Stefan von Breuning who lived just across the street. Beethoven had set aside a goodly sum of money in bank stock for Carl. Although he now was in real want of food, he would not touch any of it, thinking of it as already Carl's. Instead, he wrote to the London Philharmonic Society asking them to arrange a subscription concert of his works and to advance him some money on it. The London Philharmonic promptly sent a generous sum, and Beethoven took heart again.

"Now we can have many good days yet," he said.

He ordered a fine dinner brought—such as he had not had for many days. But he was too ill to taste it. He could only make the friend who was with him eat every bit and watch his enjoyment of it. Ten days later, he died in the midst of a great thunder storm which seemed to mark the passing of the last of the giants of music.

RECORD LIST — CHAPTER VII

Beethoven, Ludwig van (1770-1827)
        Bagatelles and Ecossaises (piano)
        Contra Dances and German Dances (orchestra)
        Piano Concerto No. 5 in E Flat, Op. 73 ("Emperor")
        Violin Concerto in D, Op. 61

Missa Solemnis, Op. 123
Overtures: Consecration; Coriolan; Egmont; Fidelio;
   Leonore No. 3
String Quartet No. 1 in F, Op. 18, No. 1
String Quartets Nos. 7, 8, 9, Op. 59 ("Rasoumovsky")
   (Any one of the three)
Piano Sonata No. 8 in C Minor, Op. 13 ("Pathetique")
Piano Sonata No. 14 in C Sharp Minor, Op. 27, No. 2
   ("Moonlight")
Piano Sonata No. 21 in C, Op. 53 ("Waldstein")
Piano Sonata No. 23 in F Minor, Op. 57 ("Appassionata")
Violin Sonata No. 9 in A, Op. 47 ("Kreutzer")
Symphony No. 3 in E Flat, Op. 55 ("Eroica")
Symphony No. 5 in C Minor, Op. 67
Symphony No. 6 in F, Op. 68 ("Pastoral")
Symphony No. 9 in D Minor, Op. 125 ("Choral")
Trio No. 7 in B Flat for Violin, Cello, and Piano,
   Op. 97 ("Archduke")

CHAPTER VIII

SCHUBERT

BEETHOVEN AND SCHUBERT

When Beethoven trudged alone through the streets, his hat jammed on the back of his head, a thick "conversation-book" in one pocket and an ear trumpet dangling from the other, he made such a queer figure that his selfish nephew Carl was ashamed to be seen with him. Yet there was another young man in Vienna, a musician, who worshipped Beethoven as a god and would have given half the songs in his heart to share those lonely walks. Often he would eat at the same inn as Beethoven, just to be near the great master and watch him.

He was as stocky and awkward as Beethoven himself, but shy as Beethoven had never been. He never had princes at his feet, but only a circle of young friends who painted, wrote poetry, or merely loved music. He had no publishers bidding for his work. Some of his best songs brought only twenty cents apiece, and many of his compositions were given away to friends or stuffed in drawers and forgotten. He was Franz Peter Schubert, born in 1797—six years after the death of Mozart, twenty-seven after the birth of Beethoven.

EARLY LESSONS AT HOME

His father was a school teacher in the suburbs of Vienna. His mother, like Beethoven's, had been a cook. One of the earliest pleasures he could remember was being taken by a friend of his father's to a great warehouse full of new pianos to play—all so fine and different from the old "chopping-tray," as he called it, at home. The Schuberts were a large and happy family. His first piano teacher was his brother, Ignaz, twelve years older than he. Before long, Franz had told his astonished brother that he could learn no more from him. When he was eight years old, his father began to teach him the violin, but he soon outstripped the father also and was sent to the choirmaster at the church. In a short time, good Herr Holzer reported that he had never had such a pupil. "Whenever I want to teach him anything new, I find that he knows it already. I can only look at him in astonishment and silence."

AT THE CHOIR SCHOOL

As the boy had a lovely soprano voice, his father was ambitious to have him taken into the Emperor's choir and become a pupil of the choir school where the choir boys were educated. When he went to take his entrance examination, the other boys all made fun of the chubby, serious little eleven-year old in his dull gray suit and thick spectacles. But he passed the examination very easily and had the joy of changing his drab suit for the school uniform, gay with much gold braid.

When he began to play the violin with the orchestra, he at once attracted the attention of the leader, Josef von Spaun (Shpown), the oldest boy in the school. Between the young man of twenty and the little lad of eleven, a deep friendship grew. When the boy told his older friend that he loved to compose and would compose every day if only he had the paper, Spaun furnished him with paper all through his school days.

SCHOOL DAYS

As in all the choir schools of that time, not too much money was spent for food or fuel. The rooms were cold and bare, and the boys half-starved. Soon Franz was sending a letter from the school to his brother Ferdinand who was three years older than he, and always the one he loved best.

"It's all very well on the whole, but in some ways it can be improved. You know from experience that one can often enjoy eating a roll and an apple or two all the more after eight and a half hours' fast with only a poor supper to look forward to. The pennies that Father gave me are gone in the first few days. If, then, I rely on you, I hope I may do so without being ashamed (as the Bible says). How would it be if you were to send me a couple of kreuzers (kroyt-zers) a month? You would never miss them while I could shut myself up in my cell and be quite happy. As I said, I rely on the words of the Apostle Matthew who said, 'Let him that hath two coats give one to the poor.'

"Your loving, hoping, poverty-stricken—once again, I repeat, poverty-stricken—brother Franz."

Without doubt, the good and faithful Ferdinand sent money for the rolls and apples. In spite of the scanty meals and chilly rooms, school days were happy days. When Franz could get over his shyness, he was jolly and fun-loving. The boys who had laughed at him at first became his firm friends, not only for school days, but for life. Through them, also, he met the later friends who made such a happy and devoted circle.

THE SCHOOL ORCHESTRA

In the school orchestra, he was playing all the best overtures and symphonies—Mozart's "Figaro" and "Magic Flute" overtures being the favorites. Before Franz had come to the school, the orchestra had been taken to play before the great Beethoven, and Franz could never hear too many times the boys' stories of the visit to his hero. When a friend tried to encourage him on his compositions, he said, "Sometimes I have dreams. but who can do anything after Beethoven?"

Yet, during school days, he wrote much music on the paper so kindly provided by Spaun—songs on poems which struck his fancy, variations, a sonata, a cantata for his father's birthday, an octet for woodwinds to mourn the death of his mother, and at last a symphony in D for the school orchestra (2 violins, viola, cello, 2 oboes, 2 clarinets, 2 bassoons, 2 trumpets and drum) to celebrate the birthday of the director.

When he was sixteen, his voice broke and he had to leave the choir school. Then, as now, war and fear of war were everywhere abroad. Every lad had to serve three years in the army unless he had good reason for exemption. School teachers were exempt, and Franz, who had no leaning toward a military life, became an elementary teacher in his father's school.

THE HOME ORCHESTRA

Life at home was pleasant. His father had married again a good and kind woman who became truly a second mother to her husband's children. In the evening, more often than not, there would be a family quartet. Ferdinand would be leader with the first violin, Ignaz at the second, Franz at the viola, and the father—a bit clumsy—at the cello. When he made too many mistakes, Franz would say gently, "Father, there must be something wrong *somewhere*."

Franz wrote many quartets which were played in his home almost before the ink was dry. Probably the reason Schubert's quartets are so well-loved by players and listeners alike is that they were not written for professional musicians, but for men who played for pleasure.

FIRST SYMPHONIES

One by one, different friends of Franz's joined the family group until they had a little orchestra. The humble Schubert home could no longer hold them all, and they had to meet at a larger house. They disbanded only when they would have had to hire a hall. For this orchestra, he wrote several charming symphonies which are not often played now because they were written for just the instruments he had, rather than for full orchestra. One is even for orchestra without trumpets and drums.

He still kept in touch with the choir school and old school friends. The great Salieri, who was one of the directors of the school, gave him lessons for several years after he had left. Salieri was now too famous and too old to be jealous of Schubert as he had been of Mozart. He knew that he would probably be dead by the time Schubert could win fame. Even so, when Schubert later applied for a certain position as organist, Salieri wrote a letter for him, but recommended another man more highly so that Franz did not get the place.

Yet while Schubert was his pupil, Salieri could not praise him enough. "He can do everything. He is a genius! He composes songs, masses, operas quartets—whatever you can think of!"

SCHUBERT'S FIRST MASS

At this time, his first mass was sung in the parish church. His proud and happy father gave him a grand piano to take the place of the "old chopping-tray," and the present must have meant a great sacrifice to the poor school teacher with thirteen children. Among the many compositions Franz wrote while he was living at home and was teaching in his father's school were two of his most famous, "Gretchen at the Spinning Wheel" and "The Erl-King."

"THE ERL-KING"

One day his old school friend, Spaun, called at his home and found the lad in a fever of excitement over a poem he had just read—"The Erl-King" by Goethe (Geh-ta). Goethe,

the Shakespeare of Germany, might be called the musicians' poet, because no other has ever inspired so much music by his writing. Two of Beethoven's grandest overtures had been composed to Goethe's poems of Egmont the hero, who tried to free his people from tyranny; and Prometheus, who stole fire from the gods for the people on earth. Now seventeen-year old Schubert was all aglow over Goethe's wild ballad of the elf king who snatched children from their parents' arms and carried them off to his strange unearthly kingdom.

As always, whenever Franz read a poem that touched his heart, it turned to music. He worked with fiery haste, and that same afternoon he ran to the choir school with the song in his hand. The news spread through the school like lightning that Franzl (as they called him) was there with a new composition, and the concert room quickly filled with teachers and pupils. A little friend of Schubert's with a lovely voice sang, while Schubert himself played the accompaniment. They performed with such beauty and spirit that the audience clamored for it a second time. "Of all good things there are three," the students then shouted, and the singer and composer had to repeat it again.

"The song pleases me, too," Schubert modestly said, "if only it were not so very hard to play."

ART–SONG

"The Erl-King" is an example of the German Lied (leed) or art-song, as we call it. Schubert's name is connected with this form of music, as Haydn's is with the symphony. Art-songs are different from the older folk or stanza type of song in which the melody is in binary or ternary form and the same tune is used for many verses or stanzas.

In the art-song, the accompaniment does not simply help the singer by filling in chords and melody. It paints a musical scene or background and makes the accompanist nearly as important as the singer. For example, the heavy, pounding triplets and the wild minor bass melody that Schubert found "so very hard to play" suggest the galloping horse in the wind-swept wood. The music for the singer follows every feeling in the words. It expresses the coaxing and commanding of the Erl-King, the comforting tones of the father as he tries to calm the wailing of the frightened child he carries before him on his horse, and at last, the spoken words of horror, "The child was dead."

ART–SONGS AND FOLK SONGS

Art-songs are like little musical plays or stories, with the music ever changing to fit the moods expressed by the words. They are more interesting to hear than the old song form in which all the verses, glad or sad, are sung to the same tune which may be repeated so many times that we tire of it. At the same time, art-songs are much harder to learn to sing. They are more for trained singers and listeners than for many people singing together. So there is a place in music for both kinds of song, for as long as we all love to sing together, whether or not our voices are trained and beautiful, we will sing the old and simple songs.

No one ever wrote so many songs as did Schubert in his short life—about six hundred. From "The Erl-King," which was one of the first, to the "Serenade," which was one of the last, they are all lovely and beloved. For a long time there was no one to publish them and no one to sing them because Schubert was absolutely unknown, and had no rich and power-ful friends. All the other musicians, like Bach and Mozart and Beethoven, had been famous for their playing first, and their fame as performers had advertised their compositions. Young Franz Schubert was the first composer who was not also a great virtuoso. He could play the piano, violin, and viola well enough, it is true, but no better than a dozen other young

men in Vienna. Indeed, he once broke down in the middle of
one of his own sonatas, and after trying it a second time,
jumped up, saying, "The devil himself couldn't play such stuff."

Yet he gave up his place in his father's school so that he
could give his whole time to music. Through his old friend
Spaun, he met a university student named Schober who invited him to share his rooms. There he lived until Schober's
brother came to take his place when he went to room with a
young poet, Mayrhofer, who worked in the custom-house.

Now he always had a roof over his head, but how he managed to eat and be clothed, no one knows. Every morning he
composed—songs mostly, hundreds of songs. He wrote songs
to the noble poems of Shakespeare and Goethe and songs to
the poor poems of his friends who would never be remembered
if it were not for Schubert's lovely music. He even wore his
spectacles to bed so as not to lose any time. "As soon as I
finish one thing," he said, "I begin another."

SCHUBERT AND THE ESTERHAZYS

Still he had few or no pupils and no position at all except
one summer when friends got him a place as music teacher
to the two young daughters (Caroline—eleven and Marie—
thirteen) of Count and Countess Esterhazy who were related
to the Esterhazy princes whom Haydn had served. They took
Schubert with them to their fine country estate in Hungary.
Of course, he was lodged with the servants, as all musicians
were then, except the mighty Beethoven, who was the first
to hold himself greater than princes. His letters home tell
more of his friends in the servants' hall than of his noble em-
ployers. "The cook is a merry fellow; the housemaid very
pretty; the nurse somewhat ancient. The two grooms get on
better with the horses than with us.—The young ladies are
good children. I need not tell you who know me so well that
I am good friends with everybody."

There were pleasant hours at the Esterhazy estate. Franz loved the countryside and the stirring music of the Hungarian gypsies. The Esterhazys and their guests were musical, and he enjoyed hearing them play his chamber music and sing his songs. Still, he was homesick for his gay young friends, and was not sorry when it was time to go back to the less safe, but more exciting life in Vienna.

IN VIENNA

When his work for the day was done, he liked to stroll with his friends through the pleasant suburbs of Vienna, sometimes stopping at an inn—if they had money enough —for coffee and rolls. One day, someone had brought a volume of Shakespeare. Schubert idly opened it and came upon the verse, "Hark, hark, the Lark!"

"If I only had paper here," he cried, "I have just the right music for this poem."

One of the friends ruled staff lines on the back of a bill of fare, and Schubert wrote his lovely song in twenty minutes.

SCHUBERT AND HIS FRIENDS

His circle of friends grew wider, including young poets, artists, musicians, and music-lovers. They formed a sort of society called Schubertiaden (Shu-bair-tee-áh-den) in Schubert's honor. If anyone had any money, they would dine in state and go to the opera. If not, they could be just as merry on a crusty roll. Sometimes they went on picnics to the country, and sometimes they spent a jolly evening at someone's house with dancing and games, and always Schubert's latest songs and waltzes. They all had nicknames, and Schubert was called "Kann-er-vas," because whenever a new member was brought into the circle, he would always ask, "Kann er vas?" which is German for "What can he do?"

Though Schubert's friends were many and faithful, they

were not rich or important enough to help make his music famous. They did what they could. They sent his "Erl-King" to Goethe, the world-famous author of the poem, who paid no attention to it at all. They sent some of the songs to a music publisher who returned them to another Franz Schubert. Sometimes they would find him a chance to present his compositions in the drawing-room of a noble. But he cared nothing for the society of noblemen and would slip bashfully out of the room as soon as he left the piano.

SCHUBERT AND VOGL

At last, Spaun and Schober persuaded the great court tenor, Michael Vogl, to call upon the young composer and look over some of his songs. As a schoolboy, Schubert had seen Vogl at the opera, singing the words of heroes and striding the stage in grand, rich costumes. Perhaps he had always dreamed of writing songs for Vogl's splendid voice. Now when he was pushed forward to meet the famous singer, he could hardly stammer a word. Vogl was courteous enough, but a bit over-grand in manner. As he left, he tapped the shy young man on the shoulder, saying, "You have some good stuff in you, but you don't play the part of composer. You waste your fine ideas."

But the singer could not forget the lovely songs—especially "The Erl-King." Soon Vogl was touring the country singing Schubert's songs with Schubert himself as accompanist. He even selected poems for Schubert to set to music for his remarkable voice. Everywhere the tall handsome singer got all the applause, while the meek little bespectacled composer at the piano went unnoticed. Then Schubert was known only as the man who wrote songs for the great Vogl. Now Vogl is remembered only because he once sang Schubert's songs.

These tours from town to town as a wandering minstrel

with Vogl and other musical friends were among the happiest days of Schubert's life. There were pleasant visits in the homes of music loving families, with plenty of pretty daughters and "picnics, musical parties, dances, and a whole round of outdoor and house amusements such as Schubert had probably never before enjoyed." The honor which the great city of Vienna would not give him he found in these friendly little towns.

THE "UNFINISHED" SYMPHONY

He had wanted to be a member of an honorary music society in Vienna, but his application was refused. The townspeople of Gratz elected him to their music society, and he was so grateful that he wrote for them the beautiful "Unfinished" Symphony—so called because it has only two movements instead of the usual three or four. No other symphonic music is so well known and liked as the melody of the second theme of the first movement—except perhaps the *largo*, or slow movement of Dvořák's "New World" Symphony. Yet it was too hard for the little orchestra at Gratz to play, and Schubert never had the joy of hearing it. It was not until many years after Schubert's death that it was rescued from the dust of a forgotten corner and performed for the first time.

FIRST COLLECTION OF SONGS

When Vogl had made Schubert's songs known and loved, his friends thought that if they raised enough money to have one collection published, the sale of that might pay for publishing the next, and so on. The plan worked well. A hundred copies of "The Erl-King" were subscribed to after just one evening's concert. For several years Schubert had a small, but sure income from the royalties (a certain sum for every copy sold) on his songs. Then a greedy publisher offered him a lump sum for all his rights in his songs. The money seemed a great deal to have all at once, and he accepted without consulting his friends who had better heads for business. With his generosity and love of pleasure, the money was soon spent, and he was left as poor as before.

FAILURE OF OPERAS

The Italian, Rossini (Ro-sée-nee), was winning an unheard-of fortune and the worship of crowds everywhere with his operas. Encouraged by friends, Schubert tried to do likewise. But most people then thought that Italian opera was the only good opera. Besides, the good-natured Franz read mostly books written by his friends. While the friends were good, the stories were so poor that even Schubert's music could not make them succeed. After tremendous labor and sickening hopes and fears, the operas—one after another —all failed. Music and time were wasted. All that is ever heard now is the ballet music from "Rosamunde."

It was when he was discouraged, poverty-stricken, and really ill that he spent his second summer at the Esterhazy estate. Six years had passed, and Caroline, the younger of the two "good children," was now a beautiful girl of seventeen. Music teacher and fair young pupil must have spent many hours in pleasant walks about the estate and many more at the piano, their fingers saying in music what their lips could never speak. One day Caroline asked him why he had dedicated none of his lovely music to her.

"Why should I?" he answered, "when everything I ever did is dedicated to you?"

Perhaps Caroline returned his love, for she did not marry until sixteen years after his death. But no other words of love could a poor young musician—little better than a servant— dare to speak to a lady of rank and fortune. He could only let his heart speak through his music, and probably it is due to his love of Caroline and his delight at playing by her side that he has given us more fine piano duets than any other composer.

FIRST VISIT TO BEETHOVEN

It was with a piano duet dedicated to the great Beethoven that Schubert paid his first visit to his adored master. The duet was in the form of that great test of musicianship— variations on a theme—in this case, a French song. Though Schubert had often worshipped Beethoven from afar in some coffee-house and perhaps bowed timidly now and then, he never would have dared to go to him alone. The music publisher, Diabelli (Dee-ah-béll-ee)—on one of whose waltz themes Beethoven himself had written thirty-three variations —went to introduce him.

Schubert was never at his best except among his old and dear friends. In the presence of the gloomy-browed, deaf old man, he could neither find voice to shout into the ear-trumpet or words to write in the conversation-book. He shyly put the "presentation copy" of his duet in Beethoven's hand. Beethoven looked it over and came upon a mistake in harmony which he pointed out to the young composer, adding kindly that it was not a deadly sin. Embarrassed and ashamed, Schubert fled to the street without a word. Later he was happy to hear that Beethoven often enjoyed playing the variations with his nephew, Carl.

It was not until Beethoven lay dying that Schubert had the courage to visit him again. When Beethoven was too ill to work, a friend who also knew Schubert brought him a collection of Schubert's songs. The great master who had not known more than five songs of Schubert's before could hardly believe that Schubert had already composed more than five hundred. If he was surprised at their number, he was still more astonished by their beauty. For several days,

he could not tear himself away from them, crying with joy,
"Truly in Schubert, there is the divine spark."

THE FUNERAL PROPHECY

Several times Schubert was a welcome caller at the bedside of the dying master, and once when he was with a musical
young friend, Beethoven said, "You, Anselm, have my mind,
but Franz has my soul." At Beethoven's funeral, Schubert
was one of the thirty torch bearers in full mourning with
bunches of roses and lilies fastened to their crepe arm bands.
Afterwards, when he gathered with his friends at an inn, he
drank a toast to the great man who had just gone. Then he
proposed one "to the first who shall follow him." It was
Schubert himself.

For a time it seemed as if the spirit of Beethoven had truly
come to him. His friends had been urging him to work more
slowly and take great pains as Beethoven had done. Now he
wrote a Symphony in C Major of which Beethoven himself
might have been proud. Like the famous "Unfinished" Symphony, he never heard it played. As he was in sore need of
money, his friends arranged a subscription concert of his
works, such as those that Mozart used to give. The new
symphony was to be presented then, but the orchestra
found it too hard and played one of his earlier symphonies
instead.

EXTRAVAGANT GENEROSITY

The concert was a success and brought in a sum of money
which should have kept him in comfort for many a day. But
at that time Vienna was wild over the great Paganini (Pah-
gah-née-nee) who could do amazing, unheard-of things with
the violin. If a string or two broke during the concert, he
could keep right on with the strings that were left so that no
listener could have told the difference. Prices for his concerts

were sky high—and Schubert not only went himself, but took friends who "had not a penny, while with him money was as plentiful as blackberries."

But like blackberries, the money did not last. He sent songs to the publishers so thick and fast that they would give him only twenty cents apiece for them. He now planned more large works like symphonies, but felt that he should have a better knowledge of counterpoint. He bought some books and was to study with a famous teacher, but he suddenly fell ill with typhoid fever. He was taken to the home of his faithful brother, Ferdinand, who cared for him tenderly during his last days.

He died November 1, 1828. No other great musician died so young; no other did so much in such a short time. Even Mozart, who died at thirty-six, did much of his best work in the last five years of his life. Had Beethoven died like Schubert at thirty-one, his name would hardly be known today. During the last hours of his life, Schubert spoke constantly of his beloved Beethoven and his wish to be with him. Poor faithful Ferdinand, after his brother's death, spent all his small savings to buy Franz a grave near that of the great master he had adored. There Schubert was laid to rest and on his grave were placed the words of a friend, "Music has buried here a rich treasure, but still richer hopes."

Record List — Chapter VIII

Schubert, Franz (1797-1828)
  German Dances
  Marche militaire in D, Op. 51, No. 1
  Mass in G
  Moments musicaux, Op. 94 (piano)
  Overtures: Magic Harp; Rosamunde
  Rosamunde—Ballet Music

String Quartet No. 14 in D Minor ("Death and the Maiden")
Quintet in A for Piano and Strings, Op. 114 ("The Trout")
Songs — various, including "The Erl-King" and "Gretchen at
    the Spinning Wheel"
Symphony No. 1 in D
Symphony No. 2 in B Flat
Symphony No. 8 in B Minor ("Unfinished")
Symphony No. 9 in C (old No. 7) ("The Great C Major")

CHAPTER IX

ROMANTIC MUSIC

THE only worldly goods left by poor Franz Schubert—besides his clothes and bed linen—were listed as "a quantity of old music—10 florins"—or less than five dollars. Yet this time-stained old music and the tattered manuscripts given by Schubert to various friends in payment of debts have made a treasure trove for musicians to seek out of garret and closet ever since. For many, many years no musician visited Vienna without feeling that he might stumble upon some lovely song of Schubert's waiting for some eye to discover and some voice to sing it.

A TREASURE HUNTER

The first of these treasure-hunters was a young man from Leipzig. He had come to Vienna to win fame with a musical journal—a paper that would teach people to know and love the best in music and would bring praise and recognition to good new music so that no other young genius like Schubert need die poor and unknown. He paid a visit to the lowly home of Ferdinand Schubert in 1838—just ten years after Franz's death.

Meek little Ferdinand was delighted to talk with someone who loved the music of his adored brother, the only great man he had ever known. He brought out the dusty old

papers left by Franz. Trembling with excitement, the young
visitor unearthed the score of the great C Major Symphony,
then never heard by man. He promised the middle-aged
schoolmaster, struggling to support his eight children, that
he would find a publisher who would pay a good round sum
for it. He also promised Ferdinand that it would be performed at the famous Leipzig Gewandhaus (Ge-vant-house)
concerts (so-called because they were held in the ancient
Gewandhaus or armory) under the direction of the great
young conductor and composer, Felix Mendelssohn. And he
kept his word.

The young man was Robert Schumann, born in 1810 in a
quaint, steep-roofed house in the Saxon town of Zwickau.
His father was a bookseller and publisher, already an invalid
from overwork; and his mother, the daughter of a physician,
was a gloomy woman, full of fears and strange, sad thoughts.
Robert was the youngest of five children—the baby—his
mother's pet; and her wish to settle him in a safe career nearly
lost the world a great musician.

Like most German boys, he began piano lessons very young
and learned so quickly that at seven he was writing little compositions and at eleven played the accompaniment for an
oratorio which his teacher conducted. As soon as he could
read, he learned to love poetry and would steal away to the
attic to dream over books of courage and beauty and love
and death. He liked to get his schoolmates together in his
home and conduct concerts or produce little plays he had
written.

His father favored his love of music, and from the time
Robert was nine, took him to hear all the famous pianists
who came to Zwickau or nearby towns. But by the time he
had finished school in Zwickau, his father was dead. His
mother, like Handel's father, had set her heart on having
a lawyer in the family.

A STUDENT OF LAW

Schumann, who loved his mother so dearly that he would follow her wishes in anything, entered the University of Leipzig as a law student. Yet the mother was not a hard, selfish woman set on turning her son from a career he loved. She simply thought that a lawyer led a safe and comfortable life while that of a musician was wandering and uncertain. She was always worrying about her youngest and best beloved. And she was always fearful, sad, brooding.

Sadly enough, Robert inherited his mother's fears and fits of dreaming. Often when he received a letter from his mother, if the first paragraph was gloomy, he would not read the rest for days lest it tell of some family misfortune or death.

Though he dutifully studied law, he spent more time reading the romantic poets and studying piano with the famous teacher, Wieck (Veek) whose little nine-year old Clara was already a concert pianist. Even when Schumann left Leipzig to go on with his law studies at the University of Heidelberg, he practiced his beloved piano sometimes as much as seven hours a day. Life at Heidelberg was happy with many friends, pleasure trips, and even a journey to Italy. Still, he came to hate the law studies so much that he ended by begging his mother to let him give up law for music.

At last, she agreed to leave the decision to Schumann's old teacher and wrote to Wieck, "I know that you love music. Do not let your love of music plead for Robert, but think of his age, his means, his strength, and his future. Let me know what he has to fear or to hope."

SCHUMANN AND CLARA WIECK

Hope and music won. Robert went back to Leipzig to live at Wieck's house as resident student. Few have ever loved children more than Schumann. He and little Clara

Wieck became the dearest of friends. He made up games and riddles for her, told her ghost stories. When she was away on concert tours, he wrote her the most charming letters in the world—saying how he would fill a balloon with thoughts for her or catch butterflies to send as his messengers to her.

ROMANTIC MUSIC

Old Wieck wanted Schumann to study harmony, but Robert thought it a waste of time, although he composed some piano music—chiefly "Papillons" which Clara brought out at a concert. At this time, he thought that the old masters, to whom music was sweet sounds cleverly built into artistic form, did not have the highest ideals of what music should be. He thought that the chief object of music was to express the feeling in the heart of man, and if these feelings were strong and true, the form did not matter much. This new idea of music as a means of expressing thoughts and feelings, and even sights and stories, is called *romantic*, while the earlier view of music as an art in itself and for itself alone is called *classic*.

Schumann did not invent romantic music. When Beethoven composed his "Eroica" and "Pastoral" Symphonies, he was writing romantic music to express his thoughts, to paint a picture, or tell a story. Schubert's symphonies and chamber music are *absolute music*—that is, they have no story or purpose except to be beautiful and so follow the *classic* idea of music. But when Schubert composed his art-songs with music to fit every word and mood of the poem, he was certainly writing romantic music. And already a composer of opera—von Weber—had written the first romantic opera, "Der Freischütz." Schumann, however, gave voice to the new way of music against the old, and made the difference between the classic and romantic *idea* of music seem nearly as great as the earlier difference between polyphonic and homophonic *form*.

THE INJURED HAND

Probably another reason that Schumann was not eager to spend hours over books of rules and exercise papers was that it made him impatient to see how far ahead of him little Clara was in playing. He had to make up the long years spent in law study. He practiced wrist and finger exercises early and late. He invented a contraption of weights and pulleys to strengthen the third finger of his hand. Instead of strengthening it, he lamed it, and the lameness spread to his whole right hand. In vain, he tried electricity and all kinds of cures. His hand was crippled forever.

STUDY OF COMPOSITION

His hopes of being a *virtuoso* or master pianist were gone. As he had given up law for music, he would not change. He turned from the piano to the strict study of counterpoint and composition which he once had scorned. He had not given up the *romantic* idea of music—that the feeling was more important than the form. But now he was old enough to see that a knowledge of form could be a help in expressing feeling in music, just as a poet should know grammar and poetic meter.

It was well for him that he had a small income left by his father, and did not have to depend on music for his bread and butter. He spent a quiet winter at home in Zwickau, and wrote a symphony, which was never published, but was performed at one of Clara Wieck's concerts there. Then he went back to Leipzig, which was as great a center for young musicians as Vienna was for the old.

The famous and youthful leader of the Gewandhaus concerts, Felix Mendelssohn, had attracted quite a circle of bright young men to the city. There were young men who were famous, and young men who would become famous, and young men who wanted to be famous. Evenings they would gather in some inn or coffee house, and talk and talk about music. They would tell angrily of how Bach's music had lain forgotten for years, and how Schubert had been allowed to die poor and unknown. They spoke of how an old chapel master could win fame with music dry as dust and empty of feeling as long as it was perfect in form, while a young musician could starve for a chance to be heard.

THE MUSICAL JOURNAL

What a fine thing it would be, they thought, to start a musical journal to encourage young and unknown genius and to teach people to know and love new music! Schumann, with his poetic mind, was wild about the idea, and founded the "Neue Zeitschrift (Noya Zite-shrift) or "New Journal" of music. His friends—and the friends of new music—were made into an imaginary band called Davidsbundler or Society of David. The name came from the Biblical story of David's battle with the Philistines. The little group fighting for the finest and best in music represented David against the Philistines who were those who knew little about music, but thought they knew everything and thought that whatever was new must be bad. He gave them all fanciful names; he himself was Florestan when gentle, Eusebius when aroused. Old Wieck and Clara were Master Raro and Chiara. His famous young friend, Felix Mendelssohn, was Felix Meritis—or "Deservedly Fortunate."

During these years, he was composing some of his finest piano music—the famous "Fantasie-Stücke" or fantasy-pieces and the "Davidsbündler-tanze" and the best-known and best-loved of all his music—the "Scenes from Childhood."

All this time Clara was growing from a child-wonder to a lovely young woman, one of the most famous pianists in Europe. She had always adored the young man who had brightened the strictness of her home life and the dull, long practice hours with his little games and fairy tales. He had loved her as a little girl and now he loved her as a woman. "I am quite clear about my heart," he wrote. "Fate always intended us for each other. Perhaps your father will not refuse if I ask him for his blessing."

Father Wieck not only refused his blessing. He would not give his consent. He would not think of allowing his famous daughter to marry a young man with none too much money and—as Wieck thought—even less future. So Schumann said farewell to his "glorious girl" who promised to wait for him forever, and took himself and his musical journal to Vienna. He hoped that if he won fame in that great old musical city, perhaps old Wieck's heart would soften.

IN VIENNA

Vienna treated him and his musical journal coldly. At the end of six months, he wrote a friend that he and his paper were "out of place" there and returned to Leipzig. He was no richer, no more famous, no nearer to marriage with Clara. Yet the trip to Vienna was not time wasted. He brought back that great treasure, the Schubert C Major Symphony. And as he was visiting the grave of the great master, Beethoven, he found on it a rusty pen—perhaps, he thought, dropped there by Schubert. This pen was a sacred relic to him. With it he wrote the review of the Schubert C Major Symphony for his journal, and it inspired him to compose the first of his really great symphonies—one truly worthy of the pen of Schubert or Beethoven.

MARRIAGE AT LAST

Still, he could not change old Wieck's mind about letting him marry Clara. In those days, no girl could marry without the consent of her father. But if the father refused his consent, the young man might take his case to court. If the court decided that he was of good character and able to support a wife, the marriage would be allowed. At last, when he saw that there was no way to change the old man's mind, Schumann brought suit and won his Clara.

The first years in Leipzig after his marriage were the busiest and happiest of his life. Never have so many great men of music been alive at one time, and sooner or later they all passed through Leipzig on their tours of the musical world. There was the Italian opera composer, Rossini, who was so famous that some opera houses were devoted to his operas alone. And there was the young German opera composer Wagner (Vahg-ner) whose ideas and music seemed so strange that not even Schumann would encourage him at first. There was Liszt, the wizard of the piano as Paganini had been the magician of the violin. And there was the shy young Polish pianist and composer, Chopin, whom Schumann hailed in his journal with "Hats off, gentlemen! A genius!" Others, too, like Berlioz, the eccentric Frenchman who used tone as painters use color, received their first praise from Schumann's journal.

SCHUMANN'S COMPOSITIONS

Much of Schumann's own best music was written at this time—symphonies, chamber music, songs which place his name with Schubert's as master of the art-song. He wrote a great cycle of songs, "Woman's Life and Love" to celebrate his marriage with Clara. But his most famous song is "The Two Grenadiers" which tells of two of Napoleon's soldiers returning sadly home to France after the defeat of his armies and uses the French National Anthem, "The Marseillaise," at the end.

SCHUMANN AND MENDELSSOHN

It was usually Mendelssohn who gave Schumann's works their first hearing. He was always a good friend to Schumann, even though he never really appreciated Schumann as a musician, but thought of him first of all as a writer. For his part, Schumann simply adored his "Felix Meritis" who was only a year older than he. He looked up to Mendelssohn as a "perfect god" and thought him "the first musician of the age."

If ever a babe were born with a silver spoon in his mouth and a good fairy by his cradle, that child was Felix Mendelssohn-Bartholdy. His grandfather was a rich Jewish banker, as was his father, who became a Christian and took the name of Bartholdy from his wife's family. Both Felix and his older sister Fanny were born with what their mother called "Bach-fugue" fingers. She gave them their first lessons—only five minutes long—when they were little more than babies. Later when they were studying with the best teachers in Europe, she always sat by with her knitting while they practiced.

Felix shared all his music lessons with his beloved Fanny, and never were a brother and sister more dear to each other. Even when they were grown up, had married, and were living apart, he wrote to her regularly to tell of his work and ask her advice about every step of his career. Fanny became an especially fine pianist and composed many delightful pieces, too. In those days no one thought that a woman could compose anything worth while. So Fanny's work was all published under her brother's name. Once when Felix was visiting England, Queen Victoria spoke of one of his songs that was her particular favorite, and he had to confess that it was really composed by Fanny.

The Mendelssohns lived in a spacious house in the midst of wide, tree-shaded lawns, almost like a park. In summer, when all was green, and the grounds were sweet with flowering shrubs, the young people used to gather there for garden parties and out-door frolics. Then the Mendelssohn children (there were Rebeckah and Paul younger than Fanny and Felix) would get out a little newspaper called "Garden-Times." In the winter, they would call their paper "Snow-and-Tea Times," and the happy gatherings would take place indoors, mostly for music.

FAMILY CONCERTS

Every two weeks there would be a concert in the great music room, at which the guests would be not only the young people, but many of the famous musicians who happened to be in Berlin. Fanny would play the piano, Paul the cello, and Rebeckah would sing. Even when Felix was so little that he had to stand on a chair to be seen, his father would hire an orchestra for him. In that way, he had practice in conducting his own compositions and those of the great masters and could learn the uses and tone effects of all the instruments in the orchestra.

As a teacher in harmony and composition, he had the old musician, Zelter. There were no strict lessons, but Zelter taught the boy as they strolled about his pleasant garden. Someone has said, "When Zelter became Mendelssohn's teacher, he just put the fish into the water and let it swim wherever it liked."

Zelter was a dear friend of the famous poet, Goethe, whose works have been put to music so many times. Zelter took young Felix to visit the grand old man several times. Felix wrote a lovely quartet and dedicated it to Goethe. In return, Goethe —who had never appreciated Beethoven and had paid no attention at all to Schubert's "Erl-King"—wrote a verse to thank Mendelssohn. Many other musicians would have given a year's work for such a favor from the old poet, as nothing else would make them so quickly noticed by the world.

BACH DISCOVERED AGAIN

Zelter was one of the first to discover and worship the works of Bach. Except for "The Well-Tempered Clavichord," they had lain neglected for more than a century. Some of the precious old Bach manuscripts had been found and given to Zelter by Mendelssohn's own father and grandmother before it was known that Felix himself would be a musician. Zelter would often show his pupils these dusty old papers saying, "Just think of all that is hidden here!" But he hoarded them like a miser and never would let Felix handle them.

The greatest treasure of all was the "Matthew Passion" which Zelter had found among some waste paper he had bought at the auction of the belongings of a cheese merchant who had died. At last, the nineteen-year old Felix persuaded Zelter to let him produce it. First, he practiced it in his home with a chorus of only eighteen singers. Then he was permitted to rehearse the *Singakademie* of from 300 to 400 voices for a public performance. People crowded even the rehearsals. Every ticket was sold, and a thousand were turned away from the door. Later, Mendelssohn said, "It was a Jew who gave back this great Christian work to the world."

YOUTHFUL COMPOSITIONS

In the concerts in his own home, at least one or two of his own compositions were always played. Many of these boyish compositions which were enjoyed by his friends and praised by visiting musicians, stand among his masterpieces and are well-loved today. The two most famous are the overtures, "Midsummer Night's Dream" and the "Hebrides" (Heb-rid-ees) or "Fingal's Cave."

"MIDSUMMER NIGHT'S DREAM" OVERTURE

The "Midsummer Night's Dream" overture was written when the composer was only seventeen years old. It pictures in music the famous fairy play by Shakespeare. Mendelssohn scarcely thought of anything else for all one year while he was studying at the University of Berlin, and spent most of his spare time working out the themes on the piano of a beautiful lady nearby. No one could write fairy music as well as Mendelssohn. His *scherzos* are all dainty and silvery enough to be the laughter of fairies. All of Shakespeare's story can be found

in the music, even to the braying of the luckless Bottom who
was given a donkey's head by Puck.

The "Hebrides" or "Fingal's Cave" overture was composed
a year or two later when Mendelssohn made his first visit to
England. While there, he journeyed to the Hebrides, those
little wind and wave swept islands off the northern coast. He
heard old wives singing old songs as they sat by their spinning
wheels in thatched-roofed cottages. He saw weatherbeaten
men tending gray sheep in barren pastures. Above all, he heard
the never-ending thunder of the sea against the rocks, especially
when he visited the cave where the legendary hero, Fingal, was
supposed to have lived many years before. In a letter to Fanny,
he sent a theme of twenty bars of music to show, he said, "how
extraordinarily the place affected me."

This theme—which speaks of the never-ending surge of the
waves—formed the opening of his great "Hebrides" overture.
Here Mendelssohn makes a new use of the concert overture.
Beethoven had written overtures as concert-pieces to illustrate
poems and plays, instead of "opening pieces" to an opera, as
they had been in the beginning. Such an overture was Mendelssohn's "Midsummer Night's Dream." But with the
"Hebrides" Mendelssohn went one step further, for this overture had no connection with a play or story, but was used to
paint a picture or give an impression in the composer's mind.
This use of the concert overture has been a favorite one with
musicians ever since.

The quiet, pleasant years at home were broken by many
happy journeys—family visits to Paris, or a trip through Switzerland with the whole household, including servants, a merry
party of ten. Everywhere they mingled with the greatest musicians, writers, and artists of the time. Young Felix was
not in the least spoiled by his genius and good fortune. He

was always so gay and kind and charming that everyone loved him.

THE WORLD TOUR

When he was nearly grown to manhood, his father sent him alone on three years of travel. He wanted Felix to learn to know all the different countries and decide where he wanted to settle down to practice his art. It was rather like Mozart's grand tour, except that poor Mozart was desperately looking for a chance to earn his bread, while Mendelssohn, sure of his bread and cake, had only to choose the place that pleased him best.

IN VIENNA

The whole world welcomed him. Vienna, usually so cold to strange and new musicians, received him with open arms. In Italy he enjoyed the landscape with its silver-green groves and age-old ruins, the gay carnivals and rich art treasures, the jolly peasant songs and the ancient chants for the worship of God. Here he rivalled Mozart in writing from memory part of the sacred Good Friday music, and here he received the inspiration for his "Italian" Symphony.

IN PARIS

Paris was full of music and musicians. Many famous musicians lived there, and all the others came there to win fame. Beethoven's symphonies were performed, and the operas of the famous Rossini and the not-yet-famous Meyerbeer. Paganini, the wizard of the violin, was giving concerts, as was also Liszt, the young Paganini of the piano. And shy young Chopin had just come to make Paris his home.

Mendelssohn lived a gay life with the other young musicians of Paris—jolly little lunches in the sidewalk cafés with Liszt and Chopin, evenings at the theatre, enchanted by beautiful actresses and the ballet; wild games of leap-frog in deserted midnight streets. He played Beethoven's piano concertos with the best orchestras. His "Midsummer Night's Dream" overture was received with wild applause, and his chamber music was played in the palaces of rich and noble music lovers.

MENDELSSOHN IN ENGLAND

He visited England first of all, and so often afterwards that it was like a second home to him. No other musician since Handel had been so well received there. His concerts were crowded, and he was a great favorite with Queen Victoria. He was honored with so many grand balls and dinner parties that some of his friends were afraid he was giving up music for society.

England was the inspiration for much of Mendelssohn's music. On his first visit there, trips to Scotland and the Hebrides brought forth the "Fingal's Cave" overture and later the "Scotch" Symphony. Because the English loved the oratorio above all other forms of music, Mendelssohn composed oratorios for them. His "St. Paul" and "Elijah" are among the greatest ever written, and as a composer of oratorio he ranks second only to Handel.

Yet when he at last settled down, it was as the director of the opera house, orchestra, or choral society of one after another of the music-loving little German towns. In the pleasant little city of Frankfort on the Rhine, he met lovely Cecile Jeanrenaud (Zhan-ren-ó), daughter of a French clergyman who had died many years before. She was as beautiful and good as a story-book lady. He loved her, and she loved him, and they married and lived happily for the rest of their lives.

MENDELSSOHN AT LEIPZIG

At last, he was appointed director of the famous Gewandhaus concerts in Leipzig. He moved with his family into a house looking out across Leipzig boulevard to the St. Thomas's school and church where Bach had labored for so many years.

At the Leipzig Gewandhaus, Mendelssohn had an orchestra much like the fine symphony orchestras in all our great cities to-day, from Boston to Portland, Oregon. That is, it was not an orchestra thrown together for just one concert, as were the orchestras with which Mozart used to have to present his symphonies. Nor was it a body of musical servants drilled to please some duke or prince, as was Papa Haydn's orchestra at Esterhaz. It was a group of excellent musicians who had rehearsed and played so long together that they were like one great musical instrument.

The conductor of the orchestra was free to choose his own programs. Felix Mendelssohn was the first to make the leadership of an orchestra an art in itself. Before his time, orchestra conductors usually played their own compositions and the most famous works of the old masters over and over again. Mendelssohn rescued the works of Bach and Schubert from the dust, and gave hearing to new composers like Schumann.

DUTIES OF ORCHESTRA LEADER

Since then, a good orchestra conductor not only has to train his orchestra to follow his direction, so that he can play upon it as if it were one instrument, of which each player is just a part, and try to give each piece the spirit of its composer; he must also make up his programs, much as an editor chooses stories and essays for a book or a magazine. First, he must have variety—not all symphonies or all overtures or all shorter pieces, but some of each. Then, he must not play the same old favorite classics over and over again. He must look for fine forgotten things—as Mendelssohn brought out the long neglected works of Bach, or give a hearing to worthy new composers—as Mendelssohn did to Schumann and many others.

Nowadays, a great orchestra leader is rarely a great player or a great composer. Mendelssohn was all three. In addition, when someone left a large sum of money to found a music school or conservatory, Mendelssohn did it as well as he did everything else. He found teachers among the players in his orchestra, and he himself and Schumann both taught piano. The Leipzig Conservatory became one of the most famous music schools in the world.

Leipzig worshipped him and it was always his dearest home. Even when he went to Berlin at the command of the King to direct the Royal orchestra and opera house, he always longed for his old work at Leipzig where everything he did was sure to please.

SORROW AND DEATH

His life had always been so full of joy that when sorrow came, it killed him. First, his father died—as he said "not only my father, but my teacher in both art and life," and then his gentle mother. But he still had his beloved Fanny to comfort him. Probably he thought he would have her love and encouragement always. Then, although still a young woman, she suddenly died at the piano as she was directing the choir of the little church near her home.

When the news came, Mendelssohn was worn out with the labor of his greatest work, the oratorio "Elijah," probably the greatest of all oratorios except the "Messiah." He fell to the floor with a shriek, striking his head. In 1847, scarcely six months after Fanny's death, he was buried beside her. When he died, all Leipzig mourned as if each family had lost a beloved son.

SCHUMANN'S ILLNESS AND DISAPPOINTMENTS

Several years before Mendelssohn's death, Schumann had left Leipzig. The strain of writing, teaching, and composing brought on the beginning of his nervous illness. He could not sleep. He was dizzy if he went above the first floor. He turned his musical journal over to someone else and gave up his work at the conservatory. Then he moved to the quieter city of Dresden to rest and regain his health. It was the first of many changes from city to city and journeys with Clara on concert tours, always in the vain hope of better health.

For a while in Dresden, he was much better. He composed his only opera "Genoveva" to a libretto he wrote himself—as he could not find any other to suit him. The story is of St. Geneviève, the patron saint of Paris.

He loved it more than any of his other works and sent it to Leipzig to be performed, but alas! his friend Mendelssohn was now dead. The new conductor made promises, excuses, delays and in the end never did produce the opera. At last, Schumann went to Leipzig and brought it out himself. It was not a great success. He wrote to a friend that, as it was warm summer weather, people would rather be in the woods than in the concert hall.

Though after this disappointment he wrote two of his great symphonies and some of his finest chamber music and songs, his mind and body began to fail more quickly. There were still happy moments in his home. He had his beloved Clara to cheer him, and he, who of all musicians loved children most dearly, had eight of his own. He loved to play games with them, and every week he would hear the lessons Clara had taught them and reward them with pennies from the glass bowl on his desk. But now as he got up to lead his orchestra, he would forget to give the first beat and stand motionless until at last the orchestra would have to start without him. Finally, the directors of the orchestra tried to get him to retire to take a rest. He felt that they were trying to get rid of him.

SCHUMANN AND BRAHMS

The last happening in his life to give him pleasure was a visit from a young musician named Johannes Brahms. Brahms came to Schumann's house on foot after a journey of many miles—as Bach had trudged to old Buxtehude at Lübeck—because he did not have money to ride. Schumann went wild over the young man and wrote that Brahms made him think of a young eagle, a grand river, a great waterfall "thundering down from the heights bearing the rainbow in its waves, butterflies around its banks, and nightingales' songs all about it." He and Brahms and another friend together wrote a violin sonata for Joachim (Wah-keem), the great violinist who had sent Brahms to Schumann. For the first time in years, Schumann wrote an article to send to the Musical Journal—an article in praise of Brahms.

LAST SAD DAYS

After Brahms had gone, Schumann's health grew rapidly worse. The sound of one note rang always in his ears. He imagined Beethoven was trying to speak to him in knocks like the rhythm of the first theme in the Fifth Symphony. He thought that the spirits of Schubert and Mendelssohn gave him a musical theme to work into a composition. He never finished it, but after his death Brahms made the "spirit theme" into a piano duet, dedicated to Schumann's daughter, Julie.

At last, realizing that he was going insane, he jumped into the Rhine. He was rescued by workmen and taken to a private hospital, where he died in 1856 at the age of forty-six.

COMPARISON OF MENDELSSOHN AND SCHUMANN

The faithful Clara devoted the rest of her life to making Schumann's music famous by her concerts. At the time of his death, his music was none too well liked, while Mendelssohn's was thought to be the greatest music of the age. Both Schumann and Mendelssohn had the romantic idea of music as a means of expressing thoughts and pictures of life. They did not call their short pieces "Preludes," as older musicians had done, but "Spinning Song," "Spring Song," "Venetian Boat Song" (Mendelssohn's "Songs without Words"), or "About Strange Lands and People," "Dreaming" or "By the Fireside." (Schumann's "Scenes from Childhood.") Even their symphonies were many times not *absolute* music, but painted pictures in the composer's minds, such as Mendelssohn's "Scotch" Symphony and Schumann's "Rhenish" Symphony which gives a musical picture of the festivities in celebration of a new Archbishop of Cologne.

Yet the music of Mendelssohn and Schumann is as different as the men themselves. Mendelssohn was a master of form, and sometimes was thought to care more for form than feeling. Very few of us can go through life with as little struggle and sorrow as Mendelssohn had. For that reason, he had no very deep feelings to express, and his music is more apt to speak of things he has read and seen—fairies and sea waves—"Midsummer Night's Dream" and the "Hebrides."

Schumann, on the other hand, always thought that feeling was more important than form. Though his music does not sound at all strange to us, now that we have our modern music with many dissonances, some people then called it the "broken crockery" school of music. But the greatest music is that which speaks most deeply to our hearts. Time, the greatest judge of all, has made Mendelssohn, the darling of his age, take second place as composer to his often neglected friend, Schumann.

RECORD LIST — CHAPTER IX

Mendelssohn, Felix (1809-1847)
        Capriccio brillant, Op. 22, for Piano and Orchestra
        Piano Concerto No. 1 in G Minor, Op. 25
        Violin Concerto in E Minor, Op. 64
        Elijah, Op. 70 — excerpts
        A Midsummer Night's Dream — Incidental Music, Op. 61
         — excerpts

Overtures — various
Songs without Words — excerpts
Symphony No. 3 in A Minor, Op. 56 ("Scotch")
Symphony No. 4 in A, Op. 90 ("Italian")
Symphony No. 5 in D Minor, Op. 107 ("Reformation")

Schumann, Robert (1810-1856)
Carnaval, Op. 9 (piano)
Piano Concerto in A Minor, Op. 54
Fantasiestucke, Op. 12 (piano)
Kinderscenen, Op. 15 (piano)
Manfred Overture, Op. 115
Papillons, Op. 2 (piano)
Quintet in E Flat for Piano and Strings, Op. 44
Violin Sonata No. 1 in A Minor, Op. 105
Songs — various
Symphony No. 1 in B Flat, Op. 38 ("Spring")
Symphony No. 3 in E Flat, Op. 97 ("Rhenish")

CHAPTER X

MORE GERMAN MUSIC MASTERS

From Symphony to Symphonic Poem

SCHUMANN helped many a young musician to fame with his praise and encouragement. But Johannes Brahms, the one he loved best and praised most highly, was for a while hindered more than helped by Schumann's kindness.

Johannes Brahms was born in 1833 in Hamburg, where his father played in the orchestra of the court theatre. Like other boy musicians, young Brahms studied with the best teachers of the town, and worked long and hard. But the first that the world heard of him was when, at the age of fourteen, he gave a piano concert, playing a composition of his own—"Variations on a Folk-Song."

CONCERT TOUR

Though the concert was a great success, Brahms spent five or six years more in quiet study. When next he came before the public, he was twenty years old and was travelling through Europe on a concert tour with the Hungarian violinist, Remenyi. Remenyi taught Brahms to know and love the folk music of the Hungarian gypsies, with its strange and beautiful melodies, and sudden changes of rhythm, sometimes fiery and heart-stirring and again dreamy with a far-off sadness. Later, Brahms himself wrote a set of Hungarian dances which are perhaps the best-loved of all his music.

BRAHMS AND LISZT

Remenyi knew most of the famous musicians in the different towns through which they passed. Once he took the young pianist to meet Franz Liszt, the great magician of the piano. Liszt finally consented to play for his visitors, choosing one of his own sonatas. It went on and on endlessly. When at last it was done, Liszt probably expected young Brahms to be overcome with wonder and applause. But Johannes, tired out from the journey, was in an arm-chair fast asleep!

In the town of Celles, our wandering musicians found the world's worst piano. They had to send for another just before the concert was to begin, and this one turned out to be a half tone below pitch. It is very hard for a violinist to tune and play to a piano below pitch, and poor Remenyi was in despair. Brahms solved the problem by playing the concert-piece—a difficult Beethoven sonata—in a key a half tone higher than it was written, so that it would match the pitch of Remenyi's violin. This he did at sight and without rehearsal—such an unheard-of feat of skill that the delighted Remenyi told the audience about it.

In the audience was the great violinist, Joachim, who was one of Schumann's dearest friends. As we have seen, he sent Brahms to Schumann, and Brahms, after a long journey afoot, played his Sonata in A Major to Schumann and Clara. They liked the young man, and admired his playing and composition. Besides praising him warmly in the musical journal, Schumann gave him letters of introduction to the greatest musicians in Leipzig (though Mendelssohn was now dead) and tried to help him find a publisher for his music.

BRAHMS AND CLARA SCHUMANN

When scarcely two years later poor Schumann died in a doctor's private asylum, Brahms hastened to help and comfort Clara. Long afterward, she wrote to her children: "Your father loved and admired Johannes Brahms as he did no other man except Joachim. He came like a true friend to share all my sorrow. He strengthened the heart that threatened to break; he uplifted my mind; he cheered my spirits when and wherever he could. In short, he was my friend in the fullest sense of the word. He and Joachim were the only people whom your dear father saw during his illness, and he always received them with pleasure as long as his mind was clear."

After Schumann's death, Brahms worked quietly for a while, teaching and composing. He was finding Schumann's kindness far from a help. His troubles were just the opposite of Schubert's. Few besides his friends knew anything about Schubert. All the musicians were watching Brahms. Whenever he composed anything, the critics would pounce on it, saying that Brahms was not worthy of the high praise Schumann had given him.

As he found composing a very uncertain way of earning a living, he decided to try his hand at being a concert pianist. He appeared in concerts in many German cities, and now the critics said his playing was too heavy, not brilliant enough.

SLOW FAME

Clara Schumann was one of the most famous pianists in Europe. She made tour after tour, playing the music of Schumann and Brahms, to try to make people know and love the work of her husband and his young discovery. She succeeded. Little by little, more of Brahms' compositions were brought out by great publishing houses. He was invited to play his newest piano concerto with symphony orchestras, finally even at the Leipzig Gewandhaus. At last he felt that he could give his whole life to composition.

OLD VIENNA

He had visited Vienna once and liked it so much that he now went back to make his home there. Schumann had expressed what is in the heart of every musician when he wrote:

"This Vienna with its tower of St. Stephen's, its lovely women, its pageantry; this Vienna with all its memories of the greatest German masters must be a fruitful field for the musician's fancy. Often when I looked at it from the mountain tops, I thought how frequently Beethoven's eyes must have wandered restlessly to that distant chain of Alps; how Mozart may oft have followed dreamily the course of the river Danube which always seems to swim in wood and forest; and how father Haydn may have looked up at the tower of St. Stephen's, shaking his head at such a giddy height."

Vienna was haunted by the memories of the great old masters. There were also many present joys for a young musician. Hungarian gypsies made their fiddles sing and sob their age-old tunes for gold in the cafés. The woodlands and pleasant villages echoed with the fresh and simple folk songs that have charmed all musicians. The mighty Beethoven expressed his love of the country and its happy songs and customs in his "Pastoral" Symphony. Brahms' own famous "Cradle Song" is thought to be an echo of some old folk song. Today musicians still like to discover some beautiful old melody and give it to the world, as our modern violinist, Fritz Kreisler, has given us "The Old Refrain" and others.

Nowhere was life so gay as in Vienna. Even for a poor shabby musician like Brahms, not invited to the glittering ball-rooms, there were glimpses of silks and laces, whiffs of perfume, and snatches of bright music from lighted windows. All the Viennese light-heartedness and love of living was put into the music of the famous Strauss waltzes.

"THE BEAUTIFUL BLUE DANUBE"

The first Johann Strauss won the hearts of all Vienna with his gay and lovely waltzes, and was given the title of "Waltz King." When his son turned to music also, old Johann was so jealous for fear the lad would take his title from him that he tried to keep young Johann from becoming a musician. But at last the son won his father's title with the greatest waltz of all, "The Beautiful Blue Danube."

Though the Strausses never tried to write serious music, even the greatest musicians enjoyed their bright waltzes. The younger Johann Strauss used to conduct out-of-door concerts in one of the parks, and Brahms was often there. Once when Brahms was old and famous, Strauss' wife timidly asked him to write his name on her fan. He wrote a few bars of "The Beautiful Blue Danube" and underneath, "Not, alas, by Johannes Brahms."

In Vienna, Brahms lived quietly and worked hard. He was not the kind of genius who can write a "Don Giovanni" overture in a single night, or compose an "Erl-King" or "Midsummer Night's Dream" at seventeen. He was over forty when he wrote his first symphony. Fame came slowly, but in his old age he found himself considered the greatest of living masters.

Brahms did not enjoy worship and glory, as many musicians did. At banquets he would take a seat at the lower end of the table with the younger musicians instead of with the mighty, like Liszt or the great Russian Rubinstein. When an adoring young pianist tried to snip off a lock of his hair as a keepsake, he exclaimed, "What nonsense!" and left the hall.

He never used a mirror because, as he said, he didn't like his looks. He usually wore a baggy brown coat and trousers, all spotted and wrinkled, and an old gray shawl when the weather was cool. He was always absent-minded and careless about his dress. When, after years of discouragement, he was invited to conduct his First Symphony at Leipzig, his friends were horrified to see him appear on the platform with his dirty old trousers under his evening coat. Worse still, as he moved about to conduct the orchestra, trousers and coat parted, showing a wide band of white.

The passing years had surely made a great change in the

musician's place in the world. Haydn was dressed in a bright uniform just like a footman or any other servant. Even the stormy Beethoven would shave, put on clean linen, and cover his unruly hair with a neat wig before playing in the drawing-room of noblemen. Now Brahms was honored like a prince, though he was as slovenly and as rude as he pleased.

And rude he certainly was! One evening a lady thought she would please him by singing several of his songs. When she stopped, expecting a compliment, Brahms said, "Singing is difficult, but it is often far more difficult to listen to it." Again as he was leaving a party, he turned at the door and said, "If there is anyone I have forgotten to insult, I beg his pardon."

It is hard to think of this gruff old man as the composer of the world's best-loved cradle song. Yet Brahms was very fond of children. Visitors would often find him on his hands and knees with the neighborhood youngsters riding on his back. He never married to have children of his own. Some say that he loved Schumann's daughter, Julie, who could not think of him as a lover, but only "good old Uncle Brahms."

LAST CLASSIC MASTER

His friendship with Clara Schumann was lifelong, and he lived only a year after her death in 1896. It seems strange that Schumann who worked so hard for romantic music loved above all others the one who became the last of the classic masters. Bach, Beethoven and Brahms are sometimes called the "three great B's." Like Bach and Beethoven, Brahms wrote absolute and not program music. The old form of the *theme with variations* was one of his favorites. Perhaps only a musician can really understand and appreciate his greatest work—the four great symphonies and chamber music. But anyone who can play in an orchestra or listen to a radio is fond of the cradle song, the tender German waltzes, and the stirring Hungarian dances.

LISZT, A MUSICAL EXPLORER

Another great musician whose best-loved work was inspired by the Hungarian gypsies was Franz Liszt. He was older than Brahms in years, but younger in musical ideas. He once said that all life changes with time, and that music and the arts should not stand still or follow old ways but should change, like everything else in life. Brahms' music is much more truly great. Liszt's work is important more for the new ways it showed to later musicians. Liszt was a musical explorer who made a new path to the music of the future.

It is no wonder that of all Hungarian music, Liszt's "Rhapsodies" best catch the gypsy fire, for his childhood was spent within the sound of gypsy fiddles. He was born in 1811—just one year after Schumann—on the Hungarian estate of one of the Esterhazy princes where his father was steward. His father was delighted when the little boy showed a love for music because he himself had always longed to be a musician.

He was an excellent pianist and taught his son so well that when the child was nine, he gave a public concert and played in the drawing-room of Prince Esterhazy. Six Hungarian noblemen raised money to send him to study in Vienna. There is a story that when he was eleven, he played before Beethoven who cried, "He will make my music loved by generations to come."

When the boy went to study in Vienna, he already could play any music written. But his teacher, Czerny (Cherny), whose piano studies are still used, made him start at the beginning again with wrist and finger exercises. At the time, he was discouraged, but later he was thankful for his sound training.

THE PAGANINI OF THE PIANO

He heard Paganini, the wizard of the violin, and made up his mind to be the Paganini of the piano. He learned to do

AN IMPRESSION OF LISZT

brilliant, impossible, miraculous things with a piano. He also
wrote music such as never had been tried on a piano before.
He believed that there was no form of music that the piano, his
beloved chosen instrument, could not express. He made piano
arrangements of almost all kinds of music ever written, from
grand opera to Beethoven symphonies.

Nowadays it seems a pity to turn the rich tones of a Beethoven symphony into just a piano piece, but it was different
then. People had no machines to give them music—no radios,
no phonographs, no player pianos. Only the large cities could
afford to have opera companies and symphony orchestras.
But there were pianos in the smaller towns, and every year
some famous pianist would stop on a concert tour. Liszt
thought that by rewriting operas and symphonies for the piano,
he could bring the lovely melodies to people who otherwise
would never have a chance to hear them.

Liszt's own concert tours began when he was no more than
a boy, and covered all Europe, from Madrid with its whirling
Spanish dances and cruel, colorful bull-fights, to the quiet
gray towns of the northern countries. Spain, Italy, Switzerland,

England, Germany—there was scarcely a town of any size anywhere that did not see the handsome Liszt glide tiger-like along some concert platform to pounce on the piano and wring from it music such as the people had never heard.

Famous musicians in Paris were as thick as robins in May, and yet Liszt became the darling of them all. The ladies adored him and strewed flowers in his path. A princess gave him freely of her fortune, and a countess eloped with him.

LISZT'S GENEROSITY

Though he was spoiled and petted, he was one of the most generous musicians who ever lived. He gave $10,000 to a fund for a monument to Beethoven in his birthplace, Bonn. He turned over all the proceeds of a concert tour to help the sufferers from a flood in Hungary. When later the grateful people there raised a sum for a statue to him, he insisted that the money be given to a struggling young sculptor. He saved a fellow musician from poverty in his old age, and he gave hundreds of lessons to ambitious youngsters without ever taking a penny in payment.

Liszt was one of the first to make musicians respected as followers of a noble art, and not thought merely entertainers of princelings and treated as upper class servants—like Haydn, Mozart, or Schubert. Once after he had returned from a concert tour, a princess asked him if he had had good business. "Your highness," he answered, "I am in music, not in business."

Music meant more to Liszt than fortune or fame. At the height of his glory, he gave up his concert tour to become director of the orchestra of the Court Theatre in the little town of Weimar. Here Bach a century before had been director of music for a prince, and here the great poet Goethe had also been a director of the theatre. Liszt thought that this position would give him a chance to bring out new works by

young musicians, works that otherwise might not have been
heard until years after their composers were dead.

ENCOURAGEMENT TO UNKNOWN MUSICIANS

Among many little known works which deserved a hearing,
he produced Schumann's one, ill-fated opera "Genoveva,"
which its unfortunate composer had liked so well. Most important of all, he gave a hearing to that greatest of composers in
the operatic world, Richard Wagner, at a time when musicians
were laughing at his work. At Weimar, Liszt himself turned
from piano compositions to works for full orchestra and composed his famous *symphonic poems*. For a long time after
they were brought out, they were not well known or liked because they were so different from the classic symphonies, or
even from the symphonies of earlier writers of romantic music.

LAST YEARS

After twelve years, he had a quarrel with the rather stodgy
board of directors of the Court Theatre over a new piece he
wished to perform, and he resigned. The rest of his life was
spent in Weimar, Paris, and Rome. In Paris, he was still the
darling of the drawing-rooms, as he had been when he was
young. At Weimar, he had a circle of worshipping pupils
nicknamed "The Swarm." These he taught without pay, en-
couraged if they had talent and, if not, sent them on their
way with the advice to the maidens to "Marry soon, dear
child."

He went to Rome to pray in the beautiful old churches
where so many artists and musicians nad done their best work
for the glory of God, and so many great men and good men
had come to worship. As a boy of sixteen, after the death of
his father, he had wanted to become a priest. But the good
father in his own parish had persuaded him that he should not
waste the great gift for music which God had given him. Now

that he was old, he turned again to the church, and for the rest of his life was known as Abbé Liszt.

Of all Liszt's music, his "Hungarian Rhapsodies" are the best known and best loved, but his symphonic poems are the most important. In them, he developed a new musical form, just as Haydn did with the symphony. The symphony was the greatest form of *absolute* music, but the strict rules by which its themes must be worked out and its movements always be placed in a certain order made it not so well suited to *romantic program music*. There was need for a long form for full orchestra by which romantic music could express its thought or tell its story.

"LES PRELUDES"

Liszt composed his symphonic poems all in one movement and used his musical themes much differently from the way they were used in the classic symphonies. His best known symphonic poem, "Les Preludes," was written to express the words of a French poem, "Is our life anything but a series of preludes to an unknown song of which death sounds the first and solemn note?" Liszt told of the different "preludes" or parts of life—love, struggle, joy in country life, and call to battle—by the way he used two lovely musical themes all through the composition. He changed the time and rhythm, broke the themes into shorter themes or added notes to make them longer, gave them softly to the strings and woodwinds for love and nature, or blared them with brasses for the call to arms.

"TILL EULENSPIEGEL"

Many later musicians followed Liszt's pattern for the symphonic poem, but not all symphonic poems are solemn and sermon-like. The German composer, Richard Strauss (not related to the waltz kings), has told in his symphonic poem,

"Till Eulenspiegel" (Oil-en-shpee-gel) or *"Till Owl's-Mirror,"* as it would be in English, the musical story of a merry, likeable rascal of German folk-lore. Till was somewhat like the English Robin Hood who robbed fat lords and friars to give to the poor and led the Sheriff of Nottingham such an exciting life. Or the impish goblin, Puck, who would come by night to curdle the cream and play all sorts of pranks on simple English milkmaids.

The composer, Richard Strauss, was one of the great musicians of his time. Although he lived to be 85, his most important compositions were written before he reached the age of 50. Strauss was born in 1864 in the old city of Munich, where his father was a French horn player in the court orchestra. Like many of the great masters of earlier times, young Richard was a child wonder.

EDUCATION OF STRAUSS

Strauss began to study the piano at the age of four. When he was six, he had composed a polka or little dance. At eight, he began to study the violin. When he was in the Gymnasium (as high schools in Germany are called), he took special lessons in composition and instrumentation, or the use of instruments in orchestral music. At sixteen, he surprised his teachers and classmates by composing a chorus for an old Greek play and a Festival overture. He was only eighteen when a famous conductor produced his first symphony, and made him known to the world of music.

At first, he cared only for the older classic forms of music and took Haydn, Mozart, Beethoven and Brahms for his only models. Later he became friendly with a musician who was a follower of romantic music. Through him, Strauss learned to know and love the work of Liszt and the great French tone poet, Berlioz. After a trip to Italy, he wrote his first program music, "Aus Italien" or "From Italy," and in the end, he wrote romantic music and tone poems in which he uses musical themes and all the instruments of a huge orchestra in ways no other musicians had ever dared.

Strauss became a great conductor as well as a composer. From the time he was twenty-two until he was twenty-six, he led the orchestra at the Munich Court Theatre, and then he was appointed conductor at Weimar. In the old town, haunted by the spirits of Bach and Goethe and Liszt, Strauss composed his great symphonic poems. He expressed thoughts and poems in music as Liszt had done. Then he went further and even turned stories into music with the symphonic poems "Don Quixote" and "Till Eulenspiegel."

STORIES IN MUSIC

At first, people did not know what to think of Strauss's stories in music and the way he used the orchestra to describe characters and adventures. But when the strangeness and the newness had worn off, they could see that here was truly great music.

Although Strauss composed operas and many lovely songs, he is perhaps best known for his symphonic poems. He himself thought that "Till Eulenspiegel" was the best of his symphonic poems. Strauss began this work with two quaint, quirky themes which describe Till as well as if they said, "This is Till Eulenspiegel, a sly, funny rascal, always up to sudden tricks. You never can tell where he will be or what he will do next, for he can stride over the country in seven-league boots or hide in a mouse-hole."

MISCHIEVOUS ADVENTURES OF "TILL EULENSPIEGEL"

Then Till is off on his adventures. The way the two Till themes are found in different shapes, alternated with new themes, makes it seem as if Strauss were finding a new use for the old rondo form. First, it is market-day in town. The

women sit around the square with their wares around them—
heaps of fruits and vegetables, pots and pans, and crates of
ducks and fine fat geese. As the market-women cry their wares
and chatter among themselves, a ragged stranger slips through
the gate to the town, leading his bony horse. It is Till. "Hop!
Eulenspiegel springs on his horse, gives a smack of the whip,
and rides into the midst of the crowd. Clink, clash, clatter!"
(Klatte's analysis of score.) Pots and pans are broken, vegetables roll in every direction, and the market-women flee. The
rascal hurries away to safety, and we can hear in the music the
jogging of his old nag in a new rhythm for the second Till
theme.

Next, Till disguises himself as a priest to fool the people.
There is a sturdy, simple tune like a German folk tune to
represent the good, believing people while the funny Till
theme on the clarinet shows how the rogue is mocking them.
But even the rascally Till isn't bold enough to wear the priestly
disguise for long. He is himself again, and at once falls in love
with the first pretty girl he sees. She will have none of him
and off he goes in a great rage—represented by a variation of
the first Till theme in a smashing passage for the brasses.

Just then, Till finds himself in the midst of some stuffy
old professors who think they know everything in the world.
He sees a chance to have some fun at their expense and asks
them a whirl of questions that they cannot possibly answer—
then dashes off, leaving them open-mouthed with amazement.

After that, we hear a gay street song interwoven with the
Till themes in different forms. In the midst of all his mischievous fun, Till begins to wonder if he had not better turn
over a new leaf and lead a sober life. But his repentance is
short-lived, and he goes on to ever wilder, wickeder things until at last he is caught by the law.

Judgment comes. "The drum rolls a hollow roll; the jailer
drags the rascally prisoner into the court-room." We hear the

judges in solemn, threatening chords on the woodwinds and heavy strings. Till answers with his quirky little theme—frightened, but still mocking the big-wigs. The game is up; he is dragged terrified off to the gallows, and the trap is sprung —choking off the saucy theme at last. The ever slowing pizzicato, or plucking of the stringed instruments, tells of his death.

At the very end of the composition, Strauss repeats the Till themes as sweetly as an old folk tune, seeming to say, "No matter what Till's faults, people will always love to tell and hear fine stories about him." And then in a mighty blare of full orchestra, "But don't forget that he was, after all, a rascal and more pleasant to meet in stories than in real life."

In an old graveyard near the North German town of Lübeck, they say that his tombstone may still be seen with an owl and a mirror carved on it. The musical story of his merry pranks will live forever.

RECORD LIST — CHAPTER X

Brahms, Johannes (1833-1897)
    Academic Festival Overture, Op. 80
    "Children's Songs"
    Piano Concerto No. 1 in D Minor, Op. 15
    Piano Concerto No. 2 in B Flat, Op. 83
    Violin Concerto in D, Op. 77
    Hungarian Dances
    Liebeslieder
    Piano music — various
    Quintet in B Minor for Clarinet and Strings, Op. 115
    Quintet in F Minor for Piano and Strings, Op. 34
    Sonatas for Clarinet and Piano, Op. 120, Nos. 1 and 2
    Songs (lieder) — various
    "Songs in Folk Style"
    Symphony No. 1 in C Minor, Op. 68
    Symphony No. 2 in D, Op. 73
    Symphony No. 3 in F, Op. 90
    Symphony No. 4 in C Minor, Op. 98

Variations on a Theme by Haydn, Op. 56A
Variations on a Theme by Paganini, Op. 35

Flotow, Friedrich von (1812-1883)
Martha — excerpts

Humperdinck, Engelbert (1854-1921)
Hansel and Gretel — excerpts

Liszt, Franz (1811-1886)
A Faust Symphony
Hungarian Fantasia for Piano and Orchestra
Hungarian Rhapsodies (piano or orchestra)
Les Preludes
Mephisto Waltz (piano or orchestra)
Piano music — various
Piano Sonata in B Minor
Todtentanz, for Piano and Orchestra

Strauss, Johann, Sr. (1804-1849)
Radetzky March, Op. 228
Waltzes, Polkas, Marches, Galops — various

Strauss, Johann, Jr. (1825-1899)
Die Fledermaus — excerpts
Waltzes — various, including "On the Beautiful Blue
Danube"; "Tales from the Vienna Woods"

Strauss, Richard (1864-1949)
Also sprach Zarathustra (Thus Spake Zarathustra), Op. 30
Don Juan, Op. 20
Don Quixote, Op. 35
Der Rosenkavalier — excerpts or suite
Salome — Closing Scene
Sinfonia Domestica, Op. 53
Songs — various
Till Eulenspiegel, Op. 28
Todt and Verklärung (Death and Transfiguration), Op 24

CHAPTER XI

FRENCH MUSIC—
TONE COLOR

THE FIRST PROGRAM MUSIC

When the German composers of romantic music first began to make spring and slumber songs instead of preludes,
and used music to express thoughts and paint pictures, people
thought they were doing something new. Yet more than a
hundred years before, French musicians had been writing little
pieces for the harpsichord with names like "The Cuckoo,"
"The Hen," or "The Battle."

FRENCH FOLK SONGS

Like the ancient Greeks, the French did not care for their
music as a joy in itself, but as something to make life and the
other arts more pleasant. The peasants sang fine old folk songs
in the provinces of France—wild songs in Normandy, graceful troubadour tunes in Southern France, old songs of Brittany,
shaded with sadness as the country was with clouds. But folk
songs played little part in the music made by musicians, for
the music of France was mostly made for the city of Paris.

Paris liked its music to go with life and action. If a French
musician was not composing music to go with a story or dance
on the stage, he was making it to paint some picture in his
mind. What is more, gay Paris did not care where her music
came from or who made it as long as it was amusing. The
stories of the two most famous French operas came from

155

foreign countries—"Faust" from Germany and "Carmen" from Spain. And the first great French musician was an Italian.

Giovanni Battista Lully was born about 1633 near the old Italian city of Florence. He grew up, a merry black-eyed lad who could sing beautifully and play the guitar. He caught the fancy of the Chevalier de Guise who was travelling through Italy. This French nobleman took the boy back with him as a present to the sister of the king.

So young Giovanni Battista became Jean-Baptiste, a scullion in the kitchen of the princess. He did not have to work hard and had plenty of time to sing, play his guitar, and learn to play the violin. This he did so well that he was made a member of the princess' band where he soon was the best violinist of them all. Then he was caught writing a saucy song about his royal mistress and was at once dismissed from her service.

He had become so skilled in violin playing that he soon was wearing the bright beribboned suit, plumed hat, and lace ruffles of the king's own orchestra. The "Violons du Roi" or "King's Viols," was made up, as the name shows, of stringed instruments—violins, violas, and basses. Soon he began to compose music for the king's ballets.

The *ballet* was a combination of dancing, poetry, and music, and was a favorite form of entertainment in the court of Louis XIV. All the nobles took part in ballets. Even the King himself delighted in strutting around the stage in the gaudy costume of a ballet dancer, and reciting verses to tell of his own greatness. A later form of ballet was called dramatic ballet, and was without words, the story being told by panto-mime, or dumb show, and music. Ballet became so well liked

in Paris that no opera could be successful unless it introduced a ballet at exactly 9:30 P.M. Some French composers wrote their best music for the ballet, and their ballet music is still heard while the operas are forgotten.

As a composer of music or airs for ballet, Lully became a great favorite of the King. Lully wished to compose and produce operas. To make sure that his operas would be successful, he had the King pass a law that all rival theatres could have only two singers and six stringed instruments. Of course, that made Lully's opera the only opera in Paris. In the end, the King ruled that no other music but Lully's could be performed in any theatre or court concert or even in church.

To be sure, Lully's operas were better than any other at that time. In his duets, he still had his voices sing one after the other instead of together. But he suited his music to his words and action better than others had, and he had made his chorus part of the play—like a street crowd, soldiers, etc.—instead of merely standing and singing. Some of his music is often heard today—especially the *Airs de Ballet*.

At rehearsals, he was a regular tyrant. He himself would

drill the performers in everything—even the expressions of their faces. He would often fly into a rage, kick the singers, and once even broke a violin over the head of one of them. His death was due to one of his wild moods. In conducting his orchestra, he beat time on the floor with a bamboo cane so violently that when he accidentally struck his foot, the blow caused a wound from which he died.

JEAN PHILIPPE RAMEAU

When he died in 1687, Bach was just two years old and the next great French musician, Jean Philippe Rameau (Rah-mó) was but a child of five. When Rameau was seven years old, he could play the clavichord and read any music at sight. Though he quickly learned organ and violin also, he would not open a book unless it was about music. So he was expelled from school. Then when he was seventeen, he fell in love with a young widow who made so much fun of the spelling in his letters that he was ashamed, and studied by himself the things he should have learned in school.

His father sent him to Italy to forget his love affair, but he did not stay long. He became first violinist in a travelling theatrical company that went from town to town all over southern France. After a few years as organist in a country church, he went to Paris. The great organist of Paris was then the Marchand who had run away from Dresden because he was afraid of a contest with Bach. At first, Marchand was kind and helpful to young Rameau. Then, when he saw that Rameau would soon outshine him, he became wildly jealous. Rameau entered a competition for an organist's position, and Marchand, who was one of the judges, gave the place to someone else.

In the end, as Rameau saw that Marchand would try not to let him get ahead in Paris, he retired bitterly to the cathedral organ in a little mountain town. It was a lonely place, and the raw, harsh weather in the winter kept him indoors much of the time. He began to experiment with harmony, and tried to find out why one chord, or combination of notes, sounded better than another, and why certain chords sounded well when they followed each other, while chords played in a different order did not. He made rules for the use of chords, and wrote his "Treatise on Harmony," which was a great help to later musicians.

He went back to Paris to have his book published. This time he managed to get a place as organist, and little by little became a favorite teacher among ladies of nobility. His first opera was not produced until he was fifty years old, but during the last twenty years of his life he composed an immense number of operas and ballets. His harmonies and orchestration were richer than Lully's. Instead of having his woodwinds play the same music as his strings, he composed separate parts for them. Like Lully, he gained all kinds of honors from his king, and when he died, all France mourned.

Now French music was well started on the way it would go. French musicians followed Rameau in working out new combinations of tone and expressing life in tone color. As the people of Paris, like Lully's king, cared only for opera and ballet, opera flourished. But the musicians who gained the most fame and fortune were not French. The famous battle of opera was fought between the Italian Piccinni and the German Gluck. For many years, the highest place of honor in French music was held by the Italian Cherubini (Kay-roo-be-ne). When, at last, the French had a truly great musician of their own, they let him nearly starve to death.

HECTOR BERLIOZ

He was Hector Berlioz (Bér-lee-os), born in 1803, the son of a country doctor. His father wished the boy to be a doctor, too, and sent him to medical school in Paris.

While there, he began to study the music of Gluck and Beethoven. He could think of nothing but music. He composed a cantata for voices and instruments, and was admitted to the Paris Conservatory. When his father heard of it, he was furiously angry and stopped young Hector's allowance.

Then came lean and bitter years. He slept and shivered in a bare and dingy attic. He lived on bread and grapes. At last, he got a job singing in the chorus of a cheap little theatre, and so managed to keep from starving. All this time, he was disliked by most of his teachers at the Conservatory, and positively hated by Cherubini, the director, because his works were so strange and different from the usual operas and pretty little ballets. He liked large orchestras with deep, rich tone combinations.

He was not allowed to compete for the longed-for Prix de Rome, which carried with it a government pension for three years of study at Rome. They said he was not fit. When, on the fourth attempt, they let him offer his work, he won. After the few peaceful years at Rome, his life went on its stormy way.

MUSIC OF BERLIOZ

He believed in program music, or music that should tell a story. His mind was wild to the point of madness. He wrote music for dances of devils, and murderers meeting punishment in the next world. It is true that he also wrote lovely and simple religious music—"The Farewell of the Shepherds" and "The Rest of the Holy Family" from "L'Enfance du Christ." But people expected wild and strange things from him, and seldom appreciated anything else that he did.

Only once did anyone at first take a fancy to his music. When his "Symphonie Fantastique" was first played at the

Conservatory, Paganini, the wizard of the violin, was in the audience. Afterwards, he came to Berlioz, fell upon his knees, and kissed his hand. The next day he sent the young composer a cheque for twenty thousand francs. That was the only help and praise that he found in France.

The very tall, grim man with the wild mop of hair, who looked "as if he would like to kill everybody on sight and yet never did anybody any harm," was made an object of fun in Paris. His operas failed. He could not make a living from his music, for in Paris there was not much music except the opera. For twenty years he had to write weekly articles for a musical paper to keep himself alive.

It made him sad and bitter to have to take time from his music for writing. Yet his articles brought him fame as one of the greatest musical critics in Europe, and his book on the use of instruments of the orchestra was a help to hundreds of young composers. The work of Berlioz has made young musicians see the importance of *orchestration*, or the art of choosing the best musical instruments for voicing special kinds of musical ideas. We can see what a difference orchestration makes in music by comparing the same piece set for orchestra by two composers—such as the Hungarian "Rákóczy March" orchestrated by both Berlioz and Brahms. Both versions may be equally good, but as different as a painting and a photograph of the same scene.

THE MODERN ORCHESTRA

Berlioz is sometimes called the "father of the modern orchestra" because his works call for practically the same sort of orchestra as that used by composers of today. Before his time, orchestras were smaller, and the combination of instruments was always changing. Mozart was the first to use clarinets in his symphonies, but he used them instead of oboes. Beethoven was the first to use both clarinet and oboe, and the opera composer, Meyerbeer, was the first to use the tuba and give an important part to the brasses.

What is more, the instruments themselves were always changing. An instrument like a queer looking serpent of Handel's time would pass out of use as other wind instruments of less harsh tone were invented. The size and shape of flutes and clarinets were always changing. But Berlioz was as much a wizard of the orchestra as Paganini of the violin and Liszt of the piano. He tried every possible combination of instruments, and later musicians have kept the orchestra about as he left it.

There are four groups of instruments in the orchestra of today. The string group contains the harp, the violin, the viola, the violoncello, and the double bass. The woodwind group contains the flute, piccolo, oboe, English horn, clarinet, bassoon and contra-bassoon. The brass group contains the horn (commonly called the French horn), the trumpet, the trombone and the tuba. Percussion instruments include the tympani, the snare drum, the bass drum, the tambourine, cymbals, triangle, castanets, xylophone, marimba, orchestra bells, and many other special noise-making instruments.

The personal life of Berlioz was as stormy and unhappy as his musical career. He was always afraid that after his death someone would write the story of his life and say mean and ridiculous things about him. So he wrote his own life, giving himself the praise that his countrymen withheld from him. When he made a tour of the different countries of Europe, the French were more than surprised to see him honored everywhere as a great man. Yet French music, as time went on, turned more and more from the opera to follow Berlioz's lead in expressing stories and pictures in tone, and seeking new and daring uses of instruments.

France has had only one great composer of absolute music, and he was born a Belgian. César Franck, born in Liége, came to Paris when he was fifteen to enter the Conservatory. He won prizes for piano, organ, counterpoint, and fugue, but did not try for the Prix de Rome, as his father wished him to devote himself to church music rather than opera. He spent all his quiet, saintly life teaching and playing the organ in Paris—as someone said, "finding joy in the service of the church and laboring devotedly through long hours of teaching every day to do his very best for every one of his pupils."

All his beautiful works were composed in the few hours he could snatch from a long day of drudgery. One of his pupils wrote: "Winter and summer he was up at half past five. The first two morning hours were devoted to composition, 'working for himself,' he called it. About half past seven after a frugal breakfast, he started to give lessons all over Paris, for to the end of his days this great man was obliged to devote most of his time to teaching.

LIFE OF LABOR

"All day long he went about on foot and by omnibus and returned to his quiet home in time for an evening meal. Although tired out with the day's work, he still managed to find a few minutes to copy or orchestrate his scores except when he devoted his evenings also to pupils. In those two early hours of the morning, Franck's finest works were conceived, planned, and written."

Although Franck composed two operas (never produced) and some symphonic poems, he did his best work in church music or absolute music, like the old masters. His church music, like that of Bach and Palestrina, was truly for the worship of God, and not to show off his own skill as a musician. His Symphony in D minor, the only truly great symphony to come from France, is now probably one of the ten symphonies most frequently played. Yet it was seldom heard until many years after Franck's death.

Someone said of Franck, "He stands out from the musicians of his time as one of another age. They seek glory; he let it seek him." While César Franck was living a life as solitary and devoted as Bach, most other French composers were travelling the beaten track to glory. Gounod (Goo-no), Saint-Saëns (San-Sahn), Bizet—all were brilliant lads at the Conservatory and composed opera and program music.

GOUNOD

Gounod was the oldest, born in 1818, five years before César Franck. He won the Prix de Rome, and during his stay in Italy thought for a while of becoming a priest. Though he expressed his love for the church in music, he is best known for his two operas, "Romeo and Juliet" and "Faust." "Faust" is so full of action and bright melodious tunes that it will always be a favorite even with people who know little about music. It seemed almost as play that he composed little program pieces like the "Funeral March of a Marionette."

SAINT-SAËNS

Camille Saint-Saëns was much younger, born in 1835. Twice he tried for the Prix de Rome, and twice lost to musicians who are nearly forgotten today. He composed many operas, because only by writing for the stage could a French musician make any money or fame. But he was at his best in music for orchestra—painting pictures or telling stories in tone. He composed a set of little pieces called "Carnival of Animals," in which he described in music some of the animals at the zoo. The best known of these pieces is "The Swan." The graceful melody floats like a swan on the rippling waves of the accompaniment.

"DANSE MACABRE"

His Symphonic Poem, "Danse Macabre" is one of the best known examples of story-telling in music. The orchestra announces the stroke of midnight with a loud note struck on the harp and strengthened by the horn. We then hear Death tuning his fiddle (solo violin). The flute gives the ghostly waltz, which is taken up by Death's fiddle while the xylophone (an instrument not often used with symphony orchestra) gives the clatter of bones as the skeletons leap from the graves and dance in their shrouds. Wilder and wilder grows the dance until at dawn the cock's crowing (oboe) is heard, and the skeletons scamper back to their graves as the birds sing and a morning service is chanted in the church by the graveyard.

GEORGES BIZET

Georges Bizet (Bee-zay), born in 1838, was the youngest of the three, and but for his early death might have been the greatest. His opera "Carmen" is one of the best of all operas, with its throbbing Spanish rhythms and wild bursts of melody to fit the exciting story of the Spanish gypsy girl. His other very famous work, "L'Arlésienne Suite," is incidental music to a French play which deals with life in the province of Arles in southern France.

BIZET AND THE SAXOPHONE

In this music, Bizet was one of the very few composers to use the saxophone with a symphony orchestra. The saxophone, a brass instrument with a clarinet reed, named for its inventor, Saxe, was always a favorite in bands and popular orchestras. Though Bizet showed how beautiful its tone can be when rightly used, it is still more or less an outcast in the symphony orchestra.

As time passed, French musicians went farther and farther, both in trying different notes together for new harmonies, as Rameau had done, and trying different combinations of instruments for tone color.

DEBUSSY

At last came Debussy (Day-byoo-see), the founder of modern music, who explored strange lands of tone which no other musician had ever discovered. Claude Achille Debussy was born in 1862. There were no musicians in his family. His father was a shopkeeper, too poor to give his son any sort of education, and he planned to make his boy a sailor. But a kind lady who had once been a pupil of Chopin took an interest in the child and gave him free lessons. He did so well that by the time he was eleven years old, he had passed the examination for the Paris Conservatory.

While he was in the Conservatory, he became pianist in the trio of a rich Russian lady and had a chance to travel all over Europe—Florence, Vienna, Venice, and at last, stayed for a while on her Russian estate. There he met some of the Russian composers who were trying to make a national music for their country from the folk music. He was very much interested in the strange scales they used, so different from the major and minor scales used by composers of other countries. These scales were found in the folk music of wild Eastern peoples.

After his year abroad, he came back and finished his conservatory course by winning the Prix de Rome, like many other great French musicians. But the music that he composed was not like other musicians' at all. He seldom used the major and minor scales as they were used in most great music. Sometimes he went back to the quaint old modes of early church music. More often he used a *whole-tone* scale.

Our major and minor scales are made up of seven notes,

five whole tones and two half tones, and the difference between the major and minor scales depends on where the half tones come. In the major scale, the half tones are always between the third and fourth, and seventh and eighth notes (mi-fa; ti-do). In the minor scale, one half tone is always between the second and third notes, but there are several different kinds of minor scales which have the second half-tone in different places. The scale Debussy liked best had six notes and no half tones at all (C, D, E, F sharp, G sharp, A sharp). So his melodies sound different from any ever heard before, and his harmonies were stranger still.

Perhaps one reason why Debussy did so many new and daring things with music was because no musician ever had such a sensitive ear. Whenever he heard a note struck, he often heard another note five tones above sound with it. At first, he thought he might be going insane like poor Schumann who always heard the note "A" ringing in his ears. Then he realized that what he was doing was actually *hearing* the first overtone.

OVERTONES

Just as a color is often made up of other colors (purple = blue and red, orange = red and yellow, etc.)—so a tone is always made up of a combination of other tones. Tones are caused by vibrations in the air, and as we saw from the Greek monochord, whether a tone is high or low in pitch depends on how fast these vibrations are. But beside the first or primary vibration which gives us the tone, there are secondary or sympathetic vibrations, just as a stone thrown into water makes not one wave, but an ever-spreading circle of ripples.

The first and strongest of these overtones or partial tones is five tones above the tone sounded. This is the one that Debussy could hear with his unaided ear. If we have a perfectly tuned piano and press down a key silently and then strike loudly the key five tones above or below it, we can often hear it sound with the other as an overtone, giving the effect that Debussy had by ear.

The next overtone is ten notes above the original tone. The higher up from the original tone the overtones are, the closer they lie together, and as a rule, the weaker they are. It is the difference in overtones that makes the difference in the *tone color* of the various instruments. An instrument, like the violin, in which the lower overtones are stronger, has a smooth and mellow tone, while one like the trumpet, in which the upper overtones are stronger, has a tone that is harsh and blaring.

It was from these tones, trembling unheard in air, that Debussy built his weird, unearthly music. Sounds that people did not even know they heard he sounded boldly for all to hear. He used different combinations of instruments in his orchestra, too, because of his sensitive ear, to give soft shimmering effects. At first people were puzzled by his music and did not know what to make of it, but once they became used to it, they liked it very much indeed.

IMPRESSIONISM

Like that of other French composers, Debussy's music is program music rather than absolute music. Sometimes the kind of music Debussy wrote is called impressionistic. He does not so much paint pictures of real life, like Schumann and Mendelssohn, as he tries rather to describe the feelings or impressions those pictures give us. There was a school of painters and poets in France called impressionists, and Debussy tried to get the same effects with music that they did with paintings. This impressionistic art really paints, not the beauty of life, but the beauty of dreams, a far-off beauty like the pot of gold at the end of the rainbow. In his use of new harmonies and tone color, Debussy was the pioneer of modern music.

RAVEL

Perhaps the most important composer to follow Debussy was Maurice Ravel (Ra-vel'). Ravel did not use whole-tone scales and strange-sounding chords quite as much as Debussy. Probably there never has lived another composer who knew better how to extract so many shades of color from the orchestra. For example, in "Bolero," the rhythm is the same throughout, and the melody is repeated over and over again. The variety and interest in this Spanish dance form come from Ravel's skillful use of dynamics (the change from soft to loud, or loud to soft), and his ingenious combinations of tone colors. Ravel also used his genius at orchestration to help tell stories with his music, as in the "Mother Goose Suite."

MUSIC AFTER WORLD WAR ONE

At the close of the First World War (1918), many of the younger French composers felt that the veiled, shimmering effects of Impressionism and the pretty tunes of Romanticism were out of step with the times. Something more virile was needed. A few of them banded together as "The Group of Six" to write and publicly perform music full of strong dissonances, clashing tone colors, and new rhythms, including American jazz. One of the best-known works to come from any member of "The Six" was "Pacific 231" by Honegger, who said, "I love locomotives the way other men love . . . animals." Full of dissonance beyond anything the old masters ever dreamed of, it expresses in a striking way the dynamic energy of a huge machine, the American steam locomotive after which it was named — steel wheels on steel rails, pounding pistons — a controlled monster hurtling across a vast country. Probably the early French composer of the pretty cuckoo piece would have been as puzzled by this music as by the locomotive itself roaring past his stagecoach. Yet after all, both composers had the same thought

— to use music to picture things or suggest ideas which had caught their fancy.

CHAPTER XII

FROM OPERA
TO MUSIC DRAMA

EVERY composer was fond of the opera, and longed to have his own music set to thrilling stories, and performed with gorgeous scenery and bright costumes. Nearly every composer tried his hand at opera, for there was more money and fame in it than in any other kind of music. Yet Mozart was the only one who succeeded in composing both great symphonies and successful operas. Most of the musicians who made their fortune from opera never wrote anything else. While the mighty Beethoven was struggling with his one and only opera, "Fidelio," and poor Schubert was working on opera after opera that failed, a gay Italian fellow named Rossini was the darling of opera houses all over the world.

ROSSINI

Gioacchino (joa-kee-no) Antonio Rossini was born in 1792 in a little Italian town on the Adriatic Sea. His mother was the baker's daughter, and his father was both town trumpeter and butcher. In Europe then, as now, it was often dangerous to be on the wrong side in politics. Father Rossini spoke his mind too freely, and found himself in jail.

The mother had a good voice. When she was left alone with her little boy to support, she went to Bologna to find a place in the opera house. In a short time, she made a success as prima donna or leading lady in *opera buffa* (bóo-fa), or comic opera. When the father was free again, he played the trumpet in the orchestra while his wife sang.

All this time, the boy was boarded with a good pork butcher at Bologna. There was not much chance for him to learn anything. He began to study the harpsichord, but his teacher could only play with two fingers himself. Young Rossini made so much fun of him that the teacher flared up in anger, and the lad was apprenticed to a blacksmith.

His mother was very sad, because she thought that all music for him had come to an end. But he soon found a better teacher, and in a few months learned to read music, play the piano fairly well, and sing well enough to be boy soprano in the church. When he was ten years old, his mother's voice wore out. The family was once more in need until the boy, too, was able to sing in the theatre and play the horn in the orchestra by his father's side.

After several years his voice broke, and then he entered the Conservatory of Bologna to study 'cello and harmony and composition. In a few months, his teacher made the mistake of telling him that while long years of study were needed to compose church music, he already knew as much as most opera composers.

"Then I need nothing more," said the boy, "for operas are all I want to write."

So he left the conservatory and all further study. He was only eighteen when he made a success with his first opera buffa. One successful work followed another until, when he was twenty-four, he composed one of his two greatest works, "The Barber of Seville." The Barber is no other than our gay friend, Figaro, the hero of Mozart's "Marriage of Figaro." The story of "The Barber of Seville" takes place before jolly Figaro's courtship of Susannah. His master, the Count, is not yet married, and the schemes of Figaro help him woo and win the fair Rosina in spite of the disapproval of her guardian.

"THE BARBER OF SEVILLE"

It takes a good story to make a good opera, and Figaro helped both Mozart and Rossini do their best work. Like all Italian operas, "The Barber of Seville" has sparkling solo songs with which sopranos and baritones will always want to show off their voices. But the gay music and the jolly story fit so well together that "The Barber of Seville" will always be heard in our opera houses as the perfect example of the Italian opera *buffa*.

OPERA BUFFA

In the beginning, the opera *buffa* or comic opera was just an interlude between the acts of the opera *seria* or tragic opera, to cheer the people up after so much sadness. Then it grew to be a form of entertainment all by itself. The opera *buffa* was full of fun and merry music, and there were no rules to keep the composer from doing his best.

OPERA SERIA

The tragic opera or opera *seria* was quite different. In the life of Mozart, we read about the battle of opera in Paris between Gluck and the Italian Piccinni. Gluck won with his "classic" opera in which the music was composed to express the feelings in the story rather than to show off the singer's voice. But he died and his idea of opera died with him, while the Italian opera went on in the old way. There were nearly as many silly rules for opera *seria* as there had been in Handel's time. It was still just a collection of songs strung together on any kind of story, and there was no thought of having the music fit the words. The villain was always a bass, the hero a tenor, and the heroine a coloratura soprano who had to have her big scene—often a mad scene as in "Lucia di Lammermoor"—in which she could show her runs, trills, and high notes.

Although Rossini made his fame as a composer of *opera buffa*, he turned to *opera seria* when he married a prima donna who could sing nothing else. He was just as successful in the new kind of work. He wrote over forty operas in all—twenty of them in eight years. He composed at break-neck speed. He did much of his composing in bed. If the sheet of paper on which he had started an aria or duet blew to the floor, he would begin another rather than bother to get out of bed and pick it up. In all his hurry, it is not much wonder that he would use some of his own musical ideas over and over again in different operas. He even absent-mindedly borrowed from other composers—such as eight bars from Haydn's "Seasons" in "The Barber of Seville" or a phrase from Beethoven's Eighth Symphony in another opera.

Yet Rossini made Italian opera much better than ever before. In his operas, there were no long stretches of the so-called "dry recitative" or words half spoken and half sung. He used the orchestra all the way through, and he was a master at mixing his tone colors. That is, if his melody or most important part were played by the horn, he would have the accompanying parts played by instruments of entirely different tone color, like the strings, so that his musical ideas sound clear and never blurred or muddy.

Seldom had there been a success like Rossini's. In Italy, more performances of his operas were given than those of all other composers put together. New composers had a hard time getting their works produced. It was the same in Vienna, where Schubert was struggling for success that never came. Leipzig, London, Paris, all the great European cities fell under the spell of the Italian so "obliging and courteous and full of wit and fun." In some opera houses, the whole season was given up to his works alone.

Rossini lived and worked in Paris for some time. The French style of opera was not quite like the Italian. In Italian opera, song was the main thing. But as French opera grew from the ballet, action was more important, and the purpose of the music was to make a stirring scene still more exciting.

"WILLIAM TELL"

Rossini studied the French style, and wrote his masterpiece, "William Tell," as a grand opera. The story is of the Swiss patriot, William Tell, who is forced by a tyrant to shoot an apple from his son's head as a punishment for refusing to salute a cap placed on a pole. In this opera, Rossini no longer wrote tunes to please the public and show off a fine voice. Every bar of music expresses the feeling of the story, from the overture to the final grand hymn of freedom. The opera is so long—lasting over five hours—that it is not often given nowadays. But the overture is one of the few pieces for orchestra that nearly everyone knows and loves.

ROSSINI AND MEYERBEER

At about the time that "William Tell" was produced, a German Jew named Meyerbeer began to win huge success with his operas. Rossini saw that he would have to work hard to keep up with this new rival, and Rossini did not like to work hard. So although his life was not half over, he retired on the fortune he had made, and never wrote another opera.

MEYERBEER

Meyerbeer became the idol of Paris by giving people what they wanted. His parents, like those of Mendelssohn, were well-to-do, and gave him the best possible musical education. His first operas in Germany did not do very well. So he changed his first name from Jacob to Giacomo, and went to Italy, where he became fairly successful as a composer of Italian opera. But rewards were richer in Paris, and so he finally settled there.

The French liked big spectacular scenes in their operas—mobs and soldiers, battles and burning castles. Meyerbeer gave them big spectacular scenes. Schumann said that Meyerbeer turned the opera over to the circus. Someone else said that he would have put the fire department or a merry-go-round into his operas if he could have made people applaud by doing so.

It is a curious fact that if a few people applaud or cheer, others will be sure to follow them. So in the opera then—and in some places even now—there was a body of men called a claque, hired by the singers and composer to start the applause. Meyerbeer used to sit with the claque, figure out the best places for applause, and arrange his numbers so as to give the hired clappers a chance to earn their money.

It is a wonder that his music is good for anything at all. Yet three of his operas are often heard today; "The Huguenots," a story of religious conflict, with Martin Luther's hymn, "A Mighty Fortress," woven in counterpoint in one of the big scenes; "L'Africaine," a story of the explorer, Vasco da Gama; and "Le Prophète" from which we hear the grand and pompous "Coronation March" so often played by orchestra and band. Meyerbeer was also the first one to use a tuba in the orchestra and to give an important part to the brasses.

CARL VON WEBER

Von Weber never became as rich or famous as either Rossini or Meyerbeer. His operas are not produced as often today. Yet few composers ever had so many new musical ideas to give to music and later musicians. Though he was eight years older than Rossini and Meyerbeer, his first great success, "Der Freischütz" (Fry-shoots) was not composed until two years after "The Barber of Seville." He led a wandering life, which kept him from getting an early start in music and kept him from making the most of his fine ideas.

He was a cousin of Constance Weber who became the wife of Mozart. His father managed a theatrical company made up mostly of his older children, and they were always travelling from city to city. He wanted to make little Carl into a child prodigy like Mozart. But he was a poor teacher himself, and he never stayed in one place long enough to give the boy many lessons with a really good teacher. A short time with Haydn's brother Michael, and two periods of study with old Abbé Vogler were the best that he had.

He became a thrilling pianist. By starting at a mere whisper of tone and working up to a mighty thunder, he could draw listeners right out of their seats. He was a gay and charming young man of whom princesses liked to take piano lessons, and he composed some very good piano music. Long before Mendelssohn composed his "Fingal's Cave" overture, von Weber composed his "Invitation to the Dance," a piece of real program music with a story. In the bass passage, we hear the gentleman asking the lady for the dance, then her answer in the treble, the delight of the dance itself, and their parting words.

Many years before Schumann wrote of the Davidsbündler in his musical journal, von Weber had made a musical society of some of his friends and they all called themselves by fanciful names, too. He even thought of starting a musical journal himself. But before he could go very far with his plans, his fortunes changed again and he was wandering once more.

Even when he was a grown man, he and his father kept travelling from place to place, trying their hands at different ways of earning a living. Once they went into the printing business. Then Carl held positions as secretary or music master to different dukes and princes. Once he was thrown into jail for playing a joke on a king. On another occasion he was sent out of a city because his servant had been caught in graft. He also held small positions in one little theatre after another, and during this time he composed about ten operas without much success.

He was nearly thirty years old before he at last found a home. Then he married a lovely young singer named Caroline Brandt. It was one of the great love stories of music. She gave up a dazzling career for him, and in the end he gave up his life for her and their children. About the time of his marriage, he was made director of the German opera at Dresden, and here he composed his masterpiece, "Der Freischütz."

"DER FREISCHÜTZ"

"Der Freischütz" was a landmark in the history of opera. The story does not come from ancient history or Greek myth, but from an old German folk legend of a demon to whom huntsmen sell their souls in return for magic bullets. Much of the music von Weber took from German folk song. He not only was the first to give Germany a national opera, but he showed composers of other lands how to make operas from the folk tales and tunes of their countries.

THE LEIT-MOTIF

What is more, he was the first to use a special musical theme to describe a character, just as a writer uses a certain word, and to have this theme played whenever the character appears. The later composer, Richard Wagner, called this descriptive musical theme a *leit-motif*, or leading motive. He made such great use of it that people are apt to forget that it was really invented by von Weber. In the wonderful overture, it is easy to pick out the music describing the good and pure maiden Agatha.

The critics did not know what to make of a work so different from the usual opera. The great French musician and critic, Berlioz, was one of the few who liked it. But the German people went wild over it. After it had been performed in Vienna, von Weber wrote, "Greater enthusiasm there cannot be! To God alone the praise!"

His next opera, "Euryanthe," had one of those silly stories with too many characters to remember. Yet because of the fine music and the fame of "Der Freischütz," it was fairly successful. Then he was offered a princely sum from London to compose and conduct an opera in English for the English people.

Already illness was upon him. His doctors told him that if he would rest, he might live for years, but that if he went to London, his life would surely be shortened. Nevertheless, he went to London in order to earn enough money to leave his wife and little children free from want.

"OBERON"

The story chosen for the English opera was one of the many quarrels between Oberon, the king of the fairies, and his queen, Titania. Sick as he was, von Weber studied English in order to know the meaning of the words he was to set to music. It is hard to realize that the bright fairy music of the "Oberon" overture was written by a man really dying for his loved ones. He managed to conduct the performances of "Oberon" with great success, and even gave a few concerts besides. But the labor and excitement were too much for him. He died before he ever saw his home again.

CARL VON WEBER AND WAGNER

As von Weber used to pass along the streets of Dresden on his way to and from the opera house, there was a small boy who watched him with something like worship in his eyes. This lad was Richard Wagner, born in 1813. When he was eight years old, he was picking out a couple of tunes from "Der Freischütz" on the piano. His beloved stepfather, Ludwig Geyer, who lay dying in the next room, asked weakly, "Can it be that the boy has a talent for music?"

However, for a long time he cared more for poetry and plays. He read the plays of Shakespeare, and the great poems about the Greek gods and heroes. He wrote a play of his own in which forty-two characters were killed and he had to bring them back as ghosts to carry on the last act.

IN LEIPZIG

After Geyer's death, the family was in sore need of money and moved to Leipzig where an older sister, Rosalie, was leading lady in the theatre and could help them. At the Leipzig Gewandhaus, he heard Beethoven symphonies for the first time, and Beethoven became his god. Now he wanted to make music—to join music and poetry together in an art greater than either alone. He got a book on musical theory and took a few lessons from a dry and stupid teacher who cared more for rules than for his pupils. And he wrote an overture which was played at the theatre—an overture in which the drum gave a tremendous thump every four measures and the use of instruments was so queer that the audience at first was puzzled, and then howled with laughter.

At the University of Leipzig, he found a really good teacher and studied with him for six months. This was all the musical education that he had, except for his loving study of Beethoven's scores. He copied them, whistled them, sang them, slept with them. He took one job after another as chorus master or conductor in little German theatres and in Russia. After two operas that did not amount to much, he composed "Rienzi" in the Meyerbeer style. It had two revolts against tyrants, plenty of slaughter, a burning castle, and a great deal of loud, splashy music.

He thought that the Paris Grand Opera would be just the place for it, and set out for Paris with his young wife and a Newfoundland dog. There were terrific storms on the way. The mountainous waves and the wind-torn sky made him think of the old legend of the Flying Dutchman with his phantom ship, who must ever be driven wildly over the sea until some maiden loves him well enough to give her life for him.

Paris was cruel, and only the famous Meyerbeer was kind. Wagner later said, "Had it not been for Meyerbeer, my wife and I would have starved." As it was, they were often hungry. Meyerbeer introduced him to the manager of the opera house at Paris, who received him politely but did nothing. During the heart-breaking days of waiting, he did all sorts of hack work to earn his bread—such as piano arrangements of popular operatic tunes. He also wrote the libretto and music of "The Flying Dutchman." The manager of the opera house did not like his music, but wanted to buy the libretto for some other composer to set to music. Poor Wagner was so hungry that he had to agree to this proposition.

SUCCESS OF "RIENZI" IN DRESDEN

When "Rienzi" was at last produced, it was at the little German town of Dresden. It was such a huge success that Wagner was appointed to von Weber's old place as conductor at the opera house. More operas like "Rienzi" would have brought him sure fame and fortune. But in "The Flying Dutchman" he turned from Meyerbeer to von Weber as his model. Here he used the leit-motif for the first time, and in the overture we can hear the weird, wild theme of the Dutchman and the simple lovely melody of Senta spinning among her maidens.

"The Flying Dutchman" was only a lukewarm success. In his next opera, "Tannhäuser," he left all his models behind him. "Tannhäuser" was a truly national German opera founded on the contests of those old folk musicians of knightly rank, the minnesinger. Now he began to work out his own ideas as to what an opera should be. "Tannhäuser" was not a success at all. Instead of going back to the easy style of "Rienzi," Wagner was brave enough to carry out his own ideas still farther in "Lohengrin." He could not even get it produced in Dresden, except for the first act.

MUSIC DRAMA

Wagner's ideas were not all new. Gluck believed that music should express the feeling of the words and that the orchestra should not just accompany the voice, but should paint a background of tone. Von Weber used the leit-motif or musical theme to describe a character. Wagner went farther than either had ever dreamed. He did not call his works opera, but music drama, a union of two arts to make one more beautiful than either. He thought that if the music was to be good, the play should be worthy of it. So he always wrote the words for his music himself. He also believed that certain kinds of stories could be set to music better than others, and that tales of gods and heroes and times of long ago could give more to music than stories of excitement.

Wagner did not use the leit-motifs simply as musical tags to describe a character then on the stage. They were used to describe things like Siegfried's sword or the Holy Grail, and were woven into the orchestral part to show when one character is thinking of another. He even chose special instruments for his different characters and thoughts. In "Lohengrin" he used the brasses for the majesty of the king, the high woodwinds—flute, clarinet, etc.—for the lovely maiden, Elsa, the low woodwinds for the wicked witch, Ortrud, and the high shimmering notes of the violin for the Holy Grail.

He also changed the orchestra at times to get special tone color. For example, when the gods pass over the rainbow bridge to their new home, Valhalla, Wagner thought that the tones of the harp would best express the glittering light. As the two harps usually used in an orchestra were not enough, he called for six harps and wrote a different part for each. Wagner never used the orchestra as an accompaniment for the human voice, but to paint the scene and the joys and sorrows of the characters. Many times he used the human voice simply as one instrument in his orchestra and did not give it the melody, but wove it in a sort of chant as only one of the many voices or parts in the mighty music of his orchestra.

He did not think that the music should be broken up into set numbers as in a concert; now a solo, now a duet. He thought that the voice should go on in an unbroken line, and this endless flow of melody he called *melos*. It was this new use of the human voice which made it so hard for singers and audiences to learn to understand Wagner's music.

"You are a man of genius," said one of his leading ladies, "but you write such queer stuff that it is impossible to sing it."

WAGNER IN EXILE

Nowadays we certainly do not think of "Lohengrin" as queer stuff. No story in opera is better loved than that of the mysterious knight who comes in a swan boat to rescue the gentle maiden accused of bewitching her young brother. Nearly every bride today marches to the altar to the music of the Bridal Chorus. Yet "Lohengrin" was not produced

WOTAN AND VALHALLA

until Liszt was brave enough to bring it out at Weimar. By that time Wagner was in exile. There had been a revolt in Dresden. The people demanded trial by jury, a free press, and other rights. Wagner took the side of the people. When the revolt had been crushed by the soldiers, Wagner slipped away to Weimar where Liszt was about to produce "Tannhäuser." In the midst of a rehearsal, he heard he was to be seized, and that night Liszt helped him slip across the border into another country.

At the time, Germany was not united, but was made up of little states, with different princes. After another unhappy visit to Paris, Wagner settled in the friendly town of Zurich. He had no means of support. He had to depend for food and shelter on the few faithful friends who believed him a genius. There he began the great work of his life, the cycle of four music-dramas called the "Ring of the Niebelungen" which tells the legends of the old German gods and heroes. It begins with the building of the great hall of the gods, Valhalla, by the giants paid with the treasure and the golden ring stolen from the Rhine maidens, and ends with the Rhine maidens recovering the ring while Valhalla burns, the old gods die, and man rules the earth.

Think of the courage of planning a work that would take four nights to produce, that called for the best singers and orchestra in the world and impossible stage effects like a rainbow bridge, a ring of magic fire, and Rhine maidens swimming under water. He might never live to finish it. He could hardly hope ever to see it produced. Yet he wrote, "If I live to finish this work, I shall have lived gloriously. If I die before it is done, I shall have died for something beautiful."

He labored over it twenty-seven years in all, and most of them were hard, discouraging years. Though his earlier works were becoming known in the United States, they were not often produced in his own country, and almost never in London and Paris. Wagner became worn out with working on something that seemed never to be finished and never to be heard. He composed the love drama, "Tristan and Isolde," calling for a smaller orchestra and simpler settings. It was accepted and then given up after fifty-seven rehearsals.

Now even Wagner lost courage. He published the poem of his great cycle without the music. In a sad preface, he said that the music probably never would be written. The young, music-loving King of Bavaria read the poem and the preface. He sent his secretary to Wagner with the welcome words, that he would give him help to finish his work.

"DIE MEISTERSINGER"

The rest is like the end of a fairy tale. He finished his work in luxury in a Swiss villa on the shores of beautiful Lake Lucerne. But before the great "Ring" cycle was done, he was so happy that he composed one of the best musical comedies in the world, "The Mastersingers of Nuremburg." The story is of one of the contests of the old guild of mastersingers at which the prize is the hand of the fair Eva. In the end, of course, Eva is won by the song of her knightly lover, Sir Walter, even if he does not know as many of the rules of music as his pompous rival, Beckmesser. Wagner used some of the real music of the old mastersingers. "The Mastersingers" was brought out in the king's court theatre, and for once Wagner had the joy of seeing one of his best works successful from the very start.

THE FESTIVAL THEATRE

During the long years that he had been working on his great cycle of music dramas, his early works were slowly becoming known and liked everywhere from Russia to the United States. In many of the large cities, music lovers formed into Wagner societies. Now Wagner had longed all his life for a theatre of his own where he could produce his work beautifully. Thanks to the contributions of the Wagner societies and the generous young king, the Festival Theatre at the little German town of Bayreuth was built for him and ready for the first performance of "The Ring." There was a revolving stage so that he could manage the most grand and glittering scenery. The orchestra was hidden from view so that the beauty of his works would seem "swimming in a sea of tone" without the sight of men sawing and puffing away on instruments.

"PARSIFAL"

For his own theatre, he wrote his last work, "Parsifal," on a legend of the Holy Grail. Before his death, Wagner supervised the first few performances of his great music-drama. The traditions of Bayreuth were carried on by Cosima, Wagner's second wife, who was the daughter of Franz Liszt. She and her son, Siegfried Wagner, carried on Wagner's work in the theatre at Bayreuth as long as they lived. Wagner Festivals are still held at Bayreuth in his memory. Wagner dreamed a great dream and made it come true.

CHAPTER XIII

MUSIC DRAMA CHANGES OPERA

WAGNER AND VERDI

THERE never has been a second Wagner, for no other man could make both great music and great poetry together. But all opera became better and more beautiful because he had lived and worked. The changes which Wagner made in the old-fashioned idea of opera are shown in the life of the great Italian opera composer, Giuseppi Verdi (Zhu-sep-pee Vair-dee). Verdi was born in 1813, the same year as Wagner, and they have often been called the twin giants of opera. Yet, like Bach and Handel, they never met. Though Verdi studied Wagner's work carefully, it is quite certain that Wagner, who was as selfish as he was great, never bothered to hear anything by Verdi.

Verdi was born in the tiny village of Le Roncole in a part of Italy forever fought over by France and Austria. When he was a tiny baby, his mother had to hide with him in the belfry of the church, as a bloodthirsty troop of cavalry rode through, burning the houses and killing the people.

His father, Carlo Verdi, kept a little inn by the side of the dusty road. An old wandering violinist who sometimes played at the inn saw how the child loved music, and advised the father to let him study. So the father bought a broken-down old spinet—the best he could afford. It was repaired free of charge by a kind-hearted workman, even when little Giuseppi in a rage had hit the keys with a hammer because he had found a lovely sounding chord once and could not find it again.

He studied with the old organist in the village church and in three years took his place. Then his father managed to scrape together pennies enough to send him to the nearby town of Busseto to get some schooling, as there were no schools in Le Roncole. Young Verdi had been to Busseto before when his father went to buy sugar, coffee, and tobacco for his inn from the rich grocer Barezzi. To the boy, Barezzi seemed one of the greatest men in the world. He could play the flute, clarinet, and horn. He owned a fine Viennese piano, and in his house there was a great room where the Philharmonic Society, an orchestra made up of the amateur musicians of the town, practiced and played.

BAREZZI AIDS VERDI

Barezzi was a true lover of music. After Verdi had been in Busseto two years, boarding with a shoemaker during the week and trudging the three miles back home to play his organ on Sundays, Barezzi heard of him. He gave the boy a job handling groceries, and took him into his home to live. Evenings, the boy studied Latin with the priest and music with the cathedral organist. He read everything he could find, practised on Barezzi's fine piano, and played duets with Barezzi's pretty little daughter, Margherita. He also composed piano pieces for himself and Margherita, anthems for the church, and marches for the military band.

At last, Barezzi managed to raise a sum of money in the town as a scholarship to send Verdi to study at the conservatory in the great city of Milan. Verdi went to Milan to take the entrance examination. He was refused. It was a cruel disappointment, but he stayed in Milan and studied with private teachers. At the end of two years, he composed a fugue in a test at which twenty-eight conservatory students had failed.

Then he returned to Busseto and took charge of Barezzi's Philharmonic Society. There he married little Margherita and set to work on his first opera, a very unimportant work, never heard now. When at last it was done, he and his eighteen year old wife and their two babies went to Milan to try to get it produced at the great La Scala opera house. There were waits and delays, and Margherita had to pawn her few little pieces of jewelry to pay the rent.

DISAPPOINTMENT AND SORROW

Finally, two of the singers liked it so well that the manager decided to bring it out. Its success brought him a contract to compose three more operas. The first was to be an *opera buffa*. During the short three months while poor Verdi was trying to write gay music for a comic opera, his whole family died—first the little boy and then the little girl and at last Margherita herself. The opera was a flat failure, and Verdi made up his mind never to write another.

SUCCESS

The manager of the opera house thought otherwise. He locked Verdi up in a room with a libretto and would not let him out until the music was done. This opera was a great success and was the first of those operas that made Verdi as much the darling of the Italian people as Rossini had been many years before.

To the Italians, opera was not just amusement, but a part of their lives. Its music took the place of folk songs. Whenever the peasant in the vineyard or the merchant in the town was in love or felt sad, he would sing an aria of some opera he had heard. In Verdi's younger days, Italy was not a united country, but was split into little states, many of them in the power of some foreign country like France or Austria. If Verdi in one of his operas wrote stirring music for a chorus of Hebrews in exile, longing for a country of their own, the Italians took the music as an expression of their own hearts. The cry, "Viva, Victor Emanuel, Re d'Italia" (Long live Victor Emanuel, King of Italy) was forbidden for fear it would stir up a revolution. But the initials of the cry made Verdi's name, and "Viva Verdi" was the watchword of young patriots everywhere.

Verdi was thirty-eight when he composed the three operas that have made him loved by all countries and all times. "Rigoletto," "Il Trovatore," and "La Traviata" are still favorites in opera houses all over the world. The tuneful "Traviata" was a failure at first because the part of the heroine who was supposed to be dying of consumption was sung by an extremely plump prima donna. When the doctor said, "She will die within a few hours," the audience roared with laughter.

People who never have heard an opera know and love the stirring "Anvil Chorus" from "Il Trovatore" where the gypsies are shoeing their horses. The quartet in "Rigoletto" is one of the greatest pieces of ensemble music ever written for opera or music-drama. In it, four different people express different feelings at one and the same time—the Duke making love to the flirting, chattering Maddalena in the inn while outside Gilda sings of her broken heart and her father vows vengeance.

WORLD-WIDE FAME

Now Verdi's fame was world-wide, and his operas were produced everywhere—London, Vienna, Paris, St. Petersburg, and even the United States and Brazil. Then the great Suez canal was opened, so that ships could sail from Europe to the rich treasure of India and China without going around the stormy coast of Africa. The Egyptian government commissioned Verdi to compose an opera for their new opera house at Cairo as part of the celebration. A famous French student of Egyptian history furnished the story of Aida (Ah-eé-da). It is a tale of conflict between the Egyptians and the Ethiopians. Aida, the daughter of the Ethiopian king, has been captured and made slave to the Egyptian princess, Amneris. The young general of the Egyptian army, Rhadames (Rah-dah-mes), is loved by the princess Amneris, but all his love is for Aida.

"Aida" is one of the best liked of all operas, for there is something in it to please everyone. For those who like big scenes, there is perhaps the biggest scene in any opera—the gorgeous triumphal march of the Egyptians with soldiers, war chariots, images of the gods, dancing slave girls carrying the treasure of the conquered, and at last the young leader Rhadames, borne aloft to receive the crown of victory from Princess Amneris. There are real horses in the triumphal procession, and at times, even elephants and camels.

For those who like a story of the human heart, there is Aida, torn between her love for Rhadames and her fatherland; Rhadames, divided between his love of Aida and his duty as an Egyptian soldier; Amneris struggling with her passion for Rhadames and her jealousy of the slave girl who has won his love.

Those who like a melodious tune have Rhadames' love song, "Celeste Aida" and the triumphal march. The chorus, "Glory to Egypt," was adopted as Egypt's national anthem. Those who love music as an art have most of all to admire. Not even Wagner could better fit the music to the story. Verdi based some of his melodies on old Egyptian tunes and gave the whole piece "the very smell of Egypt." He used the leit-motif without being a slave to it. He did not think that the same musical theme could be used to describe a character both in anger and in happiness.

No one ever was a greater master in the use of the orchestra. When Rhadames is sealed alive in the tomb as punishment for telling the secret route of the Egyptian army to Aida and her father, he finds Aida waiting to share death with him. As they sing their last duet, "Farewell to Earth," the orchestra consists only of muted violins, viola, harp, flute, and clarinets. Someone said that the effect is "not so much notes as tears."

VERDI AND WAGNER

"Aida" was praised by critics everywhere, and it made Verdi very angry when they called him a follower of Wagner. He felt that Italian music and German music must always go different ways. Italian music was inspired by Palestrina, the great master of song. Verdi, like all Italian musicians, thought the human voice the noblest of all instruments, and gave it the most important part in his works. But German music was more instrumental than vocal, because Bach with his polyphonic or many-voiced style for both instruments and organ, was the father of German music. So Wagner used the human voice as only one of the many instruments of the orchestra. Verdi felt that he could learn from Wagner without imitating him, and still be true to himself and Italian music.

GREATEST OPERAS

After "Aida," Verdi retired to his large farm, Sant' Agata, near Busseto. Here he spent quiet years tending his fruit, breeding and selling his horses, and building additions and sinking wells in times of unemployment to make work for the townspeople. He probably thought that his opera writing days were over. But he had always loved the English Shakespeare above all other poets, and when he was a very old man, he became a friend of the poet Boïto, who was the best translator and student of Shakespeare in Italy.

Together they made operas of two of Shakespeare's best plays; the tragedy "Othello" and the comedy "Falstaff" (The Merry Wives of Windsor). There is no finer poetry than Shakespeare's. There is no more beautiful music than Verdi's. At eighty, Verdi had done his best work and produced two of the greatest operas in the world.

PUCCINI

Italian opera did not die with Verdi. It will never die as long as there are voices to sing and ears to listen. The most famous Italian opera composer since Verdi is Puccini (Poo-chee-nee) who Verdi once said would follow in his footsteps. His haunting melodies flow on endlessly like Wagner's, but are sweet rather than strong. He uses strange combinations of chords that the old-fashioned rules never allowed, and makes them sound delightful. Perhaps the reason that his work is not more truly great is that he never set a really great book to music. Most of them—like "Madame Butterfly"—would have been long since forgotten except for Puccini's music.

Perhaps the most popular of Puccini's operas is "La Bohème." This is a story of young artists, writers, and musicians who lived and worked gaily in their lodgings, often cold and hungry, but ready to share their last crust or lump of coal. It is the sort of life that Puccini himself led when he was a poor student living on twenty dollars a month from the Congregation of Charity at Rome.

THE ONE ACT OPERA

One of the latest turns of Italian opera is what is called the tabloid or "blood-and-thunder" opera. These works are short —only one or two acts. They are written to stories of everyday life; that is, the characters are common people and not kings and queens and figures out of history. They bristle with violence. Though they do not sound very pleasant, two of them, "Cavalleria Rusticana," by Mascagni (Mahs-cahn-yee), and "Pagliacci" (Pahl-yáh-chee) by Leoncavallo (Lay-on-cah-váhl-lo), are given in one evening as one of the favorite opera programs.

Though Wagner's ideas and works made all Italian opera better, the opera of other countries shows even more clearly what later composers were learning from the music-drama. These changes are strongly illustrated by three of the greatest French operas. One of the most popular of all French operas is "Faust" by Gounod. This opera was produced in Paris two years before "Tannhäuser" was hissed there. It has the good story without which no opera ever lives—a poem by the great German, Goethe, about an aged scholar, Faust, who sells his soul to the devil to be young again and win the love of the maiden Marguerite. It has big scenes, a dainty ballet, and ear-tickling melodies. It will always be loved as long as people love catchy tunes, but the music might fit almost any other story as well as "Faust." It does not stir us nearly so much as the music of "Carmen" by Bizet, who was twenty-five years younger than Wagner.

In "Carmen" the music fits every word and scene of the tale of the wild Spanish gypsy, loved by a soldier and a bull-fighter. Bizet even uses the leit-motif. There is a gloomy musical phrase first heard when Carmen throws her rose to the soldier, Don José. This theme is heard again and again to tell of evil and tragedy, as in the fortune-telling scene in the smugglers' cave when Carmen reads her own death in the cards. The critics could not see that "Carmen" was one of the best operas ever written. They attacked it so bitterly that poor Bizet died young and broken-hearted.

"Carmen" has often been called the "halfway house between Wagner and French opera." The French composer, Debussy, in "Pelleas and Melisande," composed the only other work besides Wagner's that can really be called a music-drama. This strange work carries to the last degree Wagner's idea of making the music servant to the words. The orchestra makes a lovely shimmering background of tone for the love story while the words are chanted in a sort of recitative. Words, music, and action are woven so closely together and flow on in such an endless line that no part can ever be taken from the whole.

The long struggle between opera and music drama has ended forever. After a bitter fight, Gluck triumphed with his "classic" opera, which was really an early form of music drama. But when he died, his ideas died with him. Wagner won the battle for all time. Everyone now sees that it takes a good story to make a good opera. People no longer say, as they once did, "Whatever is too silly to be spoken may be sung." Modern musicians seldom waste fine music on a worthless libretto, as Mozart had done in the "Magic Flute," von Weber in "Euryanthe," and poor Schubert in all his operas.

Moreover, all musicians now know that the purpose of operatic music is not to present pretty tunes or show off fine singers, but to follow the words and express the feelings in the story. The best musician is not too proud to have his music serve some brave or tragic tale of love and courage.

RECORD LIST — CHAPTER XIII

Debussy, Claude (1862-1918)
    Pelleas et Melisande
Leoncavallo, Ruggiero (1858-1919)
    I Pagliacci
Mascagni, Pietro (1863-1945)
    Cavalleria Rusticana
Menotti, Gian-Carlo (1911-
    The Consul; The Medium; The Telephone
Puccini, Giacomo (1858-1924)
    La Boheme; Madame Butterfly; Tosca
Verdi, Giuseppe (1813-1901)
    Aida; Il Trovatore; La Forza del Destino; La Traviata; Otello;
    Rigoletto

CHAPTER XIV

NATIONALISTIC MUSIC

NOT every country has a grand old master, like Bach of Germany or Palestrina of Italy, to serve as models to its later musicians. Yet there is no land so small and poor that it has no folk music sprung from the lives of its people. Even the Hungarian gypsies, a people without country or home, could give haunting minor melodies and stirring rhythms to great composers like Brahms and Liszt.

The folk music of each country has tunes and rhythms different from any other in the world. For instance, once we come to know the music of Spain, with its exciting rhythms marked by the click of castanets and dancing heels, we never mistake it for any other. Spain is the land of the dance. The Spanish have dances to express every feeling and to celebrate every occasion. The stately sarabande used to be danced in the churches by altar boys on Holy Thursday. The bolero makes us think of señoritas swirling in gay silken shawls. The jota (hó-ta) is a lively country dance in which the men and women, as they danced, would sometimes make up funny words to go with the music—words like "Your arms are so beautiful; they remind me of sausages which are hung from the kitchen ceiling in winter."

The very names of Spanish dances—tango, jota, bolero, aragonaise, malagueña— seemed to have a charm, and the music appealed to composers of every age and nation. In the time of

Bach and Handel, the sarabande was a part of nearly every suite. Later, a Pole, Moskowski (Mos-kóv-skee), wrote a set of Spanish dances that became better known than any of his other work. The French composer, Bizet, made the music of the great Spanish opera, "Carmen," with all the bright and savage life of Spain in its thrilling scenes of gypsies, soldiers, and bull-fighters. The great tone poem "España" (Es-pahn-ya) (Spain), was composed by another Frenchman, Chabrier, who went to Spain especially to find real Spanish folk themes to use in his work.

It was a long time before native Spanish composers began to use the folk music of their own country. A few made musical pictures of their own land, but most of the musicians of Spain went to France or Italy to learn and work.

DE FALLA

Such an one is Manuel de Falla (Fáh-ya). He went first to Paris to study. He was befriended by Dukas, composer of the well known tone poem, "The Sorcerer's Apprentice," and Debussy, and he might have stayed in Paris the rest of his life if the World War had not driven him back to his own country. Then he settled in a Spanish villa in sight of the snow-capped mountains and near the Alhambra, that old Moorish fortress and palace, with its delicately carved arches, and columns of white marble, and walls of blue and gold tile. He was also not far from the famous gardens of Granada with their palms and dark cypresses, orange trees, myrtles, and flowering pomegranates, pools full of flickering gold fish and fountains gushing silver in the moonlight.

He began to draw his music from his own land. His tone poems, "Nights in the Gardens of Spain," "Fire Dance" and other truly Spanish music, made someone say that his music gives real pictures of Spain—"sometimes the pomp and glory of a Spain that is dead; sometimes the stirring action of a Spain that still lives; now a jota danced in a shady patio; now a tiny splash of water on a moonlit terrace; now a monk and now a Moor."

De Falla's music shows that no visiting musician from outside can possibly catch the spirit of a country in music as well as one who has been born there and heard its folk music even in his cradle.

NATIONALISM IN MUSIC

When a composer founds his music on the folk songs and dances of his native land or tries to express its legends or scenery in tones, he is composing what is called nationalistic music. Schumann said that it was only natural that composers should want to make their music from the songs and stories of their own countries and not keep on imitating the work of the German masters.

CHOPIN

One of the first of these composers of nationalistic music was born in the same year as Schumann himself. He was Frederic Chopin, born in 1810 in a little Polish village near Warsaw where his father, a Frenchman, taught his native language in the university. His mother was a Polish woman. She taught Frederic and his brother and two sisters the noble and tragic story of Poland—how once it had been a proud and powerful nation, standing guard at the edge of the civilized world to keep Europe and the Christian faith safe from the attacks of the Turks. Then the greedy countries around it had fought over it, seized it, and divided it among them like pieces of pie. There were tales of courage and of cruelty, of traitors, heroes, and saints.

The Chopin family lived in three rooms at the end of an annex in the manor house of a countess. They were pleasant rooms, with white-washed walls and beamed ceilings, windows curtained with snowy muslin, and with fuchsia and geranium blooming brightly on the broad sills. They contained heavy mahogany furniture, many bookshelves, and a white tiled stove in which pine logs crackled and gave forth fragrant heat when it was cold. In the largest of the three rooms stood the piano. Unlike other boy musicians, Frederic did not love the piano. He hated it, and did not want to learn to play it.

His first teacher was a queer figure, always dressed in yellowish coat and breeches, long patent leather boots, and very gaudy colored waistcoats which he said he had bought at an auction of the belongings of the last King of Poland. He always carried a long pencil with which he used to rap the heads and fingers of dull and unruly pupils. He taught Frederic to love the piano and play it so well that the boy became known in Warsaw as "the second Mozart." At the age of ten, he was taken to play before a great Italian singer, who was so pleased that she gave him a watch. A little later, the Czar of Russia heard him play and gave him a diamond ring.

Even when he was too young to write music, he would make up little pieces which his good teacher would put on paper for him. Later he studied composition and other subjects at the Warsaw Lyceum (Ly-see'-um) where his father taught French. When he was seventeen, he left school to devote his life to music. With his second published composition—a set of variations from his beloved Mozart's "Don Giovanni"—he became known outside of Poland. Schumann discovered him and praised his work with an article beginning, "Hats off, gentlemen! A genius!"

Chopin was the first composer to devote his whole life to a single instrument. Even Liszt, the Paganini of the piano, turned to works for full orchestra in his later years, and his piano pieces sound as well—or even better—when they are rewritten for orchestra. Chopin did not try to imitate an orchestra on the piano. He found the kind of music that the piano can express better than any other instrument. It was a music of delicate tone pictures, sweet and sad as his thoughts of his native land, a music of haunting phrases of melody, linked with little runs and grace notes, delicate as silver lace. Whatever the rhythm of his pieces—whether waltz or Polish mazurka or polonaise—the melody was nearly always in simple A-B-A ternary song form. His music is as different from a Beethoven sonata as a small but perfect poem is from a play by Shakespeare.

He gave two very successful concerts in Vienna, and then wished to seek fame in a wider world. After three farewell concerts in Warsaw, he set out. He had not gone far when his teacher and former fellow-students surprised him by stopping his coach and singing a cantata composed in his honor. Then they gave him a silver loving cup filled with earth from his native land so that he would never forget it. He was never to return, but he never forgot his love for the country of his birth.

He had said that he was going "to the United States via Paris," but when he reached Paris, the home of his father, he stayed there the rest of his life. It was well for him that he got no farther. Indian war drums still beat beyond the Mississippi. The only concerts were in the few cities dotting the sea-coast—Boston, New York, Philadelphia. In the many small cities and towns between the sea and the Mississippi, the only music was furnished by the minstrel shows, which were delighting the boy Stephen Foster who was to become American's first famous composer. It would have been a sad place for Chopin, the poet of the piano.

CHOPIN IN PARIS

Before long, Chopin was the most fashionable teacher in Paris. He had as many pupils as he wished, at the highest prices. He gave lessons like a prince, always wearing white kid gloves, and arriving in a carriage attended by a servant.

Liszt introduced him to Madame Dudevant, the famous novelist who wrote under the name of George Sand. Through her, he was drawn into the gay circle of artists, writers, and musicians who made Paris their home. Yet all the success and pleasure that came to him never could make him forget the glory and sorrow of Poland.

All of Chopin's compositions are little tone pictures of his feelings. Some are taken from his own life—the dreamy nocturnes or night-pieces, the little preludes written when he was visiting George Sand and her children on the island of Majorca, and the waltzes—especially the one in D flat written, it is said, after he had watched George Sand's little white dog chase its tail. But the greater part of his music grew from his love of his native land.

POLISH RHYTHMS

Many of his greatest works were in the rhythm of two of Poland's ancient dances, the mazurka and the polonaise. The polonaise was a dance of the nobility—the stately march of princes and heroes before the throne of their king. In this form, Chopin wrote some of his grandest compositions. The mazurka was a country dance which Chopin must often have seen danced by the Polish peasants as they tried to forget the hardness of their lives in lusty merry-making. The rhythm is three beats to the measure, but with the last beat accented where the dancer clicks his heels together. Chopin composed over fifty mazurkas and in this one rhythm expressed every feeling, from sadness and mystery to the joy of living.

His great Sonata in B flat minor was founded on a poem of old Poland, and his four "Ballades" tell in tones the stories of four works by Poland's greatest poet. The most popular one tells of the love of a young knight for a fair and mysterious lady. Even his "Études," or studies, were not mere exercises, but musical sketches. The great "Revolutionary Étude," which is the ambition of all students who want to be master pianists, was written when Chopin heard that once more the Poles had risen in revolt against Russia, and once more had been cruelly crushed.

Perhaps the reason that Chopin's music is so well loved is that it does not simply tell of the beauty and sorrow of Poland. It speaks to each man's heart of his love for his own country. The German poet, Heine (Hý-neh), a friend of Chopin's in Paris, once wrote, "When he sits down at the piano, I feel as though a countryman from my native land were telling me the most curious things which have happened during my absence. Sometimes I should like to question him, 'Are the roses at home still in their flaming pride? Do the trees still sing as beautifully in the moonlight?' "

The gentle little musician with the "smile of inexpressible charm, pleasant manners, and mass of fair curly hair like an angel" became the darling of the drawing-rooms of Paris. But the excitement of life in Paris broke his health. As he grew weaker, he became sensitive and irritable. After a quarrel, his ten years' friendship with George Sand came to an end.

THE MILITARY POLONAISE

All alone in his rooms, he sat at the piano to try to forget trouble and sorrow. As he played, the fever of his illness made him think that he saw a long procession of Poland's warriors riding by to battle. He feared that he was going insane and rushed out into the streets where his friends found him wandering some time later. The musical themes which caused his vision he made into the great "Military Polonaise" with the majesty and grandeur of its melody, the roll of drums and beat of horses' hoofs in the accompaniment.

His health grew rapidly worse. In the midst of a tour of England, his strength failed and he came back to Paris to die.

It was the custom for Polish noblemen to be buried in their

uniforms. Chopin was buried in full concert dress, and over his grave was sprinkled the Polish earth which his friends had given him in the silver urn so many years before.

PADEREWSKI

It was another musician, the great Polish pianist, Paderewski (Pad-er-év-skee), who at last helped Poland to regain her freedom. Even more than Chopin, he felt the sorrow of his native land. When he was only three years old, there was another revolt against Russia His village was burned, many of its people were murdered, and his father was dragged off by the soldiers into imprisonment and exile.

When he was only five years old, he began to feel around for strange and lovely sounds on the little old organ in his father's house. His first teacher was a wandering fiddler who taught him piano, but thought he would do better on the trombone. Later, a musician came out to the farm to give him a lesson once a month, but when he was thirteen, he was sent to the Warsaw Conservatory. In four years he won first prize in piano playing, and became a teacher in the Conservatory at 25 cents a lesson.

This poor young Polish piano teacher became one of the greatest concert pianists the world has ever seen. He studied with a world-famous teacher, and made his debut in a blaze of glory. Then he set out on a grand tour. At the first concerts, few were present but the critics, but they went wild with excitement at the discovery of a new giant of the piano, a second Liszt. He played in all the great cities of Europe and the United States. He won fame as great as Liszt's and fortune even greater.

Like Liszt, he was known for his generosity. Here in the United States, he gave a scholarship fund for talented young musicians, and there is hardly a country where he played but has received some proof of his kind heart. During

World War I, when Poland was once more a battlefield between Germany and Russia, he raised an enormous amount of money to help his country. After the war, it was largely due to his efforts and the friends he had made in every land that Poland was at last set free. Paderewski was made the Premier of the new Polish republic formed at that time.

Though Paderewski the musician is remembered chiefly as a pianist—especially as an interpreter of his beloved Chopin—he also wrote a number of compositions in large and small forms. The "Minuet in G," so familiar to generations of piano students, does not represent the real Paderewski. Like Chopin, he wrote Polish dances of various kinds — Mazurkas, Krakowiaks, and Polonaises. He wrote an opera, "Manru," about the people who lived in the wild Tatra mountains of Poland and had a strange music all their own. In 1909, he completed a symphony describing the tragic fate of the Polish nation as history had thus far recorded it. Paderewski the pianist, the composer, and ever the Polish patriot, was a beloved personality in his time.

NORWAY AND GRIEG

Other musicians began to base their music on the old stories and songs and dances of their native lands. One of these was Edvard Grieg, born in Bergen, Norway, in 1843—just six years before Chopin's death. He did not write nationalistic music because of any troubles of his native land, but because of his love for its beauty and the songs of its simple, sturdy people.

His parents were both well-to-do and well educated. His mother played the piano beautifully, and composed little songs that are still heard in Norway today. One day little Edvard stretched his hands up to the piano and struck two keys together, skipping one between, to make what is called the interval of the third. Then he skipped another key and added a third note, making a chord called a triad. For his last note, he pressed down the key just nine notes above his lowest note. Now he had a full four-note chord—the lovely, dissonant "chord of the ninth" as it is called. "When I found that," he said, "my happiness knew no bounds. I was then about five years old."

Soon his mother began to teach him to play the piano, giving daily lessons as she went about her household tasks. He cared for music much more than he did for school. One day when the teacher asked all the pupils to bring an essay they had written, twelve-year old Edvard brought a musical composition instead. The other children were much excited, but the teacher was not pleased. Grieg later wrote, "She shook me by the hair until everything was black before my eyes, telling me to leave that foolish stuff at home."

OLE BULL

A friend of the family was the great Norwegian violinist, Ole Bull, often called "the blonde Paganini," because he, too, could do all sorts of amazing tricks with his violin. He was as big and blond and blue-eyed as the hero of an old Norse legend, and he could tell tales of ghosts and great deeds in such a way as to charm all young listeners. He passed on to the wide-eyed boy Grieg his own love for the old, old stories, the gay tunes fiddlers played at weddings, and the sad and simple songs sung by old women at their spinning-wheels. Ole Bull also persuaded Grieg's parents to send him to the Conservatory at Leipzig so that he might study to make music his life work.

The years at Leipzig were not happy. The teachers did not know what to make of his Norwegian melodies and the strange and beautiful dissonant chords with which he harmonized them. They tried to make him pattern his music after the classic and romantic masters, as everyone else did. Then his compositions were simply imitations of others and were no better than any student could write. He worked so hard that he had a serious breakdown, but at last he was graduated with honors.

He went back to Norway and settled in Bergen on a farm that had belonged to his grandfather. A Norwegian farm is made up of many small quaint buildings with beamed walls and steep roofs and curved corner posts. Besides the shelters for man and beast, there are houses for spinning and weaving, for threshing wheat, for storing food, and for drying grain or linen. Grieg's mother fitted up one of these storehouses with desk and piano as a study for him. He married his cousin, Nina Hagerup, a singer, and they lived in a happiness broken only by the death of their little daughter.

Many of his friends still thought that he should be less Norwegian in his work and make his music sound more like that heard everywhere else in the world. Others, like Ole Bull, persuaded him that his music was really good only when it was rooted in the folk songs and stories of Norway as a tree is rooted in its native earth.

MAKING NATIONALISTIC MUSIC

His friendship with Ole Bull grew deeper. Often they would take trips together far into the mountains. They would look up to snowy peaks and down into black lakes or stormy fjords, fringed with dark firs. They would see eagles whirling over rocky chasms and reindeer cropping the moss in stony places. They would listen to the lonely songs of the saeter-girls who spent all of the bright summer alone with the cattle in the saeters, or upland pastures, until it was time to drive them back to the farms for the winter. And they would hear the jolly scraping of a country fiddler riding at the head of a wedding procession on its way back from the little wooden church in the village to the merry-making at the farm. These songs and dances and country scenes Grieg wove into the magic of his music.

Franz Liszt, always generous, was among the first outside of Norway to encourage Grieg. He wrote the young musician a letter of such warm praise that the Norwegian government gave Grieg a sum of money so that he might go to visit Liszt in Rome. But his first really great chance came when the Norwegian dramatist, Ibsen, commissioned him to write music to go with his play, "Peer Gynt."

IBSEN AND "PEER GYNT"

Ibsen, like Shakespeare and the German poet, Goethe, was one of those men so great that they do not belong to their own country alone, but the whole world. "Peer Gynt" was taken from one of the Norwegian folk tales. No one but Grieg could have written such expressive music for poor Peer's visit to the hall of the mountain-king where all the little trolls set upon him to pinch and bite him. Or the tender song of patient Solveig waiting in the lonely hut during all the years that Peer wanders over the world.

Somehow Grieg's music almost always sounds Norwegian, even when he is describing Peer's adventures in Egypt and the strange countries of the East. The piece "Morning" seems more like a musical picture of dawn in a pleasant Norwegian woodland than in a desert where a mysterious statue speaks at sunrise. The "Peer Gynt" Suite is the best-loved of all Grieg's music. Thousands of people who have never heard of Ibsen's play know and love Grieg's music on phonograph and radio.

Though Grieg became famous all over the world as well as in his own country, it was not until the end of his long life—he died in 1907—that musicians really appreciated his work. Then they found that his melodies were not simply copies of old folk tunes, but echoes in his heart of the beauties of his native land and the sturdy lives of its people. They came to see that the strange and lovely harmonies in his music were not merely queer Norwegian things, but new discoveries from which later musicians might learn to enrich their music.

FINLAND AND "FINLANDIA"

Perhaps the greatest piece of nationalistic music is "Finlandia," a tone poem made of the song and story and sorrow of little Finland, for so many years fought over by Russia and Sweden and tossed back and forth between them like a bone between two fighting dogs. Its composer is Jean Sibelius, and he and Richard Strauss have sometimes been called the two great "S's" of modern music.

SIBELIUS

Sibelius was born in 1865—one year after Strauss—in a little Finnish town where his father was army doctor to the regiment stationed there. As a very little boy, he would make up

music on the piano and later would write down pieces for the piano and other solo instruments. When he was fifteen, he took violin lessons from the bandmaster of the regiment.

In summer, he would often take his violin and be gone days and nights in the woods—those wonderful summer nights of the Northland when the sun does not set until after midnight, and it never gets darker than a mysterious twilight. He would try to express on his violin what he felt at the beauty of nature —the fragrant forest with its tall whispering trees, the silent lakes and gay little brooks, the silver-bright bird songs. He also played violin in the school orchestra and in home concerts of chamber music with his brother and friends.

Like so many other musicians, he thought of becoming a lawyer, and spent some time in law study at the University of Helsingfors in Finland. At last, he decided to give his whole life to music. He was twenty-four years old when he first left his own country to study music in Berlin. Later he went to Vienna, where the mighty Johannes Brahms praised his compositions and prophesied that he would make a great name for himself. By the time he returned to Finland three years later, he was already well known for his first great tone poem, "En Saga," which means "From an Old Tale."

Not many years before, all the ancient legends of Finland had been gathered from the singers of songs and the tellers of tales and the old folk of the countryside, and written down in that rich book of Finnish lore called the Kalevala (Kah-le-váh-lah). While Sibelius, like Grieg, did not use real folk tunes in his music, the spirit of the Kalevala breathes through it all, even the great symphonies. Most of his tone poems give musical pictures of parts of the Kalevala—such as his "Swan of Tuonela," which describes the region of death, surrounded by a black river on which a swan is always singing its sad song. The great nationalistic tone poem, "Finlandia," speaks in music of the brave tales of gods and heroes who lived in the dark forests long before the memory of man, but it speaks still more of the love and pride in the heart of every countryman.

"Finlandia" opens with a clang of majestic dissonant chords like a call to arms. As long as the Russians held Finland, they did not allow the piece played in public for fear it would incite the Finns to rebellion. When Finland at last was free, Sibelius was given a yearly pension, so that he could give his whole life to composition, and not have to waste precious hours in earning a living by teaching, like poor César Franck.

Thanks to his government allowance, Sibelius was able to give long, quiet years to the making of symphonies and tone poems, all breathing the spirit of old Finnish folklore. Through war and peace, he lived on his lovely country estate, twenty miles from the Finnish capital. He always worshipped Beethoven above all other composers. Many believe that the future will put his name beside Beethoven's among the truly great of all times.

RECORD LIST — CHAPTER XIV

Albéniz, Isaac (1860-1909)
    Iberia — excerpts (orchestrated by Arbos)
    Spanish Rhapsody

Alfven, Hugo (1872-
    Midsommarvaka — Swedish Rhapsody No. 1

Bartók, Bela (1881-1945)
    For Children — excerpts
    Hungarian Folk Songs — various
    Mikrokosmos — excerpts
    Music for Strings, Percussion, and Celesta

Chabrier, Emmanuel (1841-1894)
    Espana

Chopin, Frederic (1810-1849)
    Ballades, Mazurkas, Nocturnes, Polonaises,
        Waltzes (all for piano)
    Piano Concerto No. 1 in E Minor, Op. 11

Dohnanyi, Ernst von (1877-
    Ruralia Hungarica

Variations on a Nursery Theme, Op. 25

Dvořák, Antonin (1841-1904)
Slavonic Dances; Slavonic Rhapsodies

Enesco, Georges (1881-1955)
Roumanian Rhapsodies Nos. 1 and 2

Falla, Manuel de (1876-1946)
El Amor Brujo
Nights in the Gardens of Spain
Three-Cornered Hat — Dances

Folk songs — various nations

Granados, Enrique (1867-1916)
Goyescas; Spanish Dances

Grieg, Edvard (1843-1907)
Piano Concerto in A Minor, Op. 16
Norwegian Dances, Op. 35
Peer Gynt, Suites 1 and 2
Songs — various

Kodály, Zoltan (1882-
Dances from Galanta
Hary Janos — Suite

Milhaud, Darius (1892-
Suite Francaise; Suite Provencale

Moszkowski, Moritz (1854-1925)
Spanish Dances, Op. 12

Sarasate, Pablo de (1844-1908)
Zigeunerweisen, Op. 20, No. 1, for Violin and Orchestra

Sibelius, Jean (1865-1957)
En Saga, Op. 9
Finlandia, Op. 26, No. 7
Four Legends, Op. 22 (Lemminkainen Suite)
(—includes "The Swan of Tuonela")
Symphony No. 1 in E Minor, Op. 39
Symphony No. 5 in E Flat, Op. 82

Smetana, Bedřich (1824-1884)
The Bartered Bride — excerpts
Ma Vlast (My Fatherland) (—includes "The Moldau" and
"From Bohemia's Meadows and Forests")

Weinberger, Jaromir (1896-
Schwanda, the Bagpiper — Polka and Fugue

CHAPTER XV

RUSSIAN MUSIC

POLAND had one Chopin; Norway, one Grieg; and Finland, one Sibelius. But in Russia every musician expressed in his music the spirit of his native land. Russia is a vast country, covering one-sixth of the whole surface of the earth. In the north, flaxen-haired giants, singing lonely songs, fished in icy seas and hunted ermine and sable in frozen woods to make robes for all the princes of the world. In the south, dark-skinned men poured over the mountains from Asia, bringing their weird, barbaric dances. In old Russia, the princes and noblemen lived in palaces with walls of lapis lazuli and precious stones. The poor men, like beasts, dragged the heavily laden boats along Russia's great river highways, or worked in the fields for a bare handful of grain. Often in the long cruel winters, they would have nothing to eat but the bark from trees. There were always wars and plots and rebellion—men slaughtered bloodily, and men sent off to the cold wastelands of Siberia to die.

No Russian musician could write a note of music—song or opera, or even symphony—without making the listener think of the splendor and savagery of Russia and the old, sad songs of its people. Yet for a long time Russia had no musicians of her own. In the time of Bach and Handel, the only Russian music, aside from the folk songs, was in the churches. There, choirs in stiff robes of cloth-of-gold sang before altars ablaze with jewels. Their anthems, with no accompaniment by organ or other instruments, made such strange and lovely music that Berlioz wrote, "It seemed as though a choir of angels were leaving the earth and gradually losing itself in the uttermost heights of heaven." During the days of Haydn and Mozart, a few tinkling opera tunes were brought from Italy for the amusement of the nobles, but that was all.

GLINKA

Glinka, who is called the "father of Russian music," was not born until 1804—at nearly the same time as Berlioz, the French master of tone. When Glinka was eight years old, he saw his home city of Moscow go up in flames, burned by its own people to keep it from falling prey to the soldiers of Napoleon. Perhaps the sight aroused in him that deep love of country which made him long to make music for his native land.

Glinka came of a wealthy family. He went to Italy to study the opera and the use of the human voice, and he studied composition a short time in Germany. But in comparison with great musicians of other countries, he did not study long or thoroughly. Music to him was always a beloved hobby rather than his whole life work. His chief compositions are two operas on Russian history and legend. The first, "A Life for the Czar" was the first great Russian music.

It is right and natural for everyone to love his country better than any other, and to try to make it the best in the world. Yet through the long years of history, no one country is ever always right or always wrong. In reading of Chopin's love for his Poland, we learned how Russia held a slice of that unhappy country. But in times long past, Poland had been powerful enough to crush Russia. "A Life for the Czar" tells of the old, sad days when the Poles ruled at Moscow. The young Russian Czar was in hiding, and the Poles commandeered the peasant, Ivan Sussanine, to lead them to him. Instead, Ivan led them off into a trackless wilderness to die, even though he knew that they would kill him when they found he had deceived them. Thus he gave his life to save the Czar.

Glinka's second opera, "Ruslan and Lioudmilla," was more cheerful, as it was founded on an old Russian folk story about a wicked wizard and a princess with three suitors. In all his music, Glinka used old Russian themes, ranging from ancient church modes to a song he heard sung by his coachman. Though Glinka's operas are not produced today, the overtures are favorite pieces for orchestra and band. Little by little, Glinka's work became known outside of Russia, but in his own country he was adored by all music-lovers.

THE "BIG FIVE"

One of his greatest admirers was a young gentleman named Balakireff (Bah-lah́-kee-reff), who was known as one of the most brilliant pianists in the drawing-rooms of St. Petersburg. He also directed a private orchestra which played the great German classics, such as the Beethoven symphonies. He became fired with the idea of carrying forward Glinka's work and making a national music for Russia.

César Cui, a young artillery officer and teacher of fortification at the military academy, was one of his closest friends. Cui also was a fine amateur musician. They would meet in each other's rooms, play Beethoven and Schumann symphonies as piano duets, and criticize each other's compositions.

With other young men who gathered to hear them, they would talk and plan a great music for Russia. There sprang up the little band known in Russian music as "the Five." Though Balakireff was the leader, and Cui wrote the most about the group and its work, the most important music was composed by the other three—Borodin (Bo-ro-deen') the doctor and professor of chemistry who composed his grandly somber symphony and opera, "Prince Igor," in moments snatched from laboratory experiments; Mussorgsky, the foppish young lieutenant of the crack regiment, having wild bursts of genius in between drills, dances, and drunken sprees; and Rimsky-Korsakoff, the young naval officer who became the only professional musician of them all.

Balakireff was always the leader. Rimsky-Korsakoff was only seventeen when he was drawn into Balakireff's circle, and he wrote of it in the story of his life. "Balakireff was a marvelous critic. Whenever I, or other young men, played our attempts at composition, he would seat himself at the piano and show exactly what changes should be made so that often other people's compositions became his, and not their authors' at all.

"Young, with alert, fiery eyes and a handsome black beard, his influence over those around him was like a magnetic force. Of all his pupil-friends, I was the youngest. He should have given me a few lessons in harmony, made me write a few fugues, explained the grammar of musical forms to me. I worshipped him and would have obeyed his advice in anything. But he could not do it, as he had not studied it himself. He did not think it was necessary, and so did not send me to study under someone else."

Though Balakireff told the others when to write opera and when to write symphonies and criticized all their work, he had only studied music off and on during his university days. A Russian who had never left his native land had no chance of getting a good musical education, for there were no really fine musical schools in Russia like the Leipzig Conservatory. Balakireff had a natural ear for music, and could tell when anything was good or bad without knowing rules. So he thought rules were useless for others.

BALAKIREFF AND RIMSKY–KORSAKOFF

He never tried to teach Rimsky-Korsakoff. Instead he told the boy at their first meeting to go and write a symphony. So young Rimsky-Korsakoff, who did not even know the names of all the chords or how to use the different instruments, went to sea with a Schumann symphony and Berlioz's book on the orchestra. He wrote his symphony during a year's cruise on the battleship. It was the first Russian symphony ever written, and it was a great success in spite of the fact that the young composer sometimes mixed up his passages for trumpets and French horns, and wrote parts for the violins that the violinists could not possibly bow.

Rimsky-Korsakoff soon left the navy. "I was never seasick," he said, "and never was afraid of the sea and its danger. But I did not like sea-service. Those were the days of rope-ends and brutal blows on the mouth. Several times I had to witness the punishment of sailors with two hundred to three hundred ratline blows in the presence of the whole crew and hear the poor man cry, 'Your honor, have mercy.'"

RIMSKY–KORSAKOFF AS A COMPOSER OF OPERA

The life of a composer of operas was much more to his liking. He composed several operas on old Russian stories and fairy tales. The best known is "Sadko," from which comes the beautiful "Song of India," which is sung by an Indian merchant at the great fair of Nizhni-Novgorod to tell of the riches of his native land. "Sadko" has been performed by the Metropolitan Opera Company in New York.

Because of the success of his operas, Rimsky-Korsakoff was offered a place as professor in the new conservatory at St. Petersburg. He bravely accepted, although he still did not know the names of all the chords, had never conducted an orchestra, and had little idea of the rules of musical form. He learned as he taught, and it was not until he had been made inspector of music bands that he thought it might be well to know about the different instruments. So he took trombone, clarinet, flute, etc., to his summer home and learned to play them—probably to the great joy of his neighbors!

In the end, Rimsky-Korsakoff learned all the ways and forms of the old masters. His new knowledge was as big a help to his friends as to himself. He deeply admired the musical ideas of his friends, Borodin and Mussorgsky, and he spent as much labor and loving care on them as on his own.

Mussorgsky was the most gifted, but the least industrious of the Five. Rimsky-Korsakoff put in long hours of drudgery on orchestrating Mussorgsky's work, especially his great and grim opera, "Boris Godounoff." This deals with the story of Boris, who murdered the heir to the throne, was crowned in his stead, and finally was haunted to madness by a young monk pretending to be the slain prince.

Borodin, the chemist, always thought his test tubes more important than his music. He died, leaving his most famous work, "Prince Igor," little more than sketched out. The generous Rimsky-Korsakoff orchestrated it from beginning to end.

THE "SCHEHERAZADE" SUITE

In his own work, Rimsky-Korsakoff liked best the music and stories of the Orient which came to Russia over the wild borders of Asia. His best known work for orchestra is the "Scheherazade" (Sheh-her-az-áh-de) Suite based on the "Arabian Nights." The wicked Sultan had the sad habit of having each of his wives beheaded the day after the wedding, until he married the princess Scheherazade. She kept him entertained with stories for a thousand and one nights so that at last he gave up the idea of killing her and they lived happily for the rest of their lives.

Rimsky-Korsakoff tells in music some of Scheherazade's tales. Through them all we hear, again and again, the Sultan theme—stern and threatening—and that of the lovely and clever Scheherazade herself, played by violins accompanied by harps. Rimsky-Korsakoff not only found just the right musical themes to describe his characters and tell his stories. He also chose exactly the instruments to give the richest tone color.

In "The Young Prince and the Princess," the Princess theme is given to the clarinet, accompanied by snare drums, tambourine and triangle. When Sinbad's ship is wrecked, the rolling sea theme and the cruel Sultan theme are joined in the whistling winds of clarinet and flute passages until "the grave ship deep laden with spiceries and pearl went mad, wrenched the long tiller out of the steersman's hand—and lay, a broken bundle of firewood, strewn piecemeal about the waters."

The Five succeeded in giving Russia a music of which any country could well be proud. What is more, their music—that of Mussorgsky more than any other—taught new musical effects to composers of other countries, especially the French. Debussy, on his Russian trip, learned much from Mussorgsky's strong dissonances and use of weird Oriental scales. The modern French composer, Ravel, has set to orchestra Mussorgsky's piano pieces, "Pictures at an Exhibition" which describe in music some scenes of Russian life painted by one of Mussorgsky's friends.

RUBINSTEIN

There has only been one of Russia's famous musicians who did not make his music from the songs and stories of his native land. He was Anton Rubinstein, whose fame as a concert pianist was so dazzling that it even rivalled Liszt's. He was made court musician to the Czar, and toured all Europe with glorious success. He was one of the first of Europe's really famous musicians to come across the sea and give concerts in the new world. The people of the new country had not yet learned to know and love the greatest music of the old world.

At one of his concerts, Rubinstein found that his manager had put on the program a cheap little tune meant to tickle the public. Rubinstein not only refused to play it, but was so angry that he never came to America again, even though he was offered $100,000 for a second tour.

In his travels and success in many lands, he became so much a citizen of the world that no one country really called him its own. He himself said, "The Christians call me a Jew; the Jews a Christian. The Russians called me a German; the Germans a Russian." He thought that a composition should not express the life and musical thought of just one country, but of the whole world. He patterned much of his music on the work of the German Romantics. Perhaps the reason that his symphonies and largest works are now gathering dust in silence is that they sometimes sounded a little second-hand, like something that had been done before.

For all the great fame that was his during his lifetime, his only compositions that are heard nowadays are a handful of little pieces—the sugary Melody in F, a few Russian dances, and one of a set of piano pieces written when he was visiting a Russian princess at Kamenoi-Ostrow. Now that he has been many years gone, the most important works of his life seem to be the two fine conservatories of music which he and his brother Nicholas founded at St. Petersburg (now Leningrad) and Moscow. And perhaps the brothers Rubinstein will be remembered longest because they hindered and discouraged their most famous pupil, Tschaikowsky. He later became Russia's greatest composer and one of the greatest of all countries and all times.

TSCHAIKOWSKY

Peter Ilyitch Tschaikowsky (Chai-kóv-sky) was born in 1840 in a little mining town where his father was government engineer in charge of a rich mine. Though the little town was crude and ugly and barren, the Tschaikowsky home was like that of a prince, with many servants, and the grandest of rugs and pictures and furnishings. Yet there was no music for little Peter—only the tinkle of an old music box and the songs of his mother.

When he was eight years old, the family moved back to the great city of St. Petersburg. The shy little boy found school life hard after being alone so long in the shelter of his home. Then in a few years his beloved mother died in a terrible epidemic of cholera and left him with a sadness which shows all through his life and music.

Now music became his only joy. His father let him study music as much as he pleased. But first he had to promise that his music would be only a pleasure to him and that he would make law his life work. So he studied law, too. When he was nineteen, he finished his law course and got a small government position. All this time, he had been going from teacher to teacher, trying to learn all the music he could. As young Rimsky-Korsakoff had found, there was no way then of learning much about music in Russia. None of Tschaikowsky's teachers was at all good. At twenty-one he knew nothing about Schumann and did not even know how many symphonies Beethoven had written.

Then Rubinstein started the St. Petersburg Conservatory. For the first time, Tschaikowsky had a chance to get a good musical education. Nicholas Rubinstein became his friend. He adored the great Anton. When Nicholas founded the new conservatory at Moscow, Tschaikowsky, at last winning his father's consent, was given a place as teacher. The Rubinstein brothers did not think that Tschaikowsky would ever become a great composer. Anton kept Tschaikowsky's first symphony from having a performance by a good orchestra. Nicholas simply laughed at his great piano concerto in B flat minor.

These were unhappy years for Tschaikowsky. He was poor. His compositions, one after another, failed to bring money or fame. He loved a famous French opera singer who jilted him for a baritone. A strange girl fell in love with him so madly that the kind-hearted young composer was afraid her life would be ruined if he refused her. Therefore, he let himself be dragged into an unhappy marriage.

Then came a friendship which changed his whole life, one of the most wonderful friendships a man ever had. A very wealthy widow, Madame Nadejda van Meck, the mother of eleven children, was a great lover of music. She heard some of Tschaikowsky's works. Long before anyone else believed in him, she thought he would some day be great. She wrote to him to tell him how she admired his work. Then someone told her how he was poor and had to spend hours in teaching in order to earn his living while he composed.

At last, she persuaded him to let her give him a yearly allowance so that he could give all his time to composing. She gave him the allowance on just one condition, and that was that they should never see each other. They wrote to each other often, and Tschaikowsky told her all his plans and hopes and fears. But they never met. Even when she went to one of his concerts, they would pass each other as strangers.

Now Tschaikowsky was able to travel to Italy and Switzerland, to live in comfort and to compose—ballets, opera, symphonies. Tschaikowsky did not try to write nationalistic music —Russian music for Russia—as the Five had done. He wrote what was in his heart, but because his heart was Russian, there is the spirit of Russia in all his music, even in the six great symphonies.

His "1812 Overture" was a patriotic piece. It was written to celebrate the dedication of a new cathedral, built in memory of the burning of Moscow in 1812. This was the fire seen by

eight-year old Glinka, when the Russians burned their own city to keep it from falling into the hands of the French. The overture was played by a huge orchestra in the square in front of the church. At the end, the Russian national anthem and the "Marseillaise" were cleverly woven together, and as a climax, the church bells were rung and cannon took the place of drums. Though Tschaikowsky himself did not like the overture over much, thinking it "too noisy," it has been played more often than any of his other works by orchestras and bands all over the world.

The beautiful Andante of his string quartet came to his mind as he heard a plasterer at work under his window, singing one of the sad and lovely songs of the Russian peasants. When the quartet was played for the first time at a concert, the great Russian writer, Count Leo Tolstoy, cried, "I have heard the soul of my suffering people."

Tschaikowsky did not win fame in his own land until long after his work was known and loved in every other country, even across the sea in the new world. Though the Five were scarcely older than he—Rimsky-Korsakoff was even younger— they were great men in Russian music while Tschaikowsky was

almost unknown. For one thing, they had an earlier start.
The boy naval officer's first Russian symphony was a success
years before the twenty-seven year old Tschaikowsky's first
symphony was condemned by Rubinstein. People had got in
the habit of thinking that no one could write Russian music
but the Five.

Little by little, Russia came to know that her greatest musician was with her. One of his operas, "Eugen Onegin," was
a great success even at the Royal Opera House, and the Czar
presented him with the honorary order of *St. Vladimir*. When
he toured southern Russia, he was welcomed like a hero, and
at one concert the enthusiastic people crowned him with a
silver wreath.

Now he would have liked most of all to stay at home and
do nothing but compose. But he had to go on tours to conduct his works with famous orchestras all over the world,
so that people everywhere would learn to love them. He even
came to the United States in 1891 to conduct the concert
celebrating the opening of Carnegie Hall. The new world was
different now from the old, rough days when Chopin so
fortunately did not make his planned trip to the United States,
or the time Rubinstein left these shores in a rage never to
return. Tschaikowsky conducted concerts in Baltimore and
Philadelphia, as well as in New York. He enjoyed his visit, and
spoke well of the orchestras he had found here, and the fine
music schools that were being started everywhere.

He was never in better health or spirits than on his return.
Yet it was the last year of his life, for once more there was an
epidemic of cholera such as the one that had caused his mother's
death so many years before. In his last year, Tschaikowsky composed one of his greatest symphonies—his Sixth or Pathétique.
He also found time to accept concert engagements in Europe,
when the programs always included the immensely popular
Suite from his delightful Christmas ballet, the "Nutcracker."

This music is so gay and charming that it is hard to believe it was written to order—so many bars of soft music, now tinkling music for the lighting of the Christmas tree, and again lively music for the entrance of the children. Even the greatest of Russian composers was proud to write music for the ballet. In France, the ballet was an amusement, but in Russia, it was an art. Men and women gave up their whole lives to making breath-taking beauty out of music and motion. As little children, they would be taken into the great ballet schools. There they would be put through drills more rigid than those of soldiers. There would be hours of exercises to make them limber and graceful, a strict diet, no time for fun and play. They would grow into fairy-like creatures, dressed in gorgeous storybook costumes. The impresario (im-pres-áh-re-o), or manager of the ballet company, who arranged and invented the ballets, would get the best of artists to design his costumes and backgrounds, the most famous composers to write his music. And many times the music would be loved and remembered long after ballet and ballet dancers were gone and forgotten.

STRAVINSKY AND THE BALLET

One of the greatest of Russian composers alive today wrote his most beautiful music for the Russian ballet. He is Igor Stravinsky, the son of an actor and singer, who was brought up to know the excitement and color of life in the theatre. Though he loved and studied music, he also studied law like so many other great musicians from Handel to Tschaikowsky. And his father—like so many other fathers before him—thought that music was too uncertain a way of earning a living.

Though there were many famous musicians in Russia, Stravinsky had to go to Germany before meeting one of them. When he was twenty years old he took a trip to Germany.

There he became acquainted with Rimsky-Korsakoff, who was surprised that a young man who loved music so well and knew so much about it still was not a professional musician. He persuaded Stravinsky to give up his life to music, and took him as a pupil. Stravinsky often surprised his famous teacher with his strange sounding tone combinations. To celebrate the marriage of Rimsky-Korsakoff's daughter, Stravinsky wrote a piece called "Fireworks."

The wild splashes of tone color were different from any music ever heard before and caught the fancy of Diaghileff (Dyah-gee-lef), the most famous ballet manager in the country. His companies danced for the grand dukes of Russia, and also travelled all over the world. Stravinsky was commissioned to write the music for one ballet after another—"The Firebird," "Petrouchka," "Rite of Spring," "The Song of the Nightingale." These ballets were mostly founded on old Russian legend, such as "Petrouchka," which represents a puppet show given at a Russian Shrovetide Fair. Poor foolish Petrouchka and the bold Blackamoor both love a dainty ballet dancer. They fight over her, and Petrouchka is killed. Then, as the Russian peasants stand staring around the puppet booth, Petrouchka's ghost appears to snap his fingers at the showman.

In his ballets, Stravinsky gives us a new kind of music. It has no form, but is put together in bright bits like a patchwork quilt. Sometimes it is not even written in one key at a time like most music, but goes on with different parts in different keys, all at the same time. It is full of strange chords and realistic effects in the use of instruments—such as the tuba growls of the dancing bear and the crash of cymbals as poor Petrouchka's head is bashed in. Diaghileff and the greatest of his ballet dancers are dead and the rest scattered. Stravinsky was driven from his country by the Revolution there. He now lives in America and composes music of a less programmatic type — more like the absolute music of the old masters. But his best work is his ballet music. "The Firebird," "Petrouchka," "The Rite of Spring," and "The Song of the Nightingale" will always bring to our concert halls the spirit of the splendor of the old Russian ballet.

Like French music, the music of Russia has not been so much an art in itself as a companion to the other arts and to life. Even Russian symphonies are usually what are called program symphonies. That is, like Beethoven's "Pastoral" Symphony, they either paint a tone picture or express some thought in the mind of the composer. As in French music, the Russian composers had a strong liking for the ballet, the opera, the tone poem. But the French musician used his music to paint any scene in the world or in history that caught his fancy—an old Greek dance, a fiery story of Spain, an American railway locomotive. The Russians preferred subjects from their own history or folklore—or that of the Orient.

All the rich and colorful life of old Russia can be found in its music. When Russia was changed by one of the most strange and terrible revolutions in the history of the world, the new way of life was pictured in a new music.

The people of Russia now did their work with machines instead of the old, hand methods used in the time of the Czars. The machines gave the workers a feeling of progress and importance—they took the place of the churches, the paintings, the life of old Russia. They were worshipped like gods.

One of the most interesting examples of music celebrating the arrival of the new age in Russia — the machine age — was "The Iron Foundry," by Mossoloff. The composer described it as "a song of labor"—a song of men and machines working together. Beautiful, it certainly is not. From beginning to end, it is full of strong, jarring dissonances and conflicting rhythms. Besides all sorts of strange and clashing combinations of instruments, the score calls for beating with a stick upon a sheet of metal.

Many musicians fled from the hardness and ugliness of the
new life to other lands where they would be free to make any
kind of music they wished without governmental interference.
Others stayed behind to try to change with their country, and
keep music alive during the terror of the early years of the new
government. A few of the older musicians adjusted themselves
to the new way. Prokofieff, after wandering all over the world,
settled once more in his native land. Another was Ippolitoff-
Ivanoff, who declared, "My life has been an uninterrupted
hymn to labor." Glière, who became a professor of composition
in Moscow, attempted to make a new "revolutionary music"
for Russia.

As a composer, Glière is remembered chiefly for his ballet,
"The Red Poppy" (named for the bloody flower of the Revolution), and the folk-tale symphony, "Ilya Mourometz." It was
as a teacher that he exerted his greatest influence; most of the
young Soviet composers were his pupils. Shostakovitch, the
most famous of them, told what the new music was trying to do
when he said, "Music has the power of stirring special feelings
in those who listen to it. Good music lifts and heartens and
lightens people for work and effort. It may be tragic, but it must
be strong."

RECORD LIST — CHAPTER XV

Balakireff, Mily (1837-1910)
          Islamey — Oriental Fantasy (piano or orchestra)
          Tamar — Symphonic Poem
Borodin, Alexander (1833-1887)
          In the Steppes of Central Asia
          Prince Igor — selections or Polovstian Dances
Choral music, sacred and secular — various
Folk songs — various
Glière, Reinhold (1875-1956)
          The Red Poppy — excerpts or suite
          Symphony No. 3, Ilya Mourometz, Op. 42

Glinka, Michael (1803-1857)
    Russlan and Ludmilla — excerpts
Ippolitoff-Ivanoff, Michael (1859-1935)
    Caucasian Sketches, Op. 10
Khatchaturian, Aram (1903-
    Piano Concerto
    Gayne — Ballet Suites 1 and 2
Mossoloff, Alexander (1900-
    Iron Foundry
Mussorgsky, Modest (1839-1881)
    Boris Godounoff — excerpts
    A Night on Bald Mountain
    Pictures at an Exhibition (piano or orchestra)
Prokofieff, Serge (1891-1953)
    Classical Symphony (Symphony No. 1 in D), Op. 25
    Lieutenant Kije — Symphonic Suite, Op. 60
    Peter and the Wolf, Op. 67
Rachmaninoff, Sergei (1873-1943)
    Piano Concerto No. 2 in C Minor
    The Isle of the Dead, Op. 29
    Piano music and songs — various
    Rhapsody on a Theme of Paganini, Op. 43
Rimsky-Korsakoff, Nicolas (1844-1908)
    Capriccio Espagnol, Op. 34
    Russian Easter Overture
    Scheherazade
Stravinsky, Igor (1882-
    Firebird Suite
    Petrouchka Suite
    Le Sacre du Printemps (The Rite of Spring)
    Song of the Nightingale
Tschaikowsky, Peter Ilyitch (1840-1893)
    Piano Concerto No. 1 in B Flat Minor, Op. 23
    Violin Concerto in D, Op. 35
    Eugen Onegin — excerpts
    Nutcracker Suite, Op. 71A
    Overture, 1812, Op. 49
    String Quartet No. 1 in D, Op. 11
    Symphony No. 5 in E Minor, Op. 64
    Symphony No. 6 in B Minor, Op. 74 ("Pathetique")

CHAPTER XVI

MUSIC OF
MERRY ENGLAND

SOMETIMES the music of a country does not come so much from any special form of folk song as from the spirit of its people. It is so with the music of England, the land of pleasant meadows, bright gardens, and happy-hearted people. The gay and gentle spirit of English music shows clearly when we compare English folk songs with the wilder and more rugged songs of Wales and the sadder ones of Ireland.

MUSIC IN EARLY ENGLAND

There was always music in England. Hundreds and hundreds of years ago an old Bishop wrote, "The Britons do not sing their tunes in unison like the people of other countries, but in different parts. This they do, not so much by art as by natural habit. Their children, as soon as they begin to sing, adopt the same manner." The very earliest piece of polyphonic music, or music written in different parts, that we know, is the English "Sumer is I-Cumen In." This is in six parts and is not in the old church modes, but in the key of F. The four upper parts are in canon (like "Three Blind Mice") while the two basses, sing over and over again, "Sing, cuckoo, now, sing cuckoo."

The different peoples who conquered England—the Saxons, Danes, and Normans—were gifted in minstrelsy. There were harpers and songs at all their banquets, and minstrels played an important part in history. King Alfred, disguised as a minstrel, went into the camp of the Danes, played at their table, and learned all their secrets. There is a story that during the Crusades, when Richard the Lion Hearted was imprisoned in an Austrian castle, his life was saved by his minstrel, Blondel.

The minstrels went with the coming of the printing press. Their place was taken by the ballad singers who sang on street corners and sold their ballads for a penny. There were also jolly dance tunes in the key of F, instead of the queer old modes, and with the themes repeated as in melodies today. Even King Henry VIII composed dances—King Harry's Pavanne, the King's Mark, a Galyard, etc. Music in England rose to its greatest height during the reign of his daughter, Elizabeth.

In the "golden days of good Queen Bess," all England flowered. Brave men in little boats were carrying the British flag to far seas and distant lands. Bold Sir Francis Drake sailed around the world, plundering the heavy Spanish treasure ships, and was the first white man to set foot on strange shores on the other side of the world (among them what is today our California). The gallant stepbrothers, Sir Walter Raleigh and Sir Humphrey Gilbert, who could see into the future better than other men of their times, were vainly trying to make new-world colonies for their Queen. And the Queen's navy defeated the mighty Spanish Armada and became mistress of the seas.

In England, strolling players were bringing to the people the grandest drama since the days of the Greeks—Shakespeare, Marlowe, and rare Ben Jonson. There was poetry, too, in the age of good Queen Bess, and music. English music was far ahead of the world, although the world across the stormy English channel did not know it.

Music was taught in the great universities of Cambridge and Oxford. There were organs and trained choirs in all the cathedrals. Thomas Tallis, the father of English cathedral music, was setting the English church service quaintly in the Dorian mode, and writing his famous song of forty different parts. To him and his great pupil, William Byrd, Queen Elizabeth gave letters patent, which decreed that they alone should have the right to print music and ruled music paper in her kingdom.

MASQUES

Music was joined to poetry in the masques, which were performed at courts or in the houses of noblemen to celebrate weddings or festive occasions. The noblemen themselves took part in the masques. The greatest poets like Ben Jonson and Milton wrote the words, usually to myths of ancient Greece. The best composers set them to music, and the most famous artists designed the gorgeous costumes and scenery. They were the forerunners of opera in England.

MADRIGALES

In those days, gentlemen could sing in six-part songs more easily than they could spell. There were many books of "madrigales composed in four, five, and six parts in favor of such as take pleasure in musick of voices." These songs were gentle, pleasant songs, with such titles as "Sweet Honey-Sucking Bee," and "Now is the Month of Maying." All these songs were for voice without accompaniment. Some of the most famous musicians—Byrd, Bull, Gibbons, and others—published such a book in praise of Queen Elizabeth—"Madrigales, the Triumphes of Oriana to 5 and 6 voices composed by divers severall authors." This, remember, was about a hundred years before Bach.

The lute and virginal were favorite instruments of the time. The lute was pear-shaped like a mandolin, but played with the fingers instead of a pick. It had thirteen pairs of strings, and someone said that a lute player eighty years old had certainly spent sixty years of his life tuning his instruments. There were famous lutenists then just as there are famous pianists and violinists today. One, John Dowland, left England to become lutenist to the King of Denmark and when he returned to his native land, the poet Shakespeare wrote of him—

"Dowland to thee is dear whose heavenly touch
Upon the lute doth ravish human sense."

The virginal was a small spinet or harpsichord, and perhaps it got its name from the fact that the Virgin Queen herself was an excellent player. She must have been to play the difficult music in "Queen Elizabeth's Virginal Book," the 418 pages of music, variations on popular songs, dance music, etc., prepared for her by the best composers of her realm.

Queen Elizabeth was interested in all musicians, whether great or small. It was she who started the famous choir school for the little boys who sang in the Chapel Royal of St. James's Palace. There were never less than eight or more than twelve of them, and they were called Children of the Chapel Royal to distinguish them from the Gentlemen of the Chapel Royal who took the tenor and bass parts. They wore scarlet coats trimmed with ruffles and gold lace and blue velvet, scarlet breeches, cocked hats, black stockings and shoes, and white gloves.

They were boarded and lodged in the palace itself, and for every eight boys, there was a daily allowance of "two loaves, one mess of great meats, two gallons of ale." The Queen appointed a Master of the Grammar School to teach them. This master at one time made money out of them. He would take them to sing at public and private concerts for a half guinea (about $2.50) apiece and then pocket the money. All the boys would get was sixpence, or twelve cents, among them for barley sugar.

MUSIC DESTROYED BY PURITANS

Most of England's later musicians were trained in the school of the Children of the Chapel Royal. Even after Queen Elizabeth's death, music flourished until the Puritans came into power. They believed that music must be wicked because it was so pleasant. They tore up and burned the music books, smashed the organs, and turned out the choirs. It was even thought a sin for men to make music in their own homes. When, at last after bitter civil wars, old ways of living and government were restored, music had become nearly stamped out. New organs had to be built, new choirs trained, new music books written, mostly from memory, and in the whole land there were only five organists left alive from the old days.

PURCELL AND ENGLISH MUSIC RESTORED

One of the first Gentlemen of the new Chapel Royal choir was Henry Purcell, who was also a member of the King's Band. When he died, he left a little six-year old son, Henry, who became England's greatest musician. He became one of the Children of the Chapel Royal and even while he was a choir boy, he composed anthems. When he grew up, there was no kind of music that he could not compose.

He was organist in Westminster Abbey and wrote the noblest of church music. He also wrote songs for the "Catch Club or the Merry Companions," a collection of those English part-songs called "catches." He composed much chamber music; and also suites and sonatas for harpsichord. He made incidental music to plays and poems by Dryden and Shakespeare. He studied the Italian style and gave England many operas of its own. No king, queen or prince could arrive in England or celebrate a birthday without a song from Purcell.

He was a master of counterpoint and fugue, and all through his works there is bright English melody. He died at the early age of thirty-seven, and on his tomb was the inscription, "Here

lyes Henry Purcell, Esquire, who left this life and is gone to
that blessed place where only his harmony can be succeeded."
At the time of his death, Handel and Bach were only ten years
old.

GERMAN MUSICIANS IN ENGLAND

Had Purcell lived longer, he might have started a national
school of music and left other English musicians to follow in
his footsteps. As it was, England had no native musicians to
match the visiting Germans who came to make music there—
first Pepusch, who adapted old national and popular songs to
the words of Gay's "Beggar Opera," then the mighty Handel,
then Bach's youngest son, Christian, called "the English Bach,"
then Haydn, then Mendelssohn. For more than a hundred
years, English music lay under the spell of Germany. It was
not set free until the reign of England's second truly great
Queen, Victoria.

With Victoria, as with Elizabeth, England had a sudden
spurt of power. The British Empire spread to the far places
of the world. There was a second golden age in literature. And
at last, an Englishman made English music for English people.
In 1842, the fifth year of the reign of Queen Victoria, was
born Arthur Sullivan who broke the foreign hold over English
music, almost without knowing that he did so.

ARTHUR SULLIVAN

His father was Sergeant of the Band at a military college.
Sullivan later wrote that he had learned to walk with a clarinet.
Musical instruments were his toys. With the help of the bands-
men, he learned to play every wind instrument and sometimes was allowed to play with the band at rehearsal. The lives
of the musicians were his favorite reading. Almost from the
time he was a baby, he had longed to be one of the Children
of the Chapel Royal like Purcell.

At first, his father objected. Music had not brought him any great fortune and he wanted something better for his boy. When at last Arthur had won his father's consent, he went for his examination to the house of Sir George Smart, organist and composer to the Chapel Royal. He was trembling with fear, for there was a rule that no boy would be admitted to the Chapel Royal after the age of nine, and he was twelve. But he sang the song "With Verdure Clad" to his own piano accompaniment so beautifully that at once the rule was broken and his dream had come true. Two days later, in his bright, new gold-braided uniform, and with his father in the audience, he sang a solo part.

Days as a choir-boy brought both fun and honors. He became conductor, organist, and composer to the Chapel Royal Chorister's band, in which the instruments were books for drums, combs covered with tissue paper, and "squeakers." At the christening of a Duke, Queen Victoria was so pleased with his singing that she sent her congratulations and ten shillings. He composed two anthems, and the Dean patted his head and gave him a sovereign. The choir school was teaching him the use of the voice in music just as the band had taught him the use of instruments.

In 1856, a scholarship for study in Leipzig was offered in memory of Mendelssohn. Competition for it was open to any boy over fourteen, and Arthur had been fourteen just six months. He was the youngest boy to take the examination, and he and the oldest boy were tied for first place. There was a second examination lasting well into the evening, a conference among the examiners, and it was not until the next day that Sullivan received a letter telling him that he had won.

There were two years more in England studying German and learning more music at the Royal Academy—and then Leipzig. The gay black-haired lad became a favorite with teachers and pupils alike. He took lessons in counterpoint in the house where Bach had done his mightiest works. He met the great Liszt and made one of a table of whist with him. He learned how backward England was in music.

Like a true Englishman, he took Mendelssohn for his model. Because Mendelssohn at seventeen had composed music for Shakespeare's "Midsummer Night's Dream," Sullivan at eighteen wrote music for Shakespeare's "Tempest." Because Mendelssohn had composed a Scotch symphony, Sullivan, after he had returned from Leipzig, wrote an Irish symphony. He wrote piano pieces in imitation of Mendelssohn's "Songs Without Words" and oratorio because it had been done by all the great Germans before him.

Back home he was considered the bright hope of English music. His works were performed by the best symphony orchestras. He was invited to conduct at music festivals at the different English towns. The poet laureate, Tennyson, wrote poems for him to set to music. He went to Paris with the great novelist, Dickens, and met Rossini. He made a pilgrimage to Vienna with Grove, the editor of the great musical dictionary. There they found the lost music to Schubert's "Rosamunde" and met an old, old man who had known Beethoven and Haydn and had been at Schubert's christening.

Fame and honor did not bring him bread and butter. He took a position as church organist to earn his living and became organist at the Opera in order to learn more about the stage. In composition, he said he was "ready to undertake anything—symphonies, overtures, ballets, anthems, hymn tunes, songs, a concerto for the cello, and at last, comic and light operas."

Sullivan's most famous hymn tune is "Onward, Christian Soldiers." His best known song is a setting of Adelaide Procter's poem, "The Lost Chord," written as he watched by the bedside of his dying brother. His first successful comic opera was more or less an accident. There was a man in London who gave famous Saturday evening parties for the greatest artists, actors, writers, and musicians. Sullivan and a writer named F. C. Bernand made a one-act operetta called "Cox and Box" as part of the entertainment at one of these parties.

Everybody talked so much about it that it was given again at a performance for charity and at last was put on in a regular theatre where it ran three hundred nights. Then Sullivan met Gilbert.

GILBERT AND SULLIVAN

Gilbert, a lawyer by profession, was six years older than Sullivan, and had become known for his "Bab Ballads," with his own clever pen-and-ink drawings. The "Bab Ballads" were comical, topsy-turvy verse like the sample:—

> "Tell me, Edward, dost remember
> How at breakfast often we
> Put our bacon in the teapot,
> While we took and fried our tea?"

It was Gilbert's gay verse that set Sullivan's music free from German models. Gilbert had great ambitions to write serious plays just as Sullivan had great ambitions to compose operas and symphonies. Yet almost the only work they did which lived after them was that which they did together. They were never close friends. They were too different. Sullivan was charming and pleasant, with a genius for making people like him. Gilbert was a bit gruff and irritable and apt to rush into a lawsuit whenever he had a quarrel.

What is more, though Sullivan's music certainly would not have been composed except for Gilbert's words, critics had a way of speaking as though the music was much better than the words. Several times Gilbert's name was even left off the program. Sullivan's genius was recognized by the Queen and he became Sir Arthur Sullivan years before Gilbert was knighted by Victoria's son. So Gilbert had a few moments of feeling disgruntled, and Sullivan had many moments of feeling that he was wasting himself on comic opera.

"TRIAL BY JURY"

It was two years after they had met before a theatre manager thought of commissioning them to do a comic opera together. Though this was fairly successful, it was four years more before they did their second, the one act "Trial by Jury." In "Trial by Jury" comes the clever use of the chorus that is found in all later Gilbert and Sullivan works. It paints the background and action and describes the feelings much like the chorus of the old Greek plays. It repeats the last line of the solo very much like the church music Sullivan had sung in the Chapel Royal. Soon everybody in London was quoting bits of the verse or singing and whistling snatches of tune from "Trial by Jury."

D'OYLY CARTE

The manager of the theatre where "Trial by Jury" was first given was Richard D'Oyly Carte, two years younger than Sullivan. Out of his great enthusiasm for the work of Gilbert and Sullivan came the idea of the Comedy Opera Company to give England a national comic opera instead of that of France or Italy. He planned it for all English writers and composers, but in the end, it was Gilbert and Sullivan alone who gave England a musical form to suit the spirit of the country. For over ten years, the partners in merriment poured out the works that have added to the gaiety of life not only in England, but in all countries from then until now.

Their first, "The Sorcerer," was followed by the famous "Pinafore," which brought them across the seas to America. At first, "Pinafore" nearly failed, as there was a hot spell in London which kept people away from the theatre. Slowly its fortunes improved, partly because Sullivan, at the Promenade concerts, played selections from "Pinafore" and people liked the music so well that they wanted to see the whole opera. Then there was trouble with the directors of the theatre, and it was closed for repairs in the middle of the profitable Christmas season.

While "Pinafore" was shelved in England, it was the rage in America. It was not only produced by a good company in Boston, but was given by children, church choirs, and colored troupes, and the music was ground out by every hand organ. And Gilbert and Sullivan were not making a penny out of it all, as there was no copyright or other law to protect them. Anything that had been published in a foreign country was public property in the United States. The only way that Gilbert, Sullivan, and D'Oyly Carte could make any money out of the opera was to come to America and put on a production of their own. This they did, while the news that "Pinafore" was playing in a hundred places in the States gave it a new lease of life in London.

During "Pinafore's" successful run in New York, Gilbert and Sullivan finished a new work, "The Pirates of Penzance." This has one of Gilbert's delightfully funny stories. It is about a boy whose father wishes him to be apprenticed to a *pilot*, but his nursemaid, who is hard of hearing, apprentices him to a *pirate* instead. The victim of this sad mistake, Frederic, looks forward to his twenty-first year when his apprenticeship will be over and he will be free to leave the pirates. But, alas! he finds that he was bound not until his twenty-first year, but his twenty-first birthday. And he was born on Leap Year.

> "Though counting in the usual way,
> Years twenty-one I've been alive,
> Yet, reckoning from my natal day,
> I am a little boy of five."

From "The Pirates," which was written and produced in America, comes the scrap of tune which was adopted for the street song, "Hail, Hail, the Gang's All Here." "The Pirates of Penzance" was produced on the same night in England and New York, and from manuscript, not published copy. But even that did not solve the copyright problem here, as the court ruled that anyone who heard the opera could write it out from memory and produce it for his own benefit.

"Pinafore" and "The Pirates" made so much money that the next operetta, "Patience," was first produced in a fine new theatre built especially for Gilbert, Sullivan, and D'Oyly Carte. The theatre was called the Savoy, and even now the works of Gilbert and Sullivan are called the Savoy operas, and people who played in them, Savoyards. It was the first theatre to be lighted by electricity. It was the first to be devoted to a wholly English art. "Iolanthe" and "Princess Ida" followed, and then came the first split with Gilbert.

Sullivan had been knighted while Gilbert had not, and the Musical Review said, "It will look rather more than odd to see in the paper that a new comic opera is in preparation, the book by Mr. W. S. Gilbert, the music by Sir Arthur Sullivan. A musical knight must not soil his hand with anything less than an anthem or madrigal." Sir Arthur rather thought so himself.

He found fault with Gilbert's stories. He said he had written all the music he could to plots about magic pills (like the

"Sorcerer") or babies changed in the cradle (like "Pinafore")
or fairies (like "Iolanthe"). He wanted a "story of human interest and probability." Gilbert answered in anger. D'Oyly
Carte tried to smooth things over. Gilbert sent a plot which
Sullivan refused. At last, they came together on the "Mikado."

"THE MIKADO"

"The Mikado" is the best loved of all the Savoy operas.
It is sheer joy to eye and ear from beginning to end. Gilbert
was never more at his topsy-turvy best, but perhaps improbable
things seemed more probable to Sullivan when they happened
in Japan. Certainly, he never wrote music that made Gilbert's gay verse seem more bright and sparkling.

Someone said that Sullivan was to comic opera what Wagner was to music drama in fitting music to the meaning of the
words. He was a master at making his orchestra tell of his
characters and action. He often did not write in the orchestra parts until the opera was being rehearsed to piano
accompaniment. Thus, he often got ideas from the action,
like the clarinet swoop for the swish of the snickersnee of
Ko-Ko, the Lord High Executioner.

The scenery was all dainty cherry blossoms and gay little
Japanese houses, and the costumes a whirl of rainbow satins
and painted fans. Katisha, the elderly, ugly lady whom the
Emperor's son is supposed to marry before he flees disguised
as a second trombone, wore a real Japanese costume two hundred years old. The costume of the Mikado was just like
that of the real Mikado of ancient days, even to the gold embroidered petticoat and the cap with the queer curled bag
on top of his head to enclose his pig-tail. "The Mikado" took
the fancy of the world from Berlin to Los Angeles.

Their next, "Ruddigore," was not such a happy success.
The name reminded squeamish people too much of blood.
Many thought that the story of the Murgatroyd bound by a

curse to commit a crime a day was more grim than funny. Sullivan thought it was a failure because it ran only 288 nights while someone else's comic opera ran 500. Yet once more the break between the partners was postponed, and they set to work on "The Yeomen of the Guard."

This opera was the favorite with both Gilbert and Sullivan. To Gilbert it was a step nearer serious plays, and to Sullivan it was a step nearer grand opera.

But the Queen had said to Sir Arthur, "You ought to write a grand opera." Now he felt more strongly than ever that he wanted to write no more music to Gilbert's words. Gilbert, too, had grievances "not necessarily against Sullivan," but against D'Oyly Carte. There were bitter words, but friends brought them together for their last really rollicking work, "The Gondoliers." In this work, Gilbert and Sullivan seem to grow young again in music and in thought. Gilbert even has his mixed babies. In this case, they rule the country as twin kings because no one knows which was the real prince and which the son of the gondolier. In the end, the real king turns out to have been still another baby!

The final and fatal quarrel was over a carpet. Gilbert, Sullivan, and D'Oyly Carte were supposed to share the expense of the theatre together. During the run of "The Gondoliers," a carpet was bought, some say for scenery, but others for Carte's private office. Gilbert objected to the extravagance. Sullivan tried to be neutral, but Gilbert forced him to take sides—and he sided with Carte.

Gilbert shouted, "You are both blackguards!" and rushed from the office. He sent a notice that the collaboration was at an end, and "after the withdrawal of 'The Gondoliers' our united work will be heard in public no more." He took the matter to court.

Sullivan tried his grand opera in the Royal English Opera House built especially for him by the devoted D'Oyly Carte.

His first opera, "Ivanhoe," was a dismal failure, and the Royal English Opera House failed with it. D'Oyly Carte went back to a Savoy without Gilbert and Sullivan. For three years, Gilbert and Sullivan worked alone or with others without achieving the success or satisfaction they had found together. Then they patched up their differences and wrote two more operettas which were only feeble echoes of their former gaiety. The old spirit had gone forever. They were worn out, Sullivan especially. He had always written his bright music in moments snatched from severe pain, for he had a complaint which operation after operation would not cure. Now he was weakened by years of suffering. It was the end for Gilbert and Sullivan.

But not for the Savoy opera. There is still a Savoy company in England under the direction of a son of D'Oyly Carte, playing the operas exactly as they were played in the days of Gilbert and Sullivan. Not only are they often produced by American companies, but every year they are played in probably every state in the union by some school or choral group. They will live as long as people love to sing and be merry. And since Sullivan taught English music how to laugh, English musicians have freed themselves from foreign rule. Now they dare to express their ideas and the spirit of their country in their own way.

RECORD LIST — CHAPTER XVI

(For music of Byrd, Dowland, Gibbons, Morley, Weelkes — see CHAPTER II)

Britten, Benjamin (1913-
     A Ceremony of Carols, Op. 28
     Peter Grimes — Four Sea Interludes and Passacaglia, Op. 33A
     Serenade for Tenor, Horn, and Strings, Op. 31
     Variations on a Theme of Frank Bridge
     The Young Person's Guide to the Orchestra

Elgar, Edward (1857-1934)
 Enigma Variations, Op. 36
 Pomp and Circumstance Marches, Op. 39
 Serenade for Strings, Op. 20

Delius, Frederick (1862-1934)
 Appalachia
 Brigg Fair
 Koanga
 On Hearing the First Cuckoo in Spring

Folk songs, ballads, and dances — various

Gilbert, W. S., and Sullivan, Arthur
 The Gondoliers
 H.M.S. Pinafore
 Iolanthe
 The Mikado
 The Pirates of Penzance

Holst, Gustav (1874-1934)
 The Planets, Op. 32

Purcell, Henry (c. 1659-1695)
 Anthems and secular songs, various
 Dido and Aeneas — excerpts
 Fantasies for 3, 4, 5, 6, 7 Viols da Gamba
 Suite for Strings
 Trumpet Voluntary in D
 Tune and Air for Trumpet

Sullivan, Arthur (1842-1900)
 Incidental music to "The Tempest" and "Henry VIII"

Vaughan Williams, Ralph (1872-
 English Folk Song Suite
 Fantasia on a Theme by Tallis
 Greensleeves
 Symphony No. 2, "A London Symphony"
 Symphony No. 6 in E Minor

Walton, William (1902-
 Belshazzar's Feast
 Concerto for Viola
 Facade (declamation and chamber orchestra; or instrumental suite)
 Orb and Sceptre, Coronation March (1935)

CHAPTER XVII

MUSIC IN THE NEW WORLD

LONG before ships brought the white men from old Europe to conquer a new world, there was music in the wigwams and around the campfires of the Indians. As with all savage peoples, their music was a part of their lives. The old women of the village would come and sing to the new-born baby in its cradle, "Little baby, how tiny you are!" If the brown, bright-eyed little papoose strapped to his mother's back was fretful, she would sing a lullaby, "Little fox, I want to keep you. You are my little baby." The Indians thought that everyone should be kind and cheerful when near a baby so that it would not get discouraged and die.

Indian children played their games to music. The little girls would march around the village in a line, each with her hands on the shoulders of the girl in front of her, as they sang, "The deer follow each other." Every Indian boy at the age of twelve went out into the wilderness to prepare for his manhood. There he would stay, alone and fasting, until he had received a song from the spirits. This song was supposed to call to his aid in time of need the spirits which the Indians believed dwelt in every living thing—birds and beasts and trees.

MUSIC IN INDIAN LIFE

The braves went on the warpath with song, and when they returned victorious, there would be a war dance. In times of hunger, the tribes led by the medicine man would sing together to pray for rain or success in the hunt. The medicine men had special songs to drive the evil spirits from the sick and send the spirits of the dead to the Happy Hunting Ground.

The Indians had different sorts of flutes and whistles split and hollowed of sumac or cedar or box elder. Sometimes the flute or whistle was used by the medicine man to help him against evil spirits. Or a look-out would play a signal to warn the village of an approaching enemy, while the enemy would think the sound of the flute was only some lover playing to his maiden. Flutes were played most often by young men a-courting, and an old Indian once said, "The flute is as old as the world. There have always been flutes just as there have always been young men and maidens."

Most Indian music was singing accompanied by drums and rattles. In Indian singing, the voice glides from note to note with a nasal, wailing sound. The Indians did not put two tones together to make harmony like the white man. All their singers sang the same note in unison. Some of the songs of the Indians do not sound like tunes to us, for they do not follow any scale or mode, but simply wander among sounds. In others, the tonic and dominant—or the first and fifth notes of our scale—are heard so often that they seem to form part of some Indian scale. Still others use the five tone scale.

INDIAN MELODIES AND RHYTHMS

Indian melodies usually go slowly downward and end on their lowest note. The rhythm often changes during the song, and sometimes the drums and the singers have different rhythms at the same time, the drums playing three beats while the singers have two.

The Indians had nearly as many different kinds of drums and rattles as there were tribes. They had small hand-drums carried by leather thongs to be used while the player was riding or dancing. They had the large drum made by stretching skins over stakes driven in the ground, and six or eight players would sit around it, thumping as they sang. There were the great drums made of hollowed logs partly filled with water, which could be heard for twelve miles.

They had rattles made of gourds, tortoise shells, or rawhide; and birchbark boxes filled with pebbles of different sizes. And they had notched sticks or pieces of bone to rub together and make a rasping sound. The Indians enjoyed putting different kinds of noises together just as our musicians enjoy combining tones.

For many years, the white people knew and cared nothing about Indian music. By the time American musicians saw that the Indians could give them a rich store of folk melody, the Indian was in government reservations, fast forgetting old ways and old songs. The first comers were more interested in the Indian's pumpkin and corn than in his music.

In conquering the wilderness and the Indian, the early settler was too busy even to think about a music of his own. Certainly, the tiny ships were too crammed with pots, pans, glass, nails and needful things to hold a musical instrument. And the early settlers had little music in their hearts. Those who settled the New England coast came from the religious party in the old country which later smashed the English organs and disbanded English choirs. They brought no music but hymns with little tune and no accompaniment.

OLD BALLADS OF THE SOUTH

The English who settled in the South brought with them the ballads of the times of Queen Elizabeth. These folk songs were frowned upon during the Puritan power in England and are all but forgotten there. But in little cabins in the southern mountains, hidden away from the changing world, grandmothers still sing the old songs as they spin or quilt. So the folk music of the old world has become the folk music of the new.

WORK SONGS

At last, the people began to make folk songs from their life in the new world. These songs were not so much dance songs or love songs, like the folk music of Europe, as they were work songs. There were the sea chanteys of sailors weighing anchor on great ships about to skim around the world for the spice of India and the silk of China. There were the lonely songs of cowboys on the wide prairies. There were songs of adventurers braving a wilderness in search of gold, and songs to the thud of the pickaxe as men drew the different parts of the country closer together with shining rails of steel.

SONGS OF THE NEGRO

And there were the songs of the Negro slaves toiling in the cotton, rice and tobacco fields, looking for comfort to God and a hope for a better life in another world.—"Nobody Knows de Trouble I've Seen," and "Swing Low, Sweet Chariot, Comin' for to Carry Me Home." Unlike the Indians, the Negroes naturally sing in parts or in harmony. Their soft, sliding melodies, exciting dissonances and rhythms have made the songs of the Negro the greatest gift to American folk music.

STEPHEN FOSTER

The first really great American musician was Stephen Foster, who has been called a maker of folk songs. The story of his life shows the great difference between music in the old world and the new. He was born in 1826. It was the golden age of music in Europe, with Beethoven, Schubert,

Rossini, Meyerbeer all at the height of their fame, and Berlioz, Schumann, Mendelssohn, Liszt, Wagner and Verdi all
growing to manhood. Had he been born across the sea, he
might have entered a choir school or conservatory and become
a composer of symphonies instead of simple songs. As it was,
he was born in a little town near Pittsburgh, Pennsylvania.

A few European artists and opera companies came to Boston, New York, Philadelphia and Baltimore, but they never
strayed from the coast. Inland, what was called "classic
music" was made up of young ladies in muslin, tinkling on the
piano and singing such cheerful little ditties as,

> "Love and hope and beauty's bloom
> Are flowers gathered for the tomb—
> There's nothing true but heaven."

(From a song actually sung by Foster's sister Charlotte.)

The music teachers were mostly broken-down French or
German hacks who came to the new world because they
could not earn a good living in the old. A German named
Klebe, who ran a music store in Pittsburgh probably taught
Stephen all he ever knew of the piano and harmony. The
Fosters did not always have a piano. The father was constantly trying his hand at something new, going from one
business or position to another. Sometimes the eight Foster children—Stephen was the youngest—lived in comfortable
homes of their own. At other times, they lived with relatives
or in boarding houses while their father was trying to get
established again after his latest failure.

Father Foster could "draw a few tunes on the fiddle."
Somewhere, somehow, Stephen learned to play violin, flute,
and clarinet. Like many families south of New York, the
Fosters had two Negro servants. The Negress, Olivia Pise,
often took little Stephen with her to church. The boy learned
to love the mellow voices, fine melodies, and rich natural
harmonies of the Negro singers. The memory is echoed in

many of his songs. In "Hard Times, Come Again No More," and "Oh Boys, Carry Me 'Long," he used bits of these Negro melodies which he told a friend were "too good to be lost."

FOSTER AND THE MINSTREL SHOW

At that time, about the only form of music in which men took part was the minstrel show. Minstrel shows then were much as they are now—white men with blacked faces and giddy, flashy costumes, rags, and checked shirts to make people laugh. They told jokes in a dialect with a wrong use of long words (like "Amos and Andy") and sang sentimental and silly songs. Nowadays, minstrel shows are put on by amateurs to benefit some church or charity. Then, the minstrel companies travelled from town to town like theatrical and operatic companies. They took the place of our motion-pictures and concerts. They brought to the small towns all the entertainment and music that the people ever had. They even toured Europe to represent American music!

Minstrel shows played an important part in Stephen Foster's life. When he was nine years old, he made up a minstrel company of neighborhood youngsters and gave shows in a barn. He began to compose even during his unsettled school days when he was moving from place to place and school to school. While he was living with a married brother, the young men of the town had a club which they called Knights of the Square Table. Stephen wrote three songs for them to sing at their meetings, "Louisiana Belle," "Old Uncle Ned," and "Oh, Susannah!" He had always hung around the minstrel shows that came to town, getting acquainted with the manager and singers. Soon they began to sing his songs.

"OH, SUSANNAH"

In those days, a minstrel show would take a song from town to town and set people to singing it and wanting to buy it. While Stephen was keeping books in his brother's store in

Cincinnati, his songs were travelling over the country. At last, a Pittsburgh publisher named Peters wrote Foster for copies of the songs to publish. Stephen sent them to him with no thought of receiving any pay. But Peters sent him $100 for "Oh, Susannah!" and Stephen later wrote, "the two fifty-dollar bills I received had the effect of starting me in on my present vocation of song writer." Peters made $10,000 on the song.

There were faulty copyright laws in this country, as Gilbert and Sullivan later found to their sorrow. Any minstrel manager to whom Stephen had generously given a copy of a song could publish and sell it. Anyone who heard it sung could write it out and publish it. There were twenty different versions of Susannah published—Susannah for voice and Susannah for band, Susannah quick steps, polkas and quadrilles, and Susannah with easy variations for the piano. On only three of these did Stephen's name appear.

Negroes took Susannah to their hearts as a folk song of their own. She cheered the forty-niners on their hard overland journey in search of California gold. She even reached Germany as "Ich komm von Alabama mit der Banjo auf dem Knie." Though she brought Stephen no fortune, she did bring him fame.

In 1849, he signed an agreement with a firm of New York publishers. They alone were to have the right to publish his songs; he was to give the minstrel managers only copies already printed so that they could not flood the market with printed copies of their own; and he was to receive a royalty of two cents on every copy sold. Now the songs that had made money for others would begin to do something for him.

"OLD KENTUCKY HOME"

With contracts to show his family that his songs really would make money, he gave up book-keeping and went back home to Pittsburgh. There he married Jane McDowell, his "Jeanie with the Light Brown Hair." Soon after their marriage, they paid a visit to Federal Hall in Bardstown, Kentucky, the home of Judge Rowan, a cousin of Stephen's father. This beautiful old southern brick mansion was the "Old Kentucky Home" that Stephen put into a song never to be forgotten. The state of Kentucky has now made the "Old Kentucky Home" a Stephen Foster memorial museum.

Soon Foster settled down to the business of being a song writer. Melodies came to him as naturally as they did to Schubert to whom he has been compared—a Schubert without the help of a choir-school or a family orchestra or a Salieri. Where Schubert could use rich chords and lovely dissonances to suit his accompaniment to the melody and words, Stephen knew only a few simple chords for all his songs. Yet they were well suited to the simple melodies and homely words.

STEPHEN FOSTER'S MUSIC

His tunes were all in folk song style—ternary form with an A theme repeated a number of times, a chorus opening with a new B theme, and a return to the A theme at the close. Like folk songs, they were melodies easy to love and remember and easy to sing. Though the words of many of his songs are "Ethiopian" to be used in minstrel shows, the form and rhythm are much more like Anglo-Saxon folk songs than like real Negro music. Some of his tunes even have the old Scotch-Irish "quirk" in the rhythm.

Where song writers in Europe made music for the words of the greatest poets like Shakespeare and Goethe, Foster was either using cheap newspaper verse or writing his own. Often the tune could come to him first, and he would make words to fit it. He took a great deal of pains with his words, and his notebooks show them changed and written over and over again. In his most famous song, "Old Folks at Home," the Swanee River was at first the Pedee River. But Foster did not like the sound and hunted on a map until he had found that most musical sounding of all rivers, the Suwannee.

Most of his songs are in Negro dialect because they were used in minstrel shows. Yet like true folk songs, they speak simply of the simple things that appeal to us all, old and young, black and white—the faithfulness of old dog Tray, longing for home, grief over departed loved ones. There is beauty in the picture of "My Old Kentucky Home" before and after "hard times came a-knocking at the door." There is real poetry in such a line as "The day goes by like a shadow on the heart." And Stephen could write such jolly nonsense verse that it is a pity that he did little but "Oh, Susannah," "De Camptown Races" and the charming "Nelly Bly" with the heart "Warm as a cup of tea and bigger dan de sweet potato down in Tennessee."

"OLD FOLKS AT HOME"

Like Sullivan's friends, those of Foster tried to persuade him that the thing he could do best was not good enough for him. Accordingly, Stephen decided for a while not to publish his "Ethiopian" songs under his own name. Thus it was that his greatest song, "Old Folks at Home," was for many years published under the name of the minstrel, Christy. Christy paid him for the privilege, Foster, of course, getting the royalties.

Never did a song go to the hearts of so many people. A musical journal said, "Pianos and guitars groan with it night and day. Sentimental young ladies and gentlemen sing it. All the bands play it. The street organs grind it out at every hour. The 'singing stars' carol it at concerts and the chambermaid sweeps and dusts to the strains of 'Old Folks at Home.' "

Then Stephen Foster paid Christy back his money and had his own name put on the song. He could well be proud of perhaps the greatest "home song" in the world. Famous European singers who came to New York took it back with them, and it became probably the first piece of American music to be heard there in concert halls with the works of the old masters.

Stephen Foster's fame brought him no comfort or happiness. Like so many of the great musicians, he had little business sense. His publishers used to pay him around a hundred dollars in advance of the royalties which were expected to come in. Stephen formed the bad habit of drawing on his publishers for money for songs not yet written. When he was hopelessly in debt to them, he would repay by selling for a small amount his royalty rights in his already successful songs. It was what Schubert had done before him. The steady income which might have been his for years was gone forever.

Then his health began to fail, and with it went his genius. There were two years in each of which he wrote only one song. Then came two years in which he wrote more songs, but none were really great. At last, he moved to New York. Perhaps he thought it would help him to be nearer his publishers. Perhaps it was lonely in Pittsburgh now that his father and mother were dead and the beloved brothers and sisters had married and moved away. For one with his poor health and habits, it was the worst possible move.

LAST YEARS

His health grew worse. Some of his songs were rejected by publishers. He no longer could get any money in advance for those that were accepted. In ragged clothes and glazed cap, he took to haunting the back room of a grocery store, often making a meal of nothing but apples and raw turnips peeled with a large pocket knife. Sitting on a barrel, he would write down songs on brown wrapping paper and hawk them around at publishers and theatres, feeling lucky to get $10 or $15. In 1864 he died in Bellevue Hospital as a result of a fall in his room. From these sad years there comes just one of his really great songs, "Old Black Joe" which begins with the words, "Gone are the days when my heart was young and gay."

DVOŘÁK

As life in the new land grew less hard, there was more time for music. Opera companies and symphony orchestras sprang up in the large cities. America could well be proud of learning to know and love Wagner's work while he was still despised in his own country. Now the new country could hear and see the greatest of musicians from Rubinstein and Tschaikowsky to Gilbert and Sullivan. Though Sullivan reported that most of the players that he found in the orchestras here were German, splendid new music schools were started to train native American musicians.

To the New York Conservatory, one of Europe's most famous composers came as a teacher. He gave America his richest musical gifts, and in return America gave its best to him. He was the Bohemian Antonin Dvořák (Dvor-zhak), and his life reads like a story-book struggle for success. He was born in 1841 in the little Bohemian village of Mühlhausen, where his father was inn-keeper and butcher.

Antonin, as the oldest of eight children, was expected to learn his father's trade and help support the family. But he wanted to be a musician. The folk music of his country-people became as much a part of him as the blood in his veins. The peasants not only sang at their work. They would often begin to sing and dance after church on Sunday and keep it up without stopping until the following morning. There were more than forty kinds of Bohemian national dances.

Music was taught in the Bohemian schools, and at four-teen, Dvořák had learned to sing and play organ, violin and piano. Now he took part in the village orchestra that played for weddings and on holidays. His father still called upon him to give up music. To try to persuade his father to change his mind, Antonin composed a polka for the village band. But he did not know that trumpets were transposing instru-ments—or instruments which play music in a different key from that in which it is written. The polka was a sad failure, and he went into the inn and butcher shop.

He was so unhappy that at the end of a year, his father let him go away to the organ school at Prague. He had no money to support him. He had to play in an orchestra in a restaurant on week-days and in church on Sundays. Here he learned the uses of the different instruments and how their tones are blended together. He had little chance to hear anything but the church music and the cheap popular tunes in the res-taurant. Sometimes he coaxed the kettle drummer in a sym-phony orchestra to let him crouch behind a drum and hear a concert. Once he had a chance to hear "Der Freischütz" for four cents, but lacked the four cents. The organ school was a musty, dusty place which taught little but theory and rules. He could not afford to buy the scores of any of the great works, and there was no library where he could use them. When he was graduated at twenty-one, he still knew little of the Beethoven symphonies.

Better days came. There was a national movement in music in little Bohemia as in greater countries, and its leader was Smetana whose gay opera, "The Bartered Bride," is so popular today. He was director of the national opera house, and Dvořák got a place in the orchestra. Smetana was kind to him, lent him scores of all the great masterpieces, and en-couraged him to compose.

For ten years, Dvořák composed operas, symphonies, every

kind of music, and tore them all up because he did not think them good enough. Little by little, his courage and patience were rewarded. After being rewritten three times, one of his operas succeeded. By the time he came to America, he was famous all over the world as the composer of the beautiful "Slavonic Dances." He had received highest honors in his own country, was decorated by the Austrian government, and received an honorary degree from the University of Cambridge in England.

The Dvořák who had loved the old folk dances of his own country loved the folk music of the new—the Negro and Indian music and simple songs of Stephen Foster. Dvořák's "Humoresque" is based on the same chords as Foster's "Old Folks at Home." As a stunt they are often sung together.

Dvořák was no dry-as-dust professor like the old men in his organ school. He tried to teach the spirit as well as the rules of music. He thought that young American musicians tried too hard to imitate the music of Europe. He felt that they should be making their country a national music from their own rich store of folk melody. To show them how this could be done, he wrote his great symphony "From The New World."

The "New World" Symphony is one of the greatest of all symphonies. Dvořák did not simply copy Negro and Indian themes. He made themes of his own, inspired by the music of the Negro and Indian. In gay flashes of tune in the first and third movements, we even get a glimpse now and then of the lusty barn dances and husking bees of the American settlers. The beautiful Largo is perhaps the best known of all symphonic music. It is in the spirit of the Negro spiritual, and is often sung like a spiritual to the words "Goin' Home." In the "New World" Symphony Dvořák composed his masterpiece and the greatest piece of music ever inspired by our country.

EDWARD MACDOWELL

Many years before Dvořák's visit, one of America's greatest composers was born. It was in 1861 while Stephen Foster was starving and dying in New York. Like the boy Mendelssohn, young Edward MacDowell was fortunate in many ways. He was gifted alike in music, art, and poetry. His father had always longed to draw, but had been prevented by strict parents who thought art a silly, useless thing. So he was all the more eager to help his own little boy. He was a well-to-do merchants and could afford to pay for the best lessons. The MacDowells lived in New York where the best teachers were to be found and the best music to be heard.

EDUCATION ABROAD

Young Edward studied with two famous South American pianists who had settled in New York. He showed so much talent that his parents were advised to send him to Europe where he might get the very best musical education. When he was fifteen, he and his mother went to Paris where he easily passed the examination to the conservatory. One of his companions was Claude Debussy, and the two composers took a lifelong interest in each other's work. It was here that he was caught drawing a picture of one of his teachers, who took it to an artist. The artist offered to give him lessons free for three years, but McDowell felt he should give all his time to music.

Like a true American, MacDowell did not stay with any one school when he thought he might learn more by adventuring farther. After hearing one of Europe's most famous pianists, he felt he would never learn to play like that in Paris. So he left, and tried other schools. He applied for private lessons from a great German pianist but was rebuffed with the advice that the pianist "could not waste any time on an American boy."

At last, in the conservatory at the German town of Frankfort, he found teachers to love and admire. When his piano teacher, Heymann, retired, he wanted his talented young pupil to take his place. But the native German musicians were jealous, and a German was given the important position. He became piano teacher at the conservatory of the tiny town of Darmstadt and also took private pupils. Among the first of these was the lovely American girl, Marian Nevins, whom he later married.

Liszt, who was always generous to young musicians, heard him play his first piano concerto and got him a chance to play his first piano suite at a great German music festival. It was one of the highest honors that could have come to a young musician. Through Liszt, also, his work was accepted by a famous old publishing house in Leipzig. Everywhere critics praised him. At last, America had a musician worthy of a place beside the young composers of Europe.

After his marriage, MacDowell bought a cottage and garden in Germany. But soon he felt that his own country needed his gift of music more than Europe with its many masters. So he came back to the United States and settled in Boston to teach and compose.

Of course, MacDowell was not the only American who was teaching and composing music at that time. Boston had George Whitefield Chadwick, seven years older than MacDowell. After studying in Germany, he had returned to teach at the New England Conservatory of Music in Boston, and finally became its director. His works were performed by the best orchestras in this country. One of his pupils, Horatio Parker, who later studied in Germany, was the first American composer to have an oratorio performed at music festivals in England.

However, the real test of a man's greatness is his fame outside of his own country. MacDowell, who won success in

Europe before returning to his homeland, was the greatest of all American musicians. After he had spent some pleasant years in Boston, a wealthy woman left a large sum of money to Columbia University in New York to start the teaching of music there. MacDowell was chosen the first professor, and moved from Boston to New York.

For his summers, MacDowell bought a farm at Peterboro, in the beautiful wooded hills of New Hampshire. In the midst of the thick fragrant pines, he built a little log cabin with a fireplace and furnished it with a working table and piano. In this "house of dreams untold," he worked as Grieg had done in his Norwegian farm storehouse.

When he was in Europe, he had become a friend of Grieg, and the two composers wrote to each other for many years. He greatly admired Grieg's music, and there is something about his own music that makes us think of Grieg. MacDowell often painted pictures and told stories with his music; such as his well-known "Wild Rose" and "Water Lily" and "Of a Tailor and a Bear." His "Indian Suite" is one of the best American compositions made from real Indian music, and in such a jolly bit as "Uncle Remus" he pictures the Negro, light-hearted and gay, without using any truly Negro themes, just as Grieg caught the spirit of the Norwegian peasant.

MacDowell worked so hard to make beautiful music and to train new musicians for America that he wore himself out. During his last years his mind was under a cloud. When he died, he was buried in the shadow of a giant granite boulder on his beloved farm. In his memory, Mrs. MacDowell made the farm into the MacDowell Colony where each summer musicians, artists, and writers can go to do their best work in the quiet of little studio cabins among the pines.

Since the time of MacDowell, America has caught up with the rest of the world in music. We now have many opera companies and one, the Metropolitan in New York, is among the best in the world. The great cities from the Atlantic to the Pacific have their fine symphony orchestras. In these orchestras and opera companies, beside the best of musicians from the old world, are young Americans who have received all their musical education in their homeland. On the programs along with the works of European masters are American operas, American symphonies, American tone poems.

What is more, our country is developing a national music of its own. Many believe that this music began with the songs and dances of the American Negro. Certainly, the jolly little bands of Negro musicians, like that of Handy in the streets of New Orleans, first set everyone to singing and whistling "ragtime" and dancing to it. Soon "ragtime" and "jazz" had captured the street songs and popular dances all over the land. This "American music," as people of the old world always speak of it, was even welcomed into European ballrooms and cafes with its strange dissonances which the Negroes called "blues" and its exciting syncopated rhythm.

Rhythm, as we have seen, is a natural grouping of strong and weak beats. In syncopated rhythm, a strongly marked note is played on a weak beat, giving the effect of a shift in the rhythm. Jazz is not the only music to have syncopated rhythm. Many of the composers of former days would use it for a measure or two to add variety to their works. Some nationalistic music, like the Hungarian dance, was already marked by syncopated rhythm. The syncopated rhythm of ragtime or jazz makes a rhythmic pattern which people all over the world recognize as "American," just as easily as we can recognize Spanish or Hungarian music.

Before long, American composers came to see that from the dissonances and rhythm of jazz they could make a truly national music. Probably in the days of Bach, ladies and gentlemen danced the minuet or gavotte to silly little tunes soon to be forgotten. Bach and the other composers of the time simply used the different dance rhythms to make their lovely suites. In the same way, though much of jazz was of low caliber, composers began to use jazz rhythms and "blues" as material for music to express life in America in their time. What is more, jazz rhythms, melodies and harmonies based on a scale with a minor third and seventh, had as strong an appeal to composers of other lands as the native music of Spain and Hungary. European composers found in American jazz an inspiration for some of their music. Examples are countless. To mention just a few: "Golliwog's Cakewalk," by the French Debussy; "La Création du Monde" ("The Creation of the World"), a ballet by the French Milhaud; "Ragtime," by the Russian Stravinsky; "Koanga," by the English Delius; and "Jonny spielt auf," an opera by the Austrian Ernst Křenek, which concerns the adventures of an American Negro jazz player abroad.

RECORD LIST — CHAPTER XVII

American Indian music — see CHAPTER I

Carpenter, John Alden (1876-1951)
    Adventures in a Perambulator

Dvořák, Antonin (1841-1904)
    String Quartet No. 6 in F, Op. 96 ("American Quartet")
    Symphony No. 5 in E Minor, Op. 95 ("From the New World")

Folk songs, national songs, work songs, play-party songs and dances — various

Foote, Arthur (1853-1937)
    Suite in E for Strings

Foster, Stephen (1826-1864)
    Songs — various

Gershwin, George (1898-1937)
    An American in Paris
    Piano Concerto in F

Porgy and Bess — excerpts
Preludes for Piano
Rhapsody in Blue

Grofé, Ferde (1892-
    Grand Canyon Suite
    Mississippi Suite

Handy, William Christopher (1873-1958)
    Beale Street Blues
    Memphis Blues
    St. Louis Blues

Herbert, Victor (1859-1924)
    Operetta selections — The Fortune Teller, Naughty
       Marietta, The Red Mill, etc.

MacDowell, Edward (1861-1908)
    Piano Concerto No. 1 in A Minor, Op. 15
    Piano Concerto No. 2 in D Minor, Op. 23
    Suite No. 2, Op. 48 ("Indian")
    Woodland Sketches, Op. 51

McBride, Robert (1911-
    Aria and Toccata in Swing
    Mexican Rhapsody

Milhaud, Darius (1892-
    La Creation du Monde (The Creation of the World)

Sousa, John Philip (1854-1932)
    Marches — various

Spirituals — various

CHAPTER XVIII

TWENTIETH CENTURY MUSIC

NEVER in history has there been a period of so many rapid changes as our twentieth century. Great wars have altered boundaries and ways of thought. Science is propelling us into an unknown future at a dizzying pace. In reflecting the spirit of the times, the arts—painting, sculpture, literature, drama, music — have been bursting through old forms to try to express the new way of life. It is difficult to believe that at the turn of the century, a critic remarked that Debussy's whole-tone scale and use of overtones had the same effect on his ears as when a dentist touched the nerve of a sensitive tooth. Music, in particular, seemed to be going through a period of change as great as the swing from polyphonic music to homophonic music.

THE MATERIALS OF MUSIC

In every country, composers were experimenting with the elements of music—rhythm, melody, harmony, form. The Russian composer, Dmitri Shostakovitch, even spoke in favor of a music in which no theme should ever be repeated and every measure should be entirely different from all that had gone before.

Many composers experimented with rhythm. In setting Shakespeare's "Macbeth" to music, the Swiss-American musician, Ernest Bloch, used consecutive measures of 3/4, 4/4, and 6/4 time to match the rhythm of the words. At the beginning of his

"Pacific 231," Arthur Honegger—once a member of the French "Group of Six"—changed the time signature with every bar to match the jerky puffs of the locomotive. Another French composer, Eric Satie, wrote a barless piece of music with no rhythm pattern at all. This, however, was not the innovation it might seem to be, for the ancient church chants and polyphonic music often were in free rhythm and without any time signatures.

Other modern composers were making music in which two sections of an orchestra or chorus had entirely independent rhythms. The modernists may not have realized that such simultaneous use of different rhythms was to be found in the music of the American Indians (p. 247); however, it has not been established that the effect there was intentional.

Composers were making just as surprising changes in melody, or the arrangement of tones horizontally. Some returned to the modes of the ancient Greeks and the early church fathers (pp. 5 and 7). Other music took its inspiration from the sliding scales of the Orientals, with their quarter tones and split quarters. The grandson of Rimsky-Korsakoff even founded a quarter-tone society to foster such music, and someone has invented a piano to play quarter instead of half tones. Although this music was not developed, it did serve to make musicians more aware of chromatic music, or music that makes use of all the half tones. The best-known example of such use of chromatics is the twelve-tone scale of the Austrian-born Arnold Schoenberg. In forming a melody, each note of this twelve-tone scale (made up of all the black and white keys within one octave on the piano) is to be used once and once only. Of course, such music is not in any particular key. It is called "atonal" and is written without key signature.

There were also startling new developments in harmony or the sounding of tones simultaneously. Composers who had turned back to the ancient modes often made use of ancient harmonies as well, such as the progressions of fourths and fifths which for centuries had been considered too stiff and awkward-sounding to use. The modernists also concocted a so-called "pan-diatonic harmony," in which—to use the piano as an example—any white key could be harmonized by any combination of other white key notes..."like children banging on the white keys," as Nicolas Slonimsky has observed.

In modern music, too, we find what is called "polytonal music"—music written in two keys at once. For example, a melody or primary theme might be in the key of C, while its accompaniment or an obbligato voice might be in F♯. As for chord harmonies, nothing now limits them except the inventiveness of the composer. One of the most famous examples of a chord associated with the name of a certain composer is Scriabin's "Promethean" or "mystic" chord. Instead of the usual intervals of a third, this chord was constructed entirely of fourths. All the notes were selected from the natural overtone series. Here is the formula for the "mystic" chord; try it on your piano: C, F♯, B♭, E, A, and D—an augmented, a diminished, another augmented, and two perfect fourths. Scriabin used it to express his idea of Prometheus, the hero who stole fire from the gods for the use of men.

MODERN MUSICIANS AND AMERICAN JAZZ

Sometimes the new musical resources enabled composers to achieve an eerie sort of beauty, as, for example, Ravel's use of pan-diatonic harmonies in the "Jardin Féerique" or "Fairy Garden" movement of his "Mother Goose Suite." Yet, many of the musical experiments, like the tricks of polyphony of the Netherlands school (p. 12), seemed of interest only to other musicians. The trend which seemed to appeal both to professional musicians and the public, was American jazz.

Another characteristic of modern music was the tendency of composers to turn to the folkways of their countries as a source of inspiration. With the invention and development of means of musical reproduction and communication—phonograph, radio, television—music had no national boundaries. Such works as the two "Roumanian Rhapsodies," Opus 11, by Georges Enesco, were loved wherever they were heard. Music was on its way to becoming a great aid in the understanding of the spirit and cultures of other peoples. The Australian-born composer, Percy Grainger, stated the case very well when he said that one should feel at home in the music of all races, all periods, and all styles, but that music should have local roots. "Local sowing, universal harvest," was his summing up of the matter.

Of all the music based on national folkways, none had more widespread influence than American jazz. With its feverish rhythms and weird dissonances, it seemed, in a way, an expression of the new age. It had many features that appealed to professional musicians. Among them were the scale with flatted third and seventh which, used interchangeably with the major scale, produced startling contrasts; and the "blues" harmony—based on seventh chords with flatted third and seventh—instead of the conventional triads which hitherto had formed the basis of harmony for folk and popular music.

However, the feature of jazz that had the strongest appeal was its rhythm. Syncopation, or emphasis on an off-beat, had been known and used for centuries by most of the great masters of music. But here, in jazz, was a new kind of syncopation — "polyrhythm," or two very strong rhythm patterns sounding against each other, such as a three-beat rhythm superimposed on a four-beat rhythm. Since intricate and multiple rhythms are characteristic of the music of primitive peoples, we accept jazz rhythms as a gift to our musical life from our Afro-American friends.

We find strong examples of this three-over-four type of rhythm pattern in the popular songs, "Fascinatin' Rhythm" and "I Can't Give You Anything But Love, Baby." One of the best extended uses of the rhythms, melodies, and harmonies of jazz and blues is found in George Gershwin's "Rhapsody in Blue."

Professional musicians were also fascinated by the primitive jazz players who seldom used written music and who, in fact, frequently could not even read music. On the spur of the moment these untaught jazz players might improvise the most elaborate variations on a melody, or intricate musical embroidery to fit in a sort of counterpoint. They seemed to have revived the art of improvisation which had all but died since Johann Sebastian Bach had astounded King Frederick the Great. The early masters of improvisation had performed "solo," or alone; but here, in the jazz band, there might be half a dozen players— each with his own independent and often quite original interpretation—all somehow miraculously keeping within the same large framework of harmony and rhythm. These players had one trait in common with the classic masters of improvisation: they usually started with a theme, or a scrap of some well-known tune. Such is the jazzmen's old favorite, "When the Saints Go Marching In." It began as a Negro gospel hymn.

As jazz spread to larger bands and more educated musicians, the making of orchestrations or arrangements became a special musical trade. Though in general, jazz bands were divided into three sections: reeds (saxophones, clarinets, etc.); brasses (trumpets, trombones, tubas, horns); and percussion—the balance of instruments might be altered. Percussion could include anything from standard drums and cymbals to piano, contrabass, banjo, guitar, etc. The writing of music, and the artful use of various kinds of tone, called for more education than many players and even many composers of popular music possessed. So the arranger became of great importance in this kind of music, giving tone color, suitable harmonies, and suitable form to other men's musical thoughts.

Years after serious European composers first brought echoes

of American jazz into their music, a gifted popular pianist and song writer, George Gershwin, dreamed of bringing music based on jazz and blues into American concert halls. His first composition of the concert type—the "Rhapsody in Blue"—was patterned after the Hungarian Rhapsodies of Liszt; that is, for piano solo with full symphonic accompaniment. Gershwin later studied orchestration so that he could write what he considered the most effective instrumental parts for his compositions, but for the "Rhapsody in Blue" he called in an expert arranger to do the scoring. This arranger was Ferde Grofé, who later used his talent for orchestration to write some compositions of his own —mostly tone pictures of the American scene. His "Grand Canyon Suite" is a dazzling display of instrumental coloring used to express the feeling of the colors and moods of nature.

NEW INSTRUMENTS AND TONE COLOR

With new developments in electronics, there would seem to be no end to the invention of instruments which might add new tone colors to the music of the future. Yet, to the present writing, only one such instrument has become at all widely known, and that, just as a musical oddity. This is the theremin —an instrument named for its inventor—"designed," as Nicolas Slonimsky says, "for the electrical generation of sounds to follow the motion of the hand in space." The electrical instruments which thus far have come into wide use—the electric organ, the electric piano, and the electric guitar—are not new instruments in so far as tone color goes. The first two imitate and the other amplifies the tones of already existing instruments.

It probably will be a long time before any newly-invented instrument will take a regular place in the standard symphony orchestra. More than a century of use by serious composers like Bizet, Saint-Saëns, Debussy, and Richard Strauss has not succeeded in making the saxophone wholly respectable.

Rather than encourage the invention of new instruments for wider tonal effects, composers have asked the time-honored symphonic instruments to perform feats which no one ever thought possible. We hear of Ravel's use of a trombone glissando "pushed through all the positions in such a way that the intervals of half and quarter tones can be clearly heard." Voices, both in solo and in chorus, are used more and more as instruments of the orchestra.

The most dramatic search for new effects was in the percussion section. Once upon a time, percussion consisted almost solely of tympani, occasionally reinforced by other drums and cymbals. Now the percussion section has become a place where anything seems acceptable—a typewriter, a key sending Morse code, a hammer, Mossoloff's sheet of iron, and Schoenberg's length of heavy iron chain. Even when the percussion is confined to the accepted musical instruments, a glance at almost any orchestral program will show the startling developments that took place in less than fifty years. For instance, side by side with César Franck's "Symphony in D Minor" (first performed in 1889 and calling only for tympani as the percussion), we might find a work such as the "Sixth Symphony" by American composer David Diamond, with 1936 listed as the year of composition. Here, the percussion includes chromatic tympani, bass drum, snare drum, tenor drum, gavel, tubular bells, xylophone, glockenspiel, piano, cymbals, suspended cymbal, and large gong.

There also are compositions that feature the percussions above all other instruments of the orchestra. Edgar Varèse startled the musical world in 1931 with his composition, "Ionisation," scored for thirteen percussion players divided into two opposing groups. Many other compositions for tuned and untuned percussions have been written since that time. Experiments have also been made at tape-recording strange sounds produced by vacuum tubes and combining the results into musical pieces of sorts. Percussion and its allied effects seem to offer the best means of expression to those composers who feel, as one of them has put it, that modern music should convey "an emotion resulting from contact with daily life — its noise, its rhythms, its energy and mechanical daring."

THE CONDUCTOR AND THE AGE OF REPRODUCTION
AND COMMUNICATION

If the invention of new musical instruments has had but little effect on modern music, the development of the means of re-producing and broadcasting music has exerted an enormous influence. It has enlarged the number of listeners beyond belief. With phonograph and radio at hand, the music lover no longer had to go to concert halls to hear the music of his choice; the concert hall could come into his home—into homes far from cities — homes where good music had never before been heard.

Over the centuries of music history there has come about a change in the relative importance of the makers of music. Up to about the time of Bach, the church was the center of musical life. Then the leading musical personage in the community was the organist-choirmaster, who produced the music for worship and often added compositions of his own to the traditional mu-sic of the church. When music came to find its chief support in the palaces of princes, the director of royal music was called a chapel-master. In the days of the minuet, suite, and early sym-phony, the musician who won greatest fame and influence was the musical director who best pleased his prince and his prince's guests. Where opera was the favorite form of music, the prima donna tried to dominate — and quite often succeeded, as we learn from events in the life of Handel.

After Beethoven defied the power of princes and brought his work before the public, the concert hall became the center of musical life. At first, the concert hall was ruled by the composer, who obtained soloists and orchestras for the performance of his own compositions. Liszt, Paganini, and singers like Jenny Lind and Adelina Patti brought in the period of the touring solo virtuosos who carried music to cities too small to support a symphony orchestra or an opera company. Often, however, to attract crowds, their business managers gave them such sensational publicity that the performers seemed far more important than the music.

The passing of time and the invention of the phonograph brought in the day of the conductor who is, after all, a virtuoso on the greatest of all instruments, the symphony orchestra. Most of the early classics—the works of Bach, Mozart, Haydn, and Beethoven — were first performed under the direction of their composers, who established a tradition as to how their music should be played. But, as the late critic Olin Downes once wrote, "The tradition is ignored by the first generation, altered by the second, and quite possibly entirely forgotten by the third. And when the music has within itself the vitality that resists generations and centuries of change, it is without doubt also changed in its stylistic conception by the interpreters. Granted them to be worthy of the name, they are more than the middlemen of music. In a real sense, they are arbiters of its destiny."

Since the written notes and the tempo and dynamic markings of a composition are only the bare bones of music, a conductor has the creative function of bringing them to life with his own spirit. Conductors — and also solo performers — become famous for their interpretation of this or that composer; we hear of "the Beethoven" of one conductor or "the Debussy" of another. What is more, in the present age a special interpretation need not fade into silence at the end of a performance, to be preserved only in the memories of the hearers. Through the medium of tape recordings or phonograph records, it can be listened to again and again. Music lovers who live miles from concert halls can evaluate interpretations, and even compare the interpretations of the living with those of the dead.

Since the days of Mendelssohn, the conductor has been much

more than a mere performer. Besides being an interpreter of music, he acts as an editor in chosing which old works to repeat, and what new works to introduce to the public. As the twentieth century progresses, it has become more and more difficult to tell which new piece of modern music is a mere conglomeration of sounds, and which one really will have a message—that is, once the ears of the public have become accustomed to it. Though the public ultimately determines by its response which new compositions shall live, it is the conductor who initially decides which of them the public shall hear.

It is through his influence as program maker that a conductor leaves behind him more than a handful of phonograph records. In the first half of the twentieth century there were a number of conductors who left a very definite mark on the musical life of the United States. We shall discuss two of them.

SERGE KOUSSEVITZKY AND NEW MUSIC

From his earliest years as a conductor, Serge Koussevitzky felt the urge to give new music a hearing. He began his career as a virtuoso on the double bass. After a few years as soloist at the Imperial Theatres in his native Russia and as professor at the conservatory where he had studied, he turned to orchestral conducting. With the inspiration and financial assistance of his wife, Natalie, he founded a publishing firm for the encouragement of Russian music. All profits went to the composers. In 1910, 1912, and again in 1914, he chartered a steamer and toured the 2300 miles of the Volga with a sizable orchestra and the composer Scriabin as soloist, bringing good music to small towns that never before had had an opportunity to hear good music. Later, in Moscow, he became famous as an orchestra conductor and opera conductor with a special interest in modern music.

In Paris, where Koussevitzky went after the Russian Revolution, he commissioned Ravel to orchestrate the piano suite, "Pictures at an Exhibition," by Mussorgsky. He assembled an orchestra and directed the "Concerts Koussevitzky," which became so well known that when one of the great American symphony orchestras — the Boston Symphony — was in need of a conductor, the post was offered to him.

During his twenty-five years as head of the Boston Symphony Orchestra, Koussevitzky put into practice his conviction that music is a living and growing art. It is striking to note, in the Koussevitzky programs, the frequency with which compositions have been marked, "performed for the first time anywhere." It was characteristic of his courage that, if he believed in a modern work, he would play it again and again, regardless of adverse criticism. His judgment generally was excellent.

It has been said that no foreign conductor has done as much for American music as Serge Koussevitzky. Of course, this does not mean that without Koussevitzky, new American works would have lacked a hearing. Howard Hanson — both in the Eastman School and as conductor of the Rochester Philharmonic Orchestra — has devoted a distinguished career to the advancement of American composers and the development of American music. It is an interesting point that two of Hanson's own symphonies were given their first performances by Koussevitzky and the Boston Symphony Orchestra. If American compositions played an important part in Koussevitzky's program making, it was not because he looked upon American music either as a novelty or a cause. It was because, in any consideration of the modern music of the world, American music could claim a rightful place.

What is more, American music was beginning to dare to be American. In subject matter, program music was turning away from foreign sources of inspiration (as in "The Pleasure Dome of Kubla Khan" and "Roman Sketches," both by Griffes), to the homeland. There seemed to be no limit to the amount of music based on American life, American literature, American history and folklore, and American heroes. There were the operas, "Merry Mount," by Howard Hanson, and "The Man Without a Country," by Walter Damrosch; the overtures, "When Johnny Comes Marching Home" and "Farewell to Pioneers," and the "Folk Song Symphony," "American Creed," and "Ballad to a Railroad Man"—all by Roy Harris. There were the ballets, "Billy the Kid," "Rodeo," and "Appalachian Spring," and "A Lincoln Portrait" for symphony orchestra with narrator —all by Aaron Copland.

Increasing numbers of composers turned for inspiration to scenes and events of their own days. From time to time during the first half of the twentieth century, such works came forth as "Flivver Ten Million," by Frederick Converse; "Filling Station," by Virgil Thomson; and "Newsreel in Five Shots," by William Schuman. Between 1915 and 1926, American audiences heard first performances of "Adventures in a Perambulator" ("a street scene viewed through baby's eyes"); "Krazy Kat" (a comic strip turned into a ballet); and another ballet, "Skyscrapers"—all by John Alden Carpenter, who was described by Walter Damrosch as "the most American" of the composers of the time.

WALTER DAMROSCH AND MUSIC EDUCATION

Walter Damrosch was another conductor to leave a permanent imprint on American music. He already had had a distinguished career as a composer and as conductor of the Metropolitan Opera and the New York Philharmonic, when the development of radio gave him a vision. Music audiences were going to increase a thousandfold—indeed, almost a millionfold. It was well known that the most appreciative audiences of good music are those who have learned what to listen for in music. Therefore he would use the radio, not only to bring good music to the people, but also to help them enjoy it.

For adults, he arranged weekly concerts with interesting commentary on the music to be performed. But as the devoted father of four children, he also was very interested in bringing good music to other children. His idea of sending good music into the schoolroom by radio led to his series of radio concerts for children, featuring selections carefully graded for the greatest enjoyment by various age groups. These concerts were planned to show the tone colors of various instruments, and to help the children to a greater understanding of how composers used the materials of music. They have served as models for music educators and makers of musical programs for children ever since. John Tasker Howard, in his book, "Our American Music," gave proper credit to this innovator when he wrote that Walter Damrosch will always be remembered as one who did more than his share in helping to make America musical.

One has only to compare music education in the schools before and after the time of Walter Damrosch to realize his influence. Of course music education did not begin with Damrosch. Over a century before, against much opposition, Lowell Mason had introduced the teaching of music into the schools. But it was singing only, and a hundred years later, except in the larger cities, music education had not advanced much beyond Mason's singing school. And how could it? It is impossible to appreciate music without hearing it. The phonograph, in its initial stages, could not reproduce the quality of the full orchestra. Moreover, in most communities, a phonograph for the classroom was seldom considered essential to education. But through national broadcasts, picked up on borrowed radios in the classrooms, the Damrosch series spread over the land and music education was vastly extended.

In the large cities, more and more orchestras featured children's concerts with programs patterned on the pioneer work of Damrosch. The phonograph eventually came to be considered a desirable, if not a necessary, part of school equipment. The hearing of instrumental music stimulated the playing of instrumental music. In the larger cities where musically gifted children had been given private lessons, school bands and orchestras had been established. Gradually, the class teaching of band and orchestra instruments — either for a very small fee or free of charge — became a well-established procedure in the schools.

The highest objective of music education in a democracy is to create an opportunity for everyone to enjoy music to the utmost of his ability. This ideal is gradually being realized. Nowadays, in most schools, children hear good music on records and sing good music. The younger ones play in rhythm bands; their older brothers and sisters may play in school bands and orchestras. It is hoped that in the near future, such musical opportunities will spread to every school in the land.

The increased musical activity in the schools has led to an interesting feature of American musical life: the formation of amateur or semi-amateur civic symphony orchestras, in which young and old, doctor, teacher, salesman, and truck driver may play good music together. There are, at the present writing (1958), close to seven hundred such orchestras, and the number increases yearly. Community choruses and bands are also on the increase. Observers of the social scene point out that, as machines take over more and more of man's work, a wise and happy use of leisure time may become one of the problems of the age. If this is true, more and more people may find in music the answer to their recreational needs.

Music education, moreover, is not confined to schools. It is extended to adults by way of lectures, newspaper reviews of concerts and records, magazines, books such as "What to Listen for in Music" and "Our New Music"—both by Aaron Copland, and the countless volumes on how to start a record library. The healing effects of music are used in what is called "music therapy"—which is really music education for the ill and the handicapped. Not only are music's soothing strains employed to relax shattered nerves, but the playing of specially constructed instruments helps to repair damaged muscles.

MUSIC AND MODERN INVENTION

The various means of reproducing and communicating music — phonograph, radio, moving picture, television — have been with us long enough for us to evaluate their early promises.

For a time, it seemed as though radio was going to fulfill all the expectations of Walter Damrosch. Good musical programs, broadcast from coast to coast, were numerous. They ranged from the so-called popular classics to symphony and grand opera. The national radio chains commissioned new works and offered prizes for compositions to be broadcast. To name just a few examples, RCA Victor offered $25,000 for a symphonic work. The prize was shared by four of the best-known musical figures of the day: Aaron Copland, Ernest Bloch (already a prize winner with a symphony called "America"), Robert Russell Bennett (then better known as an arranger than as an original composer), and Louis Gruenberg, composer of "Emperor Jones" — one of the few successful modern operas. The Columbia Broadcasting System commissioned a "Third Symphony" from Howard Hanson; a piece from Aaron Copland which he called simply, "Music for Radio"; and a radio opera from Louis Gruenberg. CBS also gave early encouragement to Gian-Carlo Menotti by broadcasting his radio opera, "The Old Maid and the Thief." It seemed almost as if radio might replace the church, the palace, and the concert hall as the principal support of musical activity.

Then television appeared as competition in home entertainment, and many good musical programs began to disappear from radio for lack of support. Among the live broadcasts of popular classics, casualties were just about as numerous. Radio stations turned to the phonograph record, the electrical transcription, and the tape recording for their daily music. The era of the disc jockey had arrived.

With the modern tendency to specialization, the broadcasting of the best music has become more and more confined to FM radio, which requires a special receiving set and can be picked up only within a limited distance from the broadcasting station. Since FM transmitters are almost always located in or near large cities, people who live a considerable distance from those cities do not have access to FM broadcasts and the good music they transmit.

Thus, the phonograph—the earliest of the modern inventions for reproducing music—is still the most widely used. About the time that Edison was experimenting to make his dream of a "talking machine" an actuality, one writer (Edward Bellamy, 1850-98) declared that the utmost in human happiness would be attained if only there existed "…an instrument for providing everybody with music in their homes, perfect in quality, unlimited in quantity, suited to every mood, and beginning and ceasing at will." The invention of "high fidelity" techniques in recording and reproducing processes brought about a vastly improved quality. Any kind or combination of instruments now can be recorded on disc or tape and reproduced in the home with much of the fullness and richness of the concert hall. The listings of the thousands of available records encompass music from the early Netherlands school of counterpoint to the twelve-tone scale… from a Palestrina Mass to the Menotti television opera, "Amahl and the Night Visitors."

The moving picture which, next to the phonograph, is the oldest of the modern means of entertainment, has had the least musical influence. When sound first was added to pictures, a few films were produced—such as those featuring the late Grace Moore—which brought vivid glimpses of grand opera to tiny towns thousands of miles from an opera house. From time to time there have been pictures—unfortunately somewhat inaccurate—that created interest in the lives and works of composers such as Schubert, Chopin and Grieg. Virtuoso performers of the caliber of Paderewski, Iturbi, and Heifetz have been featured. The picture, "Carnegie Hall," offered some of the world's finest music and musicians. In "Fantasia," Walt Disney and

Leopold Stokowski made the interesting experiment of combining music with visual effects, making program pieces such as Dukas' "Sorcerer's Apprentice" a delight to thousands who otherwise might never have stopped to listen to them.

Offerings such as these, however, have been comparatively few and infrequent. Of all the music composed especially for films, only a negligible amount is able to stand alone, that is, as music worth hearing for its own merits. The few exceptions have been composed, not for commercial pictures, but for documentary films. In this category fall Virgil Thomson's music for "The Plow that Broke the Plains," and Richard Rodgers' music for "Victory at Sea"—a picture designed to be telecast. The motion picture performs its greatest service in bringing the best works of the New York theater to the farthest corners of the land. And it is in the field of music for the theater — the development of a distinctive form of musical comedy—that the United States is making perhaps its greatest contribution to music.

AMERICAN MUSIC OF THE THEATER

In reading about the history of music, we learn that the various kinds and forms of music we now take for granted did not come into existence through deliberate planning. Like nearly everything else in the world, they are the result of evolution. Thus, the symphonic form is the result of a long search for new music to please the guests of German and Austrian noblemen. Composers of several generations had a hand in developing it; Beethoven brought it to final perfection. On another level, the delightful waltzes that filled a need in the social life of imperial Vienna evolved from the humble "ländler"—an Austrian peasant dance. Here again, many composers contributed to the foundation on which the Strausses, father and son, erected such glittering structures. In our own country, it is only recently that serious musicians have become aware that an indigenous musical style is evolving—a truly democratic kind of music that can be tooted and thumped by amateurs, or appear with dignity on the programs of concert artists.

Perhaps it all began when the young Irish musician, Victor Herbert, sailed to America to take a position as 'cellist in the orchestra of the Metropolitan Opera House, where his wife had been engaged as a singer. He soon turned to conducting and composing. His ambitions were serious. He composed symphonic poems and suites, and two grand operas that were produced at the Metropolitan. Trying his hand at operetta, he found the gift for creating light music of such charm that its continued popularity seems assured. It is true that nowadays his theatrical works are seldom performed in their entirety (as are the light operas of Gilbert and Sullivan, for instance), and the reason may be that Herbert lacked a gifted librettist. An opera or operetta seldom achieves immortality on the strength of its music alone. Victor Herbert's fame rests chiefly upon selected songs and orchestrated medleys from his operettas.

Other composers of operetta and musical comedy followed whose song hits are still widely performed more than two generations after they were first heard on Broadway. Then the formula for a successful musical show gradually changed. There came about a tendency to make musical comedies from books or plays that had already shown signs of merit or popularity. One of the first musical entertainments of this type was "Show Boat," by Jerome Kern, based on the novel by Edna Ferber. Its songs had such lovely melodies that one symphonic conductor had them arranged as a concert suite for orchestra. "Old Man River," the biggest song hit in the show, has come to be regarded almost as a folk song.

"Show Boat" illustrates a tendency of musical comedy to turn more and more to the native American scene. Subject matter might concern half-legendary figures like Annie Oakley ("Annie, Get Your Gun"), historical episodes ("The King and

I"), or even modern industrial life ("Pajama Game"). Foreign stories were transplanted, such as "Carousel," which was moved from Austria to Maine. Classics were given a native twist. Shakespeare's "The Taming of the Shrew" became "Kiss Me, Kate"; "Romeo and Juliet" was transformed into "West Side Story." Books were adapted which featured Americans in strange situations—for example, Mark Twain's "A Connecticut Yankee" and James Michener's "Tales of the South Pacific."

Of course, there were exceptions to the rule. To the makers of musical comedy, a good book was a good book wherever it might be found. They might turn to something as exotic as "The King and I" or as typical of another country as "My Fair Lady"—which had been adapted from Shaw's "Pygmalion."

"My Fair Lady" was one of the most extreme examples of another trend in the creation of musical comedy, and that was specialization. Credits for creative work, listed on the recording of the show, include: "Book and Lyrics by Lerner, adapted from Shaw's 'Pygmalion'; Music by Loewe; Musical Arrangements by Robert Russell Bennett and Phil Lang; Choreography by Hanya Holm; Dance Music arranged by Trude Rittman." Thus, instead of a partnership between librettist and musician, modern musical comedy calls for considerable teamwork involving the author of the original work, the writer who "makes the book" or dramatizes it, the composer who creates the melodies of the songs, the lyricist who writes the verses, the arranger who orchestrates the music, and a choreographer who creates the movements of the dances.

Occasionally, one person will perform several functions: a composer may write not only the songs, but the music for the dance numbers as well; a writer may do both book and lyrics. Some song writers create their own lyrics, as did Irving Berlin for "Annie, Get Your Gun." The relationship is closest between song writer and lyricist. Certain partnerships have become famous, as the team of Rodgers and Hart—later, Rodgers and Hammerstein; and the Gershwin brothers, Ira and George, whose "Of Thee I Sing" won a Pulitzer prize.

The late George Gershwin, who brought jazz and blues into the concert hall with his "Rhapsody in Blue," "An American in Paris," and "Concerto in F," also started the American musical show in a new direction. Music critics took note of the situation in articles which said, in effect, "What is happening to our musical comedy? It is not comic any more." It has, in fact, been evolving into a special sort of music drama to which no one has as yet given a name—not quite grand and not quite comic.

On the one hand are the works of the gifted Gian-Carlo Menotti, who creates both libretto and music. He has had an opera, "The Island God," performed at the Metropolitan. His greatest success, aside from the classic "Amahl," has been in music drama for the theater. "The Medium," "The Telephone," "The Consul," and "The Saint of Bleecker Street" all take a place among the finest music dramas of our time. In contrast to these serious works are the more commercial and conventional musical comedies, which show greater depth than did their predecessors and even recognize the occurrence of death, as in "Carousel" and "The King and I." This form of music has presented a challenge to many serious musicians. For instance, Leonard Bernstein — a recognized conductor and pianist, and composer of symphonic pieces such as "Jeremiah"—entered the musical comedy field with "On the Town," and followed this with the more serious "Candide" and "West Side Story."

However, it was Gershwin's "Porgy and Bess" that led the musical theater into ways of greater depth and meaning. "Porgy and Bess" is based on a touching story by Du Bose Heyward, set to music echoing the jazz elements of the 1930's. Its poignant music is, on the whole, very singable — a quality which some later composers in the jazz idiom were apt to disregard. The beautiful air, "Summertime," like Kern's "Old Man River," has become a universal favorite. "Porgy and Bess" deals with one aspect of the American scene and can be called a true American folk opera. It is quite fitting, therefore, that "Porgy and Bess" was one of the first productions to be sent abroad on a cultural mission to represent the music of America.

MUSIC AND ONE WORLD

In studying the evolution of musical life in the United States, it would be most interesting to make a chronological comparison of events here and in Europe. While Palestrina was composing his masses in the old city of Rome, there were few white settlements in what is now the United States, and they were only temporary. A permanent foothold had not yet been established. The only other human habitations were scattered hogans, wigwams, and the pueblo structures of the Indians in the Southwest. In the days of Bach and Handel, the songs of settlers in isolated cabins, and the drone of unaccompanied hymns in meetinghouses, constituted practically the sole musical activities. More than a hundred years later, in 1850, when Liszt was giving Wagner's "Lohengrin" a first performance in Weimar, the American circus manager P.T. Barnum was showing the great singer, Jenny Lind, up and down the land as a sort of musical stunt woman.

Up through the early years of the twentieth century our musical traffic with Europe was a one-way affair. Our students went abroad to study under the great masters they revered. Europe's artists came to the United States as conquering heroes, to gather fame and wealth. Sometimes they stayed on to fill musical positions of the greatest importance, such as the conductorships of our best orchestras. Now conditions have changed. A foreign diploma is no longer necessary to success in music and the other arts. More and more young musicians born and educated in the United States are being assigned to positions of great responsibility — positions that formerly were filled exclusively by artists trained abroad.

The center of musical training in college and conservatory has moved from Europe to the United States. To some extent this change can be attributed to the insecurity of life in Europe during World War Two and the subsequent periods of internal upheaval. Great musicians of the Old World fled to our country for freedom to create and teach: Stravinsky, Schoenberg, Hindemith, and Milhaud, to mention just a few. Some of those seeking temporary refuge decided to make our land their homeland, and became American citizens. The musical tide has turned to such an extent that we now find young European musicians traveling to this country to complete their educations. Such a one is the opera composer, Gian-Carlo Menotti, who came as a youth from Italy to study at one of our great musical institutes.

Now that we can take our part in the world of music on a footing of equality, our State Department uses music to help cultivate friendly relations with other nations. We send abroad not only our folk opera companies and our jazz artists, but also our best symphony orchestras, which speak an international musical language.

This particular phase of progress is due in part to advances in the field of transportation, whereby an orchestra of a hundred players can be whisked by air from place to place as if on a magic carpet. Transportation has had an influence on music that is second only to advances in communication and reproduction. Modern musical compositions may show tendencies toward nationalism, but in the areas of performance and appreciation we are becoming more and more international. We send symphony orchestras to friendly countries and to some not so friendly. We welcome outstanding soloists, orchestras, ballet and opera companies from abroad. We delight in the native dancers and the fascinating music that come to us from Asia and Africa. Music seems to be the one area in which all nations of the world may advance together in peace and good will; we can but hope that its influence will spread.

MUSIC OF THE FUTURE

By observing certain tendencies in the music of the present, we can forecast to some extent the music of the future. Some of the current trends that may influence the music of the next generation are:

1. Experimentation with new forms of melody, rhythm, harmony, and instrumentation, mirroring the dynamic impact of new forms of energy and new mechanical inventions upon life now and in the future.

2. Greater emphasis on the national character of music, accompanied by a wider international audience, leading to greater understanding between the peoples of all nations.

3. The ever-growing audience potential, through continued advances in means of transportation, communication, and musical reproduction.

4. The expansion of music education, not only to assist the musically gifted to reach their highest development, but also to enable every one of us to share in the glorious adventure of the music of the future.

RECORD LIST — CHAPTER XVIII

Addinsell, Richard (1904-
    Warsaw Concerto

Barber, Samuel (1910-
    Adagio for Strings
    String Quartet No. 1, Op. 11
    Symphony No. 1

Barlow, Wayne (1912-
    Rhapsody for Oboe and Strings, "The Winter's Past"

Bartók, Bela — see CHAPTER XIV

Bennett, Robert Russell (1894-
    Suite of Old American Dances

Berg, Alban (1885-1935)
     Concerto for Violin and Orchestra
     Wozzeck — excerpts

Berger, Arthur (1912-
     Serenade Concertante

Bernstein, Leonard (1918-
     Fancy Free
     "Jeremiah" Symphony
     On the Town

Bloch, Ernest (1880-
     Concerto Grosso for String Orchestra and Piano
     Nigun, from "Baal Shem" Suite
     Schelomo — Rhapsody for Cello and Orchestra

Britten, Benjamin — see CHAPTER XVI

Carpenter, John Alden — see CHAPTER XVII

Casella, Alfredo (1883-1947)
     Five Pieces for String Quartet
     Scarlattiana

Chavez, Carlos (1899-
     Sinfonia India
     Toccata for Percussion

Copland, Aaron (1900-
     Appalachian Spring
     Billy the Kid
     In the Beginning
     Quiet City
     Rodeo
     El Salon Mexico

Cowell, Henry (1897-
     Piano music — various
     Suite for Wind Quintet
     Symphony No. 11

Debussy, Claude — see CHAPTER XI

Delius, Frederick — see CHAPTER XVI

Diamond, David (1915-
     Music for "Romeo and Juliet"
     Rounds for String Orchestra

Dohnanyi, Ernst von — see CHAPTER XIV

Falla, Manuel de — see CHAPTER XIV

Fine, Irving (1914-
        Music for Piano — excerpts
        Partita for Woodwind Quintet

Francaix, Jean (1912-
        Concertino for Piano and Orchestra
        Serenade BEA

Gershwin, George — see CHAPTER XVII

Griffes, Charles Tomlinson (1884-1920)
        Poem for Flute and Orchestra
        Sonata for Piano
        The White Peacock (from "Roman Sketches") (piano or
           orchestra)

Grofé, Ferde — see CHAPTER XVII

Gruenberg, Louis (1884-
        Concerto for Violin and Orchestra

Hanson, Howard (1896-
        Songs from "Drum Taps"
        Symphony No. 2, "Romantic"
        Symphony No. 5, "Sinfonia Sacra"

Harris, Roy (1898-
        Sonata for Violin and Piano
        Symphony No. 3

Hindemith, Paul (1895-
        Kleine Kammermusik, Op. 24, No. 2 (for five wind
           instruments)
        Sonata for Clarinet and Piano
        Sonata for Flute and Piano
        Symphonic Metamorphosis on Themes by Weber

Ibert, Jacques (1890-
        Escales (Ports of Call)

Kern, Jerome (1885-1945)
        Scenario for Orchestra on Themes from "Showboat"

Khatchaturian, Aram — see CHAPTER XV

Kodály, Zoltan — see CHAPTER XIV

Krenek, Ernst (1900-
        Concerto for Violin, Piano, and Small Orchestra
        The Lamentations of Jeremiah, Op. 93

Lecuona, Ernesto (1896-
    Andalucia
    Malaguena

Liebermann, Rolf (1910-
    Concerto for Jazz Band and Orchestra

Loeffler, Charles Martin (1861-1935)
    A Pagan Poem (After Virgil), Op. 14

Mahler, Gustav (1860-1911)
    Das Lied von der Erde (The Song of the Earth)
    Songs of a Wayfarer
    Symphony No. 1 in D

Menotti, Gian-Carlo (1911-
    Amahl and the Night Visitors
    Amelia al Ballo (Amelia Goes to the Ball)—excerpts
    The Consul
    The Medium; The Telephone
    The Saint of Bleecker Street
    Sebastian Ballet Suite

Milhaud, Darius (1892-
    Le Boeuf sur le Toit
    La Creation du Monde
    Scaramouche Suite
    Symphony No. 4, "1848 Revolution"

Moore, Douglas (1893-
    The Devil and Daniel Webster

Mossoloff, Alexander—see CHAPTER XV

Nielsen, Carl (1865-1931)
    Maskarade — excerpts
    Symphony No. 5

Orff, Carl (1895-
    Carmina Burana
    Catulli Carmina

Pinkham, Daniel (1923-
    Concertante for Violin, Harpsichord, and Strings

Piston, Walter (1894-
    The Incredible Flutist
    Symphony No. 3

Poulenc, Francis (1899-
    Le Bal Masque
    Concerto for Piano and Orchestra

Thompson, Randall (1899-
   Alleluia
   The Peaceable Kingdom
   The Testament of Freedom
Thomson, Virgil (1896-
   Filling Station
   The Louisiana Story—Acadian Songs and Dances
Varese, Edgar (1885-
   Ionisation (for two groups of percussion players)
Vaughan Williams, Ralph — see CHAPTER XVI
Villa-Lobos, Heitor (1887-
   Bachianas Brasileiras, Nos. 3 and 5
Walton, William — see CHAPTER XVI

INDEX

INDEX